THE KILLING GAME

David DeMello

**Outskirts Press, Inc.
Denver, Colorado**

This is a work of fiction. The events and characters described here are imaginary and are not intended to refer to specific places or living persons. The opinions expressed in this manuscript are solely the opinions of the author and do not represent the opinions or thoughts of the publisher. The author represents and warrants that s/he either owns or has the legal right to publish all material in this book. If you believe this to be incorrect, contact the publisher through its website at www.outskirtspress.com.

The Killing Game
All Rights Reserved
Copyright © 2005 David DeMello

This book may not be reproduced, transmitted, or stored in whole or in part by any means, including graphic, electronic, or mechanical without the express written consent of the publisher except in the case of brief quotations embodied in critical articles and reviews.

Outskirts Press
http://www.outskirtspress.com

ISBN-10: 1-59800-068-3
ISBN-13: 978-1-59800-068-9

Outskirts Press and the "OP" logo are trademarks belonging to
Outskirts Press, Inc.

Printed in the United States of America

PART I

1

Hank Garrison's light green eyes drifted towards his cellphone if only for a second.

"Hank, stop looking at that damn phone," his wife said. "It's not going to ring, and so help me God if it does you are sure as hell not going to answer it. You're on vacation for Christ's sakes. *We're* on vacation." She slowly turned around and smiled at her two kids in the backseat.

"It's not like that, Carol," Hank replied. "I know we're on vacation…I know it…but…well it's just…ah nevermind." He realized he had lost the argument as soon as it had begun.

"You and your neverminds, one day they will get you in trouble," Carol responded.

Hank ran his hand through his salt and peppered hair then brought it down over his forehead, eyes, nose, and goateed mouth before giving Carol a smirk. Slowly he took her hand off the wheel and placed it on his cheek before softly kissing it.

"Okay Carol, I promise you this vacation will be a great one." He kissed her hand again then placed it back on the wheel. "I promise."

He glanced at his phone one more time then took it and turned it off.

"Thank you," Carol replied with a smile.

"No dear, thank *you*. Now let's stop with this nonsense and continue with the game," Hank said. "We still have seventeen hours of open road ahead of us and I'd like to have some sort of fun. It would certainly make this trip go by faster." He let out a sarcastic laugh.

"Well then stop talking and play dad," his daughter chanted from the back.

Hank turned his head to the back and focused on the young brown-haired girl that sat behind him. "I was about to Anna. Hold your horses."

Anna smiled, her dimples showing, and winked at her dad.

Hank winked back.

"It's Keith's turn." Anna turned to her older brother sitting beside her.

"Ugh," Keith snarled. "This is a stupid game and it will not get us to Florida any faster, especially with mom driving. A dead man could drive faster. Why didn't we just fly?"

"Well first off Keith," Hank started, "That was an awful analogy and secondly, flying would give us less of a chance to play these *stupid* games."

"Very funny dad," Keith harped. "How about this analogy; you could drive faster than mom and you have a gimp leg."

"Better," Hank said laughing. "But your mother is very cautious on these unrelenting six lane highways that go on for miles and miles and she feels as if going five miles below the speed limit will teach us all good defensive driving skills." Hank could barely spit the sentence out without laughing wildly.

Keith joined in on the laugh.

Carol looked at Hank. "Stop with your sarcasm, it

gets on my nerves. And I am not driving below the speed limit. I'm actually going faster than it says." She looked into the rearview mirror, back at Keith. "And now that you two are done having a father son laugh, at the expense of me, let us continue with the stupid game. Keith we're on letter 'R.'"

Keith rolled his eyes. "My name is Roger and my wife's name is Rose. We are from Roswell and we sell rifles."

2

The shanty, little, second floor apartment reeked of urine and alcohol. It was almost completely empty, save for a ripped up pullout couch whose gray and black plaid design was no less than thirty years old. Numerous newspaper cutouts were strewn on the wood floor, many beginning to yellow with age. The various headlines read: *Another Murder Solved, New Age Sherlock Holmes Sends One More Criminal to Jail, America's Greatest FBI Agent Outdoes Himself,* and many more. Each article seemed to carpet the lifeless room and yet, ironically enough, each one was about death.

To the left of the empty room was a bathroom, but unlike the newspaper-infested space, it was immaculate. A white towel was gently placed over the top of the door and a business suit was hung on the knob. The shower had all the amenities one would need and the sink was glistening clean. Above the sink was a mirrored medicine cabinet that contained the usual: a razor, shaving cream, hand soap, toothpaste, and toothbrush.

Across from the bathroom was the kitchen. Reminiscent of the living room it contained very little, solely a refrigerator, an oven, and a small one-chaired table. However, the room was rather clean, not unlike the bathroom. The only thing that littered the place was a few dishes placed carefully in the sink.

The final room was down a little hall where more yellowing articles could be used as a walkway into the space. The room was extremely small and was used more as a storage closet than anything else. Upon entering one would get a chill down their spine. It was dark and cold and inside various tools and weapons were piled on the floor. There was a small cleared out space not far from the door where another newspaper cut out lay. This time the article was freshly white and probably no more than a day or two old. It was held securely to the wooden floor. A newly sharpened arrow pierced the top of the paper and an even sharper axe held the bottom.

The headline read: *FBI Agent Hank Garrison Shot and Injured and Takes Leave of Absence.*

3

"My name is Yvonne and my husband's name is Yes. We're from Yellowstone and we sell yams," Anna said happily.

"Very good," Hank said. "But who would ever name their son Yes?"

"Well dad who would ever name their son Hank?" Anna jutted back.

"Hmmmm…good question. Nice rebuttal. Looks like only your mother lacks my sarcastic wit and charm in this family." Hank smiled and batted his eyes at his wife, making sure she saw.

Carol tried not to laugh. "Sarcastic you sure are. Witty and charming is another story."

"Ouch honey. Did I sense some sarcasm in your voice?"

"No." Carol smiled. "I was being serious."

Hank chuckled. "It's family moments like these that make me all warm and toasty inside. And speaking of toasty, turn the heat lower. I feel like my eyes are melting. It's hotter than the halls of Hades in here and I swear at any moment the devil is going to start dancing on the dash."

Carol knew she had something good brewing inside. "Oh Hank, honey, we both know the devil can't dance." She looked at Hank before continuing, "He has a gimp leg."

Hank thought for a moment then gave up. "Touché. My name is Zachary and my wife's name is Zula. We're from Zaire and we sell Zebras."

Some solitary clapping erupted from the backseat. "Good we're finished," Keith huffed.

"Finished with that game." Hank glanced at the clock and saw that it was 4:30, and then continued, "But there are others." Hank smiled back at Keith.

Keith remained quiet.

"We still have a good ten hours left. We'll stop to get food in a half an hour then drive until around ten before checking into a hotel. We should be in at least South Carolina by then," Hank said.

"Dad we should play the license plate game," Anna shouted happily.

"Maybe we should play that when we're closer to Florida Anna, because at this point we may not see much of a variety of plates." Hank tried to reason with her.

"Not true dad," she responded. "I've seen a lot of states already."

"Well I'll tell you what honey you should take a piece of paper and a pen," Hank handed her a pen from the front. "And write down as many states as you see and at the same time you can play the next game with us. It's an easy game."

"Okay, but we will play the plates game later, huh?"

"Yes we will. When we are closer," Hank compromised. "The next game is a play on words game. It makes the time go by fast and you'll like it Anna." Hank turned to Carol. "Remember this game Carol? We played it when we went skiing in Maine awhile ago."

"Yes I remember, although it's not nearly as much fun as you and Billy made it out to be."

"Well it's fun to me because I created it."

"Sure you did Hank."

"Trust me."

"Let's just play the new stupid game," Keith chimed in.

"Okay then," Hank took a deep breath. "It's best to explain by you two just following me and your mother. We'll do a demonstration. You'll understand as soon as we're finished. The object of the game is to get back to the original word. So we'll start with the word 'game.'"

"Show," Carol called out.

"Okay good. See guys." Hank turned to the back. "I said 'game' and she said 'show' so that's 'gameshow.' Now I would be using the word 'show' and I'd say 'down.' So you have the word 'showdown.' And eventually we'd get back to the original word."

"Sounds fun dad," Anna said as she hurriedly wrote a state down on her piece of paper.

Hank smiled. "Okay so I'll start. The word is 'dog.'"

"House," Anna screamed.

"Good one Anna, see you know how to play," Carol said. "Go Keith."

"Ugh...house...," he stammered searching for a good word. "House arrest."

"Oh...a big one." Carol thought for a moment then smiled as she spotted a road sign ahead. "Arrest area in one mile."

"Wow Carol a whole sentence, I like the usage of 'arrest,'" Hank said sincerely. "So my word is 'mile.'

Um…well if you can make a sentence so will I. *Mile run in the rain.*" Hank crossed his arms in excitement at the game he believed he had created.

"So dad, I use the word 'run'?" Anna asked.

"No honey you use the last word, which was 'rain,' and you don't have to use a sentence if you don't want to," Hank replied.

"Okay then, just 'bow,' like 'rainbow,'" Anna said. "Keith your turn."

"I know. I know," Keith remarked. "Bow and arrow."

Carol smiled again before responding. "Arrow of flowers I planted by hand."

Hank chuckled. "Well how else would you plant them Carol? By foot?" Hank turned to Carol and kissed her cheek then softly muttered, "Hand axe."

4

Robert Anderson left the Orlando airport and glanced at his watch.

It was 1:37 p.m.

"Well I lost three hours fast," he said to himself quietly before hailing a cab. A taxi quickly pulled up to Anderson. He opened up the door and slumped into the backseat then turned his watch's dial three hours ahead to 4:37 p.m.

"Take me to the Vandermeer Hotel please," he told the driver.

"No problem," the mustached driver said. "What brings you to Orlando?"

"Business I suppose. We're filming the pilot episode of a new crime drama series." Anderson yawned and rubbed his eyes. "I'm cast as the lead detective."

"Oh so you're an actor?"

"I plan to be. If all goes well with this show, if the pilot gets picked up, then yeah I guess so. Right now I'm a struggling actor. I hope the struggling part ends soon."

"You look more like a body-builder if you ask me," the driver responded, looking at Anderson in the rearview mirror.

Anderson flashed the driver a flexed bicep. "That's

what I'm told. I'll be one mean ass detective."

The driver smiled at the 6'4", shaved head, muscled actor sitting in the back. "I bet you will be."

About ten minutes later the taxi pulled into the front of the Vandermeer Hotel. "Well here it is sir, need any help with your bags?"

"No thank you, I only have one." Anderson held up a small black bag. "I figure if I make it big I can always buy more things here."

"I suppose that's true sir. I wish you luck. Have a great time in Orlando."

"Oh I will." Anderson handed the driver a hundred dollar bill. "Keep the change." He opened the door and got out of the cab.

Anderson walked into the hotel and up to the check-in counter. "Hi. Robert Anderson checking in."

"Oh yes, Mr. Anderson," the young blonde-haired girl behind the counter said smiling. "Room 506 sir." She handed him a keycard. "Breakfast is every morning from 5-10 a.m. and checkout is before 12 p.m. We also have a restaurant down that way and to the left," she said pointing behind Anderson to a lounge. "I hope your stay here is a wonderful one."

"Oh I am sure it will be…Miss…"

"Miss Calverly," she said blushing. "Miss Katie Calverly."

"Well Miss Calverly it was nice meeting you," Anderson said with a wink.

"Oh you too Mr. Anderson," Calverly said quickly. "And if there's anything else we can do for you here just give us a call."

Anderson paused for a moment. "Well actually I would like a wake up call at 6:30 tomorrow morning. And you can call me Robert." Anderson winked again.

"6:30," Calverly said with a smile as she typed the

time into the computer. "It was nice meeting you Robert."

Anderson walked towards the elevator with a smile on his face. He nodded his head and said softly to himself, "It will only be easier when I'm famous."

He got into the elevator and pressed number 5.

Ding...

The elevator doors opened. Anderson got out and looked for room 506. Once there he inserted the card into the door.

It didn't open.

"Oh shit," Anderson said angrily before trying again.

Still it did not work.

"Fuck this shit!" Anderson gently tried the keycard one more time. A green light flashed on the panel and he turned the handle.

It opened.

"About fucking time," he said loudly.

Anderson quickly checked out the room. It was nothing fancy. Inside was the usual; a king-sized bed, a television, a nightstand with a lamp, and a little chair with a table at its side.

"No little bar," he said aloud.

He threw his black bag on the chair and walked into the bathroom.

"Not bad," Anderson said, referring to the very clean, yet small, bathroom.

Immediately he turned on the shower, took off his clothes, and got in. The heat quickly fogged up the mirror.

"Ahhh, so refreshing," Anderson chanted.

In fifteen minutes time he was done. He turned off the shower and grabbed a towel from the rack above the toilet. He dried himself off and then turned to the fogged up mirror and toweled it off so he could see. He stared into the mirror at his naked reflection.

"Only the best," he said as he flung the towel over the bathroom door.

"Only the best," he repeated.

5

"Carol pull into this quaint little diner." Hank pointed to a small hut-like restaurant just off the road named *Mama's Place*.

"Oh dad," Keith began sarcastically, "You really know how to pick them."

Hank turned around and smiled at Keith. "Only the best Keith. Only the best."

"I'm sure they have everything we would want and we'll get something later tonight before we get to the hotel," Carol said as she pulled into a space among the many vacant ones and put the car in park.

"Looks closed dad," Anna said in a sympathetic tone.

Hank shrugged off her remark. "Nah, these old diners like it dark. It makes for a nice atmosphere."

"I'll check it first Hank." Carol opened her car door. "If it's closed we'll just go to the next place we see."

"Well then," Keith said looking at his mother. "I hope it's closed."

Carol walked up to the door and pulled the handle.
Locked.
She noticed a piece of paper taped to the glass.
Mama Barkley is on vacation until the 14th.

Mama's Place will be closed until then. Thank you.

Carol smiled. "That settles that," she muttered before returning to the car.

"It's closed," she said to everyone. "The owner is on vacation." Carol smiled some more. "But we could always come back on the fourteenth." She pulled out of the lot and got back onto the road.

Keith put his hand on his father's shoulder. Hank turned and looked at him. "Dad, usually darkness and a barren parking lot means closed."

"Well then," Hank said as he looked at the clock. It was 5:28 p.m. "The next restaurant is probably a little while away, so I hope you all can wait."

"Yes," the two children said in unison.

"And since it will be rather late, we cannot have a dinner before the hotel." Hank's stomach growled.

Anna laughed loudly.

Hank pretended nothing happened. "Munch on some of the snacks we brought." He opened a bag of chips, took a few out, and wildly placed them in his mouth. Crumbs fell to his lap. A small piece of chip remained on his upper lip, stuck in his goatee.

6

'*Bang. Bang. Bang.*'

The knock at the door made Anderson jump. He rubbed his heavy eyes and then glanced at the clock beside the bed where he was sprawled.

5:30 p.m.

"Who the fuck is this?" Anderson asked loudly. "Can I get no peace and quiet?"

The knock at the door sounded again.

"I'm coming. Hold on." Anderson grabbed the towel flung over the bathroom door and wrapped it around his waist. He pulled open the door and stared at the familiar looking man in a white uniform, standing in the hall.

"Do I know you?" Anderson asked.

"Not that I know of sir," the man replied. "I'm here to give you a message."

Anderson nodded. "Who's it from and what's it say?"

"It's from a Miss Katie Calverly, sir. She wants you to meet her in the downstairs lounge at seven."

"Oh," Anderson said as he took a deep breath. "Well thank you. You *sure* that I don't know you?"

"No sir," the man began, "But I'm *sure* I don't know you."

"Not yet anyway." Anderson smiled ear to ear. "Thanks again for the message, but next time call first." He shut the door slowly, but then quickly opened it again. "Wait."

The man's back faced Anderson. He turned around slowly.

"Hold on a second." Anderson walked quickly to the chair that held his black bag, almost losing his towel in the process. He propped up the towel again and tightened it more securely around his waist then placed his hand in his bag and took out a twenty-dollar bill. He walked back to the man. "Here."

The man smiled and took the money. "Thank you sir." He looked at Anderson for a moment. "You have something on your lip sir."

Anderson rubbed his mustache and took out the small crumb that rested there. "Well I guess I do. Potato chips in bed." Anderson smiled. "Wouldn't want Miss Calverly seeing that now would I?"

"No sir, I don't believe you would."

Anderson started to close the door. "Thanks again."

The man smiled and turned around.

The door shut.

"Is it really this easy," Anderson questioned himself. "Just think when I'm famous. How great will that be? A new girl every night."

He took off his towel and flung it over the bathroom door again. He glanced at the clock.

5:45 p.m.

"Plenty of time." He dropped to the floor and started doing pushups.

Another knock at the door sounded.

"Are you fucking serious?"

Anderson got up off the ground and grabbed his

towel. He walked to the door and opened it angrily. "What is…"

He didn't finish his sentence as he went quiet and his face dropped.

7

"Fastfood next exit mom," Keith shouted.

"I can see that," Carol replied.

"Well it's almost six now," Hank said after looking at the clock. "We'll get some food in our systems, some gas for the car, and in about four hours we'll be in a hotel."

"When are we going to get to Florida dad?" Anna asked as she wrote down another state on her paper.

"I'm guessing around three or four tomorrow. Depends when we leave the hotel in the morning."

"No dad, it depends on how fast mom drives in the morning," Keith chimed in.

Carol looked into the rearview mirror at Keith and gave him a cold stare.

Carol took the next exit and pulled into the first fastfood restaurant off the ramp.

"You guys go in and I'll fill up the car," Carol said. "Get me a number four without onions."

Hank and the kids got out of the car. Keith ran inside quickly while Anna stayed by her father's side, grabbing his hand.

"I'll help you walk dad," Anna said smiling.

"Thank you honey. Maybe you should help Keith learn how to be nice too."

Carol pulled aside a gas pump, got out of the car, and inserted a credit card into the slot on the pump.

"You on vay-kay-shone," a thick accented man said from behind her.

Carol looked nervously at the man, but said nothing.

"I noticed your plates. I ah-zumed you were on vay-kay-shone cuz of the Mazz plates." The man wouldn't stop talking although Carol pretended to not even notice him.

She picked up the hose and looked at him for a second then shook her head. She took the gas cap off and inserted the nozzle into the tank.

"I get bawed so I play road games sometimes and I was playin' one where you gotta find as many dif-fur-rant plates as you can. I hadn't seen Mazz plates yet. I'm on vay-kay-shone too. I'm goin' to Flaaa-ree-dah." The man continued, despite Carol's eyes still focused on the pump. "I'm from Kin-tuckee," he pointed to his red truck. "As you can prob-bab-lee see by my plate. Good 'ol DeWitt, a place like no otha." He pointed to his truck again and smiled. "At least that's what tha bumpa sticka sez."

Carol didn't understand how the man continued to speak despite her obvious disinterest. She remained quiet, but flashed a polite smile just to appease him.

"But I figured I'd spend some time with my fam-a-lee. They have a house nea Orlando. You eva bin to Orlando?" He asked.

She didn't answer.

"It's a love-a-lee place." He walked closer to Carol, holding out his hand. "I'm Walter Dunfellow. Nice to make your acquaintance."

Carol backed off a bit then finally gave in and shook the dirtied hand. "I'm Carol."

"That's a love-a-lee name ya know."

"Thanks." The nozzle jumped. She pressed it a few more times to make the price even. She closed the cap. "I have to get going, my family is waiting for me." She placed the hose back. "Nice to meet you."

"You too Carol."

She hurriedly got into the car and drove away.

Dunfellow just stood still where he had been and waved goodbye.

8

"Goodbye guys," Katie Calverly said, waving to her co-workers behind the desk.

"Bye Katie," another young girl responded. "Wait. What are you doing tonight? Want to go see a movie; we could catch a nine o'clock show. I get out in a half an hour."

Calverly looked at her watch.

6:33 p.m.

"I have to pick Tom up in Clermont. His car is having trouble, something about his radiator. I'll call you later about the movie though," Calverly replied, smiling at the girl.

"Oh no problem, I don't want to be a third wheel or anything."

"You wouldn't be, plus you could always get Ken to come too," Calverly said, pressing her friend for some gossip.

"Um...well Ken is probably not going to want to do that. But maybe I could get hooked up with that cute, strong guy you checked in today." The girl laughed and then blushed.

"He thought he was the hot stuff. I pretended to flirt with him for a tip. Damn tightwad. He doesn't seem like your type anyway."

"I was only kidding Katie. I would never ask him out. How strange would that be?" She smirked. "But because you checked him in I will continue to check him out." She laughed.

"Nice Jen." Calverly laughed too.

She glanced at her watch. "Oh I have to go. Tom expects me to be at his house by 7:15. That's not going to happen." She started walking to the exit. "I'll call you later."

A lady approached the desk. "Okay. Talk to you later then." Jen turned her attention to the woman. "May I help you?"

"Yes," the woman answered. "Tracy Barkley checking in."

9

Hank turned off the radio. "Here we are guys. This will be our hotel for the night. This time tomorrow we'll be watching the fireworks from the theme parks outside our hotel suite in sunny Florida."

Keith looked at the hotel his mother was pulling into. "If we can afford a suite in sunny Florida why do we have to stay in a sour in South Carolina?"

Carol laughed.

Hank turned to his son, a slight smile on his face. "We'll appreciate the Florida hotel even more if we stay here tonight."

"Why not stay at that one dad?" Anna asked, pointing to a large hotel that could be seen about an eighth of the mile down the road from their own.

Hank looked off into the distance and saw the hotel's bright lights. "That's a Vandermeer Hotel honey. That's just like the one we will stay at tomorrow." Hank patted his daughter on the head. "I'll go in and get the room."

Hank got out of the car and methodically limped toward the hotel entrance. Once inside he walked to the check-in desk and rang a small bell.

No one responded.

He rang it again.

Shortly after the second ring a slender old man with dark bags under his eyes came over to Hank. "May I help you?"

"Yes. I would like a double room please."

"Cash or credit?"

Hank pulled out his wallet. "Cash."

"That will be forty dollars."

Hank handed the old man two twenties.

"It will be room twenty-eight. Enjoy your st...ayyyy," the man's voice cracked.

Hank held back a chuckle. "We shall."

Hank left the hotel office and limped back to the car. "The nice old man gave us room twenty-eight. Sound familiar Carol?" Hank nudged her and winked.

"No," she answered. "Should it?"

"Well of course it should. That's the same number room we got at the hotel we stayed at on our honeymoon."

"No, Hank," she said, slightly angered. "We had room twenty-one."

"Oh." Hank tried to think of a joke. "I remember now. Room twenty-eight was seven doors down from ours. That's why I was confused." He took Carol's hand and kissed it.

"Not good enough Hank," she firmly replied as she parked in front of room 28.

10

"How old is the victim?" Detective Charles Gale asked a heavy detective while walking into the Vandermeer Hotel lobby.

"Twenty-eight sir," the heavy detective responded quickly. "A Mr. Robert Anderson, originally from Anaheim, California. He was here for the shooting of a television show. Some crime drama oddly enough."

"Oh an actor, huh?" Gale asked walking with the detective to the elevator.

"Yes sir." He pushed number 5. "Not a big name yet, but who knows if he could have been."

"Oh his name *will* be big Dan," Gale replied and then paused. He started again, "As soon as this gets out his name will be *real* big."

"It's quite a scene sir," Dan replied as the elevator doors opened. "The body is messed up pretty badly. One of the worst murders I've seen."

The two slowly walked down the hall towards the large crowd of police officers cramped near room 506.

"Weapon used?" Gale asked.

"Well *weapons* sir. There were two," Dan replied in less than a hurry. "An arrow and an axe."

They approached the room and Gale pushed some officers out of the way. "Detective Charles Gale coming in. Move away. Let me see the vic..." Gale stopped and gasped as he saw the dead man lying naked, sprawled out on the bed with a bloodied towel covering his face.

Blood painted every square inch of the room and the putrid smell of feces, innards, and blood filled the air. A few men were gagging at the sight, covering their mouths and noses.

Anderson's stomach and intestines were strewn all over the room. His entire stomach seemed to have been ripped open and his insides thrown out. A long piece of his small intestines draped over the bed like a rope. His lungs were atop the nightstand, his liver and kidneys found on the small table near the window, and his heart was in the bathroom sink.

Anderson's legs were spread open, but it was hard to see any part of his lower torso or groin. His body was completely slashed open. An axe was wedged deep in between his legs splitting his pelvic bone. His rib cage had been torn apart revealing what was left of his inside.

It was pretty much empty.

Everything seemed to have been thrown around the room as if Anderson's body was a suitcase and someone was looking for a prized possession.

Gale walked over to Anderson trying to avoid the blood and innards that carpeted the ground. He looked at the arrow that pierced through Anderson's trachea leaving a gaping hole in his neck. Gale began to slowly lift the towel that veiled Anderson's face.

11

'Beep. Beep. Beep. Beep.'
Tracy Barkley quickly awoke to the beckoning of her annoying alarm and peeled her eye mask off her face. She turned to the monotonous ringing at the side of her bed and pressed the 'off' button.

7 a.m.

Barkley yawned and stretched her arms in the air. She slowly sat up and flung her legs off the side of the bed.

"Why am I waking up so early?" She asked herself. "This is my vacation."

Regardless of her own questioning she was able to get herself out of bed, put on her slippers, and walk into the bathroom. She turned on the shower then turned toward the mirror.

She looked at herself and smiled then huffed at her appearance. She drew her face closer into the mirror and wiped the crust from her eyes.

She spun around and reached into the spraying water of the shower to check its temperature. "Just right." She took off her nightgown and got into the refreshingly warm water.

Grabbing one of the small bars of soap from the side of the shower she began lathering up her full-figured, mocha skinned body. "I feel like a damn giant holding these little soaps." She grabbed the small, one-use bottle of shampoo and poured some in her hand then massaged it into her straight black hair.

'Bang. Bang. Bang.'

There was a knock at the door.

"Come back later," Barkley tried to shout, but the water drowned her voice.

Another knock.

Barkley yelled again.

Barkley turned off the water with still a good amount of shampoo in her hair and running down her face.

She could hear the hotel room door opened.

Barkley grew quiet. "Who's there?"

'Bang. Bang. Bang.'

Now the knocks came from the bathroom door.

Barkley quickly reached her arm out of the shower, over to the knob and locked it. She took a deep breath. "Who's there?"

12

Gale took a breath as he continued to carefully draw the towel away from Anderson's face. He let out a sigh of relief when it was finally removed. Nothing was destroyed on Anderson's face. It was just as if nothing happened. Aside from the glossy, bloodshot eyes, he almost looked alive.

Gale started to speak, "It would seem as if the assailant stabbed the victim in the throat with the arrow weakening his ability to scream or call out for help." Gale stopped for a moment and placed the towel back over Anderson's face.

"Now by no means would Anderson just sit here and let the murderer kill him all too easily. Anderson is a big man. He probably charged at the assailant before the other weapon, the axe, was used. The wound starts at Anderson's sternum and runs all the way down to his pelvic bone. This certainly could not be done in one swift motion because no axe would be powerful enough and definitely no person would be powerful enough to wield such a force." Gale turned to the other officers who were in awe at the detective's skill.

"The uneven edges of the torn skin and different patterns of the broken bones in Anderson's rib cage would lead me to believe the murderer swung the axe at

Anderson numerous times. *Most* when he was already dead." Gale took a deep breath.

"I want to know everything you can tell me about this crime scene. Fingerprint every last inch of this place. Leave nothing unturned," Gale growled.

He continued, "I want to know why, when, and who killed this man." Gale walked towards the door side-stepping through the entrails on the floor.

"Detective Gale," Dan started.

Gale stopped and turned toward Dan.

"What do you think of this?" Dan held up a black bag.

"What's in it?" Gale questioned.

Dan slowly unzipped the black bag and looked inside. "Papers, sir. Lots of old papers."

Dan pulled out some of the yellowed newspaper clippings. One fluttered in the air like a leaf before eventually landing on his foot.

He looked down.

The paper read: *Garrison Solves Another Crime.*

13

The sun just started to peep through the blinds and into the room. A line of light just reached Hank's eyes. He clenched his eyes shut as if to ward off the sunlight, but it continued to fight back. Finally he arose from his sleep, threw off the covers, and walked over to the blinds to close them further, before the ray of light was able to reach the sleeping Carol.

With everyone else still asleep Hank got back under his covers and placed his head on his pillow. He closed his eyes and tried to get in a couple more hours of rest, but the sun's damage had been done. Now that he was up he had no choice but to remain up.

He looked at the phone on the side of the bed and thought about calling his office, but shook his head, remembering how he promised Carol he wouldn't. He gently pulled the covers off again and placed his feet on the floor. He sat up, leaned over, and propped his elbows on his knees and put his face in his hands. He massaged his face, rubbing his forehead and temples in a circular motion.

Hank rolled up his pajama pants to the knee and looked down at his leg. A large scar ran down the front of the kneecap to the halfway point of the calf. He reached over to the nightstand and grabbed the knee-brace that lay atop it. Carefully he wrapped the brace around his knee then put on his sneakers that lay at his feet. He slowly got up. Limping to the door Hank opened it slowly and then closed it quietly. Everyone still remained asleep.

The clock beside the bed flashed a glowing red 7:15 a.m.

Not knowing what to do until the last leg of the Florida drive began, Hank limped over to the motel lobby to get the morning paper.

"Good morning," a soft voice sounded from somewhere close by.

Hank, a bit startled, turned toward the sound and saw an old woman smiling behind the lobby's desk, her mouth vacant of teeth.

"Oh, good morning," Hank replied. "You have the paper?"

"Yes," the old woman replied as she reached under the desk. "It's the town paper. We don't have any big name papers."

Hank was confused. "Oh you don't?"

"No, they haven't been delivered yet," she replied.

"That's weird. It's not too early. They usually deliver papers real early in the morning, right?" Hank asked as he limped over to the counter.

The woman nodded. "Usually, but today it hasn't come yet."

"Well I have no choice," Hank said with a smile. "I'll take the town paper."

"Twenty-five cents," she replied.

Hank handed her a quarter. She handed him the paper.

"Thank you," Hank said smiling.

"You're very welcome."

He left the lobby and looked down at the paper he

just bought. The date on the top of the page was two days old. Hank let out an almost silent laugh then tucked the paper under his arm and limped toward the room.

He quietly opened the motel room door and peered at the others. They still slept. He sat down on the bed perching his back up against the headboard, a pillow placed behind him for support. He bent over and kissed Carol on the forehead. She smiled and turned over.

Hank glanced over the front page of the paper.

Nothing exciting, he thought. *At least not two days ago.*

"Honey," his wife said in a tired voice. "Why are you up? We're not leaving for another…" She squinted at the clock. "Three hours."

"Oh I know. Just habit I guess. Usually I go to work about now. Go back to sleep."

"I will." She kissed his arm. "I drove this whole way. This is my reward." She closed her eyes and drifted off to sleep again.

I wish it were that easy, Hank thought, referring to how quickly Carol fell back to sleep.

Hank looked over to the other bed where his children slept. They looked peaceful. Hank smiled and began reading the paper again.

14

"Room service," a lady's voice from outside the bathroom door answered.

Barkley let out a low, embarrassed laugh. "I didn't order room service."

"I know ma'am. It's compliments of the hotel to show our appreciation for your extended stay."

"Oh, well thank you. Leave it on the table." She was still shocked.

"Yes ma'am."

Barkley heard the patter of feet walk over to the end of the room and place the room service on the table. "Have a good day ma'am."

The door shut before Barkley could reply.

"Strange," she uttered. She turned the shower back on.

Washing the rest of the shampoo from her hair she grabbed the small bottle of conditioner and poured the gel-like substance into her palm and massaged her scalp with it. After all the soap was rinsed away she turned off the water, grabbed a towel, and dried herself off. She wrapped one big towel around her body, tucking one end into the other above her breasts, then grabbed a second towel and wrapped it around her head like a turban.

Barkley opened the door slowly as if afraid the room service lady would be waiting outside. She bent over and picked up her suitcase that lay on the floor and threw it onto the bed. Glancing over at the small table she saw the breakfast items that were brought to her room. An omelet, orange juice, toast, and some bacon adorned the tray. Barkley lifted the glass of juice and sipped some before turning to the window. She noticed the blinds weren't drawn and went over to shut them. The flashing lights below tempted her to look down at the street.

Barkley was amazed at the number of police cars outside the hotel. "Hmm," she huffed before closing the blinds.

She walked back over to her suitcase, unzipped it, and grabbed a pair of underwear and a bra from the top. Barkley hurriedly pulled on her underwear, still with her towel around her body. She dropped the towel to the floor and clasped her bra then looked inside her suitcase for shorts and a shirt.

Once dressed Barkley sat in the chair and began eating the breakfast that lay at the table. "Finally someone gets to cook for me," she said smiling. She brought the glass of juice up to her lips and looked outside again.

What is going on here? She thought.

15

Keith awoke about an hour and a half after Hank had. "Hey dad," he said, rubbing his eyes and turning to his father, who was still propped on the bed, now watching television with the sound muted. "What time is it?"

Hank looked at the clock then at Keith. "Almost nine. You got up right on time. We're going to leave in about an hour. Go take a shower before your mom or sister steal the opportunity from you."

"No problem." He hopped out of bed and walked into the bathroom, closing the door behind him.

Hank picked up the phone beside his bed and dialed the lobby. The voice on the other end said, "Hello, how can I help you?"

"I would like room service delivered to room twenty-eight please," Hank answered.

"What would you like?" The voice asked.

Carol awoke to see Hank on the phone. She glared at him. "I hope that's not who I think it is Hank. You promised me no phonecalls to work, remember?"

Hank shushed her and then covered the receiver with his palm and turned toward her. "It's room service honey."

16

"So what new information have we got?" Gale questioned Dan in his office while leaning back in his leather chair.

Dan moved closer to Gale's desk and sat down. "Not much sir. Forensics found virtually nothing. No fingerprints, no bootprints, nothing," Dan responded.

Gale's face got serious. "There's got to be something. There's no such thing as a perfect crime."

"The only thing that was a bit odd sir was the black bag full of newspaper clippings," Dan said as he leaned in even closer to Gale's desk. "Each one pertained to Agent Garrison."

Gale smirked. "Oh yes, Hank Garrison, the famed FBI man."

"Yes, sir," Dan said with a nod. "Each article was about him, some repeats, but for the most part each one was about the crimes he solved. The Rose murders, the Hunter murders, the…" Gale stopped Dan from continuing.

"I know all the murders he solved. I read about them too," Gale replied in a harsh tone. He paused and his voice softened, "A smart man. A very smart man. I worked with him about twelve years back on a murder case in New England. He knows how the criminal mind works. Scary, but certainly necessary." Gale scratched his cheek.

"Oh," Dan replied, a bit dumbfounded by Gale's walk down memory lane. "So you were Agent Garrison's partner?"

"No. It was one case. We worked apart, but together, I guess you could say."

"Why New England, sir?"

Gale looked at Dan. "Well I was originally from Maine and I believe Garrison was from Massachusetts." Gale paused and thought. "Yeah, he was from Mass. Gloucester I think it was. One of the murders took place in Garrison's jurisdiction and another in my own. After some time we realized they were connected, helped each other find the lowlife murderer. If I remember correctly before he was found seven New England residents had been brutally murdered, not unlike the victim today. Not long after that case I moved to Orlando and started this job and Garrison became an FBI man."

Dan looked stunned. "Well sir, I guess there is a lot to learn about you. I didn't even know you were from Maine."

Gale huffed. "Yep. Good old Gorham, Maine. Born and raised. It just goes to show you, there's a lot to learn about everyone. But first thing's first, let's learn more about Anderson. I'm sorry we got sidetracked."

"No sir it's actually a good thing."

"How so?" Gale asked with lifted brows.

"Well whoever murdered Anderson has some connection to Agent Garrison," Dan said excitedly as if he figured out some big piece of information.

Gale bit his lower lip. "What kind of connection?"

"Maybe friend. Maybe admirer. Maybe it was

Garrison himself. Just something." Dan thought he was on to something.

"What kind of sick shit would admire the type of man set out to get him?" Gale rhetorically asked. "And although it would be quite poetic for Garrison to be the murderer it also just doesn't seem to fit, he's not even around here."

"Well you did say Agent Garrison knows the minds of criminals," Dan said.

"True, but on the other hand, Garrison is no criminal," Gale protested. "But you are right about a connection. It would only make sense, especially with the clippings. It would be too easy to assume it was Garrison because of the clippings, and criminals are never too easy, but whoever murdered Anderson is trying to tell us something. These psychos always are."

"True sir. So what about a friend of Agent Garrison's?" Dan asked, hoping at least part of his criminal evaluation would have some legitimacy.

"Well where was Anderson from again?" Gale questioned.

"Anaheim sir, according to our records, but apparently he was renting a place in L.A. He got an audition at a casting call and was cast as a lead in that crime drama I was telling you about earlier. He flew into Orlando yesterday. The hotel records say he checked in at 4:58 p.m.," Dan responded quickly.

"How was he found?" Gale asked.

"Well you saw how he was found sir, everything was left as is."

Gale smiled a bit. "I mean *who* found him?"

"Oh, sorry sir. The manager found him. Anderson requested a wake up call at 6:30 a.m. He didn't answer the calls, so the manager went to wake him up. As soon as he saw Anderson he called the police," Dan said, a little embarrassed.

"Well I want everyone who spoke with Anderson, who saw Anderson, who even smelled Anderson from the time he arrived until the time he died to be questioned," Gale ordered loudly.

"I'll get on that sir." Dan shot up from the seat.

"Oh by the way Dan," Gale started, "What part did Anderson get in that crime show?"

"Lead detective I believe sir." Dan knew what Gale was thinking before he even finished his sentence.

"Strange coincidence, Dan. Very strange coincidence." Gale looked down at his desk. "You may go."

Dan turned around and walked out of Gale's office.

17

'Ring. Ring. Ring.'

Tom rolled over to answer the ringing phone.

"Hello," he answered in a gruff, tired voice.

"Is Katie Calverly there?" The voice on the line asked.

"Yeah, hold on a second." Tom cleared his throat and rolled back over, closer to where Katie slept. "Katie." He nudged her shoulder. "Katie wake up."

Katie turned her head to Tom. "What is it?"

"Someone's on the phone for you."

"Tell them to call me back. I'm tired." She returned to her pillow and closed her eyes.

Tom put the phone against his ear. "She wants you to call her back. She's sleeping."

"This is important. It's the Orlando police. We need to speak with Ms. Calverly now." The voice sounded mad.

"Hold on again," Tom replied, a bit confused.

He nudged Katie.

She made a grunting sound, but did not respond.

"Katie it's important," Tom said, nudging her again.

"Who is it? My mom? My dad? Jen?" She questioned angrily.

"None of those," Tom answered. "It's the cops."

18

Hank took his last sip of orange juice and placed the empty glass back on the tray. "Not a bad meal," he said sarcastically. "The bacon was just slightly older than the man who checked me in last night and this juice was freshly squeezed by the toothless lady I saw this morning."

Keith and Anna laughed.

"It wasn't *that* bad Hank," Carol said as she dried her hair with a towel.

"The eggs are good dad," Anna said as she scooped another spoonful into her mouth.

"That's because they aren't eggs," Hank responded with a smile.

"Oh stop it dad." A piece of egg flew from Anna's mouth and into Keith's plate.

Keith looked down. "Well I'm not eating anymore."

"You don't have to," Hank replied. "I hardly ate *any*…nevermind the *more* part."

"Everyone ready to go?" Carol asked.

"Yeah," the three replied in unison.

"Well let's get out of this place," Carol said as she started walking to the door.

Keith and Anna were right behind her. Hank

limped his way over.

Before exiting the room Hank scanned the area just in case something was forgotten.

Nothing.

He closed the door slowly and looked at his watch.

9:54 a.m.

Good timing, he thought as he hobbled towards the car.

19

Calverly took the phone from Tom's hand and placed it against her ear. "Hello," she nervously answered.

"Is this Katie Calverly?" The phone voice asked.

"Yes, this is her. Is there a problem?" Her eyes were still half shut.

"No Ms. Calverly. There isn't a problem. Nothing to be alarmed about. We just need you to come down to the Orlando police station, the one across from Keller's garage. Do you know where that is?"

"Yes I know. Did I do something wrong?" Calverly asked nervously.

"No, not at all. We would just like to question you about some things pertaining to a Mr. Robert Anderson." The voice was calm.

"I don't even know the guy," Calverly replied into the phone as she looked at Tom.

"You talking about me?" Tom mouthed to Calverly.

"No," she mouthed back.

"Oh we know that you do not personally know him, but we would still like to speak with you. You live in Clermont, correct?" The voice asked.

"Yes I do."

"So could you be here in about an hour? Around

eleven?"

"I will try."

"Okay, I will see you then."

"Okay." She gave the phone to Tom without saying 'bye.' He hung it up slowly.

"What did they want?" Tom questioned her.

Calverly got out of the bed, her naked body glistening in the morning light. "I don't know. Something about some guy that came into the hotel yesterday."

Tom pressed her for more information. "Why do they need to question you?"

Calverly was becoming agitated. "I don't know Tom. Enough with the questioning. I'll get enough when I get to the station."

"I wonder what it's about." Tom ignored her plea.

"I have to take a shower," she said, walking towards the bathroom.

"Can I join you?" Tom asked.

Calverly turned around.

Tom stared at her naked body, soft tanned skin, perfectly formed breasts, long thin legs.

The body of an angel, he thought.

He moved towards the edge of the bed. "Can I join you?" He asked again with a raised brow.

Calverly smiled and put a finger in her mouth. She took it out and rubbed it down her neck slowly. She brought it around her nipple. She licked her lips and blew a kiss to Tom. Slowly she caressed her body with her wet finger. Down her stomach. Slowly she ran the finger lower.

Tom sat wide-eyed at the bed.

Calverly brought her finger down further then opened her hand and placed her palm between her legs, covering her vagina. She bit her lower lip.

Tom stood up.

Calverly put a finger in the air and waved it side to side. "Uh uh." She turned around and walked toward the bathroom.

Tom sat back down. "You can cover that up all you want because I can still see your ass," he said as the bathroom door shut. He shook his head. "What a tease."

20

Walter Dunfellow's battered red truck pulled into the concrete driveway. He put the car in park and turned off the ignition then stuck his head out the window and smiled.

He stared at the Florida house that stood before him. It was painted light blue and the windows were gigantic. He looked at the roof to see the Spanish style design. "Ha," he huffed. He followed a little walkway that led to the front door. Two large white pillars stood in front of the small tiled veranda. Dunfellow tapped on one of the pillars. "Ha," he exclaimed again.

He approached the solid oak door, formed his hand into a fist, and then rapped it against the wood.

No one answered.

He put an opened hand above his forehead and pressed his face against the window beside the door. He couldn't see inside because the glare was too bad.

He rapped on the door again.

Still no answer.

He searched on the side of the door for a doorbell. He spotted one. *Am I that blind I couldn't have seen that before?* He thought.

He stuck out his index finger and brought it towards the bell.

The door opened before he could press the button.

"That bell doesn't work Walter," the man inside said laughing.

Dunfellow let out a half-hearted laugh. "Of course not An-dee. And nee-ther does the knockin' at the door. How are ya?"

"Oh I'm doing just fine Walter. We expected you a little later. We were in the pool so we didn't hear the knocking. Come on in?" Andy waved Dunfellow into the house.

"Nice place you got hea," Dunfellow said looking at the high-ceilinged open room.

"Yeah, a little better than that dump we had the last time you showed up," Andy replied smiling. "Follow me, Kelly and the kids are in the poolroom."

Dunfellow followed Andy into the living room and to an opened door.

"I'll give you the tour later," Andy said, noticing Dunfellow's wandering eyes.

"Yes. That would be good."

Andy stopped and held out his arm. "After you."

Dunfellow walked into the fenced in poolroom. He looked at the woman who was sitting down rocking a baby. "Lit-tul sis, how are ya?"

"I'm good Wally. How are you?" Kelly answered.

"Not too shabby." Dunfellow kissed Kelly's cheek and then turned to the two kids swimming inside the pool. "Hey guys."

The two children turned away and swam to the furthest edge of the pool.

"That's how your nephews respond when you visit once in a blue moon," Kelly said laughing.

"Well I don't have the mun-nee you do. I can't take a vay-kay-shone whenever," Dunfellow answered in a slightly angry tone.

"Let's not get into this. Sit down." Kelly motioned to the chair.

Dunfellow sat.

"Hey Walter, want something to drink?" Andy asked from inside the house.

"Juice if ya have it."

Andy walked over to the refrigerator and opened it. "Is apple okay?"

"That would be fine." Dunfellow motioned to Kelly for the baby. "Let me hold the lit-tul one."

Kelly handed the baby over gently. "Make sure you support his head."

"Kel, I know how to han-dul bay-bees," Dunfellow replied, looking at his sister. "I held you when you were lit-tul." Dunfellow placed the baby in his cradled arms. "Not to men-shone I held Katie when she was lit-tul."

"Yeah I think she may have been the last baby you ever held." Kelly smiled at her older brother.

"You may be right," Andy said as he walked over to Dunfellow. He placed the glass of apple juice on the table.

Dunfellow looked up at Andy. "Thank you. Where is she anyhow?"

Andy replied before Kelly got the chance, "She's at her boyfriend's house. She said she'd be by for dinner."

Dunfellow quickly looked at Kelly. "You let her stay at her boy-fren's house?"

"She's not a baby anymore Wally," Kelly responded then turned her head to the pool. "She's almost twenty now."

"Lit-tul Katie is almost twen-tee." Dunfellow smiled at the sleeping baby nestled in his arms. "One day ya'll be twen-tee." He tapped the baby's nose.

"Time to get out guys," Kelly said loudly to the two swimming kids. "You're going to get all wrinkled."

Dunfellow turned to the kids. "Ya, how do you think I got like I yam?"

The two held their noses and dunked their heads under the water.

Kelly stood up and turned to her husband. "That's why I don't like them swimming this early. They never listen."

Andy shrugged.

Two small heads bobbed back above the water. "Get out and get dressed. We're going to get lunch soon," Kelly said with a stern face.

The two boys swam to the steps and got out.

Kelly looked at Dunfellow. "C'mon. I'll show you around."

21

The waves crashing against the shore played like a constant melody. Back and forth. Back and forth. The sun beat down hard on Daytona Beach turning its soft sand into fiery weapons that bit those who walked on them. Bikini clad woman tiptoed their way around until they found open areas to spread their towels, while their wincing boyfriends followed, trying to forget about the hot sand beneath their feet.

Barkley found a small clearing near some kids building a sand castle and pulled out her towel. She grabbed the corners and threw it up into the air then slowly brought it down. It fell jaggedly over the sand. Barkley picked it up again.

"Oh sorry," Barkley apologized to an older man laying a few feet away as a gust of wind blew some of the towel's sand into his face. The towel gently fell to the ground.

Still jagged.

"Hmm." Barkley fixed the edges and straightened out the towel not wanting to have more sand enter the eyes of the man beside her. She sat on the towel and turned to her bag on the sand.

Barkley unzipped the bag and rummaged through it. She pulled out a bottle of sun block and a book. Placing the book at one corner of the towel she pressed in the sun block cap, turned it over, and squeezed a fair amount into her hand. She lathered up her arms before applying more into her hands and rubbing it on her legs.

Barkley pressed the cap closed and put the bottle back in her bag then grabbed the book.

The Assault.

A murder mystery.

She lay back, pressing her head against the soft sand. "I could get used to this," she said quietly. She turned her head to the left and saw the older man lying on his own towel reading a book.

She turned her head to the right to see a young couple making out. The girl was wearing a pink G-string bikini and small pink top. The guy was groping her wildly. Barkley noticed his visible erection.

"Ugh." She turned back.

As far as Barkley could see lay beautiful women and gorgeous men. She thought, *I'm surrounded by models. A fat girl surrounded by models.* She turned to her left again and looked at the older man. *Models and an old white man. An old, wrinkled white man.*

She nestled her head into the sand some more before finally shooting up and grabbing her bag from the side of the towel. She placed the bag under her head and brought the book to her face. She opened the front cover then quickly flipped to where her bookmark held her spot. She took it out and stuck it in the sand beside her.

She brought the book closer to her eyes, forming a shadow over her head, blocking out the powerful sun.

Barkley began reading: *Benjamin lay still on the ground. Blood oozed from his head. He opened his eyes once more and watched in horror as the bat came back down upon his face.*

'Thunk,' the bat sounded as it smashed into Benjamin's skull.

'Thunk.' Again.
And again.
And again.

22

"Again dad. Let's play again," Anna chanted from the backseat.

"You're not tired of this game yet?" Hank spun around asking.

Keith spoke before Anna could. "I am."

Anna glared at Keith, giving him a shove. "I'm not."

"One more time, then we'll play your license plate game." Hank turned around and looked at Carol.

She glanced back at him for a moment.

"I didn't expect that they'd like this game so much," Hank admitted.

"It's not *they*, it's Anna." Carol smiled and looked into the rearview mirror back at Anna. "How many states have you found already?"

Anna pulled out the crumpled up piece of paper from her pocket. "Um…" She started counting aloud, pointing to each one on the page. "Twenty-three."

"Only twenty-three," Keith shot back. "You've been writing down stuff since we left and you *only* have twenty-three?"

Anna put the piece of paper back in her pocket.

"It's a good start Anna," Carol said without taking her eyes off the road.

"Yeah," Anna agreed. "Now let's play dad's game again."

Hank laughed. "Okay we'll start with…um 'ball'"

Anna quickly shouted, "Game."

Keith looked at Anna and smirked. "Game ball. We made it back to the original word."

"Record time Keith," Hank said without turning around.

Keith looked out the window at the passing cars. "What time is it? When will we be there?"

Carol looked at the clock. "It's almost eleven. We'll stop in an hour for lunch and we should be there by three."

Keith nestled his head into the door. "Wake me when we get there."

"Dad, another starting word," Anna pleaded.

"You sure you want to play this game?" Hank asked, already a bit tired of his own game. "We could play the 'I'm Adam I come from Alaska…dah…dah…dah…game.'"

"We'll play that one next dad," Anna responded.

"Okay." Hank paused, searching for a good word. "The starting word is 'bat.'"

23

"Excuse me," Calverly said as she approached the hefty policeman, sitting behind the station desk, drinking coffee. "I was called about an hour ago, something to do with Robert Anderson. I'm Katie Calverly."

The officer removed the drink from his lips and placed it on the table. His eyes widened.

"Oh yes. Detective Gale has been expecting you." The officer's face turned solemn. "Terrible thing to happen to such a young man."

Calverly squinted a bit. "Terrible?"

"Yes. Terrible," the officer repeated as if Calverly was only agreeing. He put his hands on his desk and pushed himself up. "Follow me."

Calverly and the officer walked down a long hall of offices, passing several police at who were typing on their computers and talking on the phones. A few men eyed Calverly.

Calverly turned her head quickly.

The officer stopped at a door and knocked.

"Come in," a voice from inside responded.

The officer's chubby hand grabbed the doorknob and turned it, pushing it open. Inside were three men.

"You must be Katie?" Gale stood up from his chair and pointed to a seat in front of his desk. "Have a seat."

The door closed.

Gale offered his hand to Calverly. Calverly took it in hers and shook it.

"I'm Detective Charles Gale and these are Detectives Daniel Eronie and Jonathon Harlowe." Gale pointed to the two men sitting beside Calverly.

Eronie held out his hand. Calverly shook it.

Harlowe dipped his head down as if to say 'hello.'

Calverly still remained silent.

Gale continued, "We're the leading Detectives on the Robert Anderson case."

"Case?" Calverly finally spoke. "What case?"

"Early this morning Anderson was found dead in his room." Gale finally sat back down.

Calverly's face dropped. "That's awful. How did it happen?"

"No need to explain that, Ms. Calverly. Not now anyway." Gale leaned back on his chair.

"Why am I here?" Calverly was a little stunned. "I don't even know him."

"Just procedure." Gale rolled his chair closer then placed his arms on the desk. "I want to talk to everyone that spoke with him since he arrived. You, I am told, checked him in."

Calverly quickly replied, "Yes I did. But I only spoke with him for a minute. I handed him his keycard and he went on his way. It was small talk."

Gale stared at Calverly. "Oh I don't doubt it was anything more than that. Just following procedure."

Calverly was still a bit confused. "You don't think I had something to do with his death, do you?"

"No, not at all," Gale reassured her. "I just want to target who could have done it. I have to retrace his steps. Apparently you were the last person to see him alive." Gale leaned back again. "Do you know when you saw him last?"

Calverly thought for a moment. "Um...not sure, maybe around five. My shift ended at 6:30 and it was over an hour before that."

Eronie and Harlowe doodled something in their notepads.

Calverly nervously glanced over at them.

"Was Anderson alone or with someone?"

"He was alone. I just checked him in. It was a one bedroom room," she replied.

"Did he look scared or nervous at all? Anything that would make you think something at the time?"

"He looked normal. Happy. If anything he was flirtatious."

"I see. What did he have with him? Any luggage?" Gale asked.

"Yes. I'm not entirely sure, but I think he had just a small bag. I see so many people check in every day that I wouldn't remember exactly how much baggage he came with."

"Okay. I can understand that. Do you remember if he took the stairs or the elevator?"

"He took the elevator. I know he was on a higher floor," Calverly answered.

"Yes, we know that too. But do you know for sure he took the elevator or are you just assuming he did because he was on a higher level? He was a strong guy so maybe he liked the exercise," Gale noted.

"No. I'm positive he took the elevator. It's rare that anyone takes the stairs. But I know he took the elevator."

"So you are entirely certain?"

Calverly wanted to ask why Gale cared so much about the elevator, but refrained from doing so. "Yes."

"Do you remember if anyone entered the elevator with him?" Gale questioned.

"I don't know. Possibly. The lobby was crowded. Whether I said 'yes' or 'no' I wouldn't be certain."

"So the lobby was crowded?"

"Yes. It usually is at around five. A lot of people are coming back from beaches or other places," Calverly responded.

"Was anyone in the lobby suspicious looking? Anyone with a big bag? Something noticeable?"

"I can't say that I recall. Like I told you, I see so many people. After awhile they all look alike, no one is more suspicious looking than the next person," she answered.

"And after Anderson left for his room you never saw him again that night?"

"No, I never did. But I suppose he may have come back down without me noticing he had."

"Okay," Gale nodded his head. "So Miss Calverly you said that you left work at 6:30?"

"Yeah," she replied quickly.

"And where did you go after work?" "To my boyfriend's house," Calverly answered in a jumpy voice, suddenly seeming more nervous than before. Her eyes were a bit glossy.

Gale looked at her and grabbed a box of tissues from his desk drawer. "Are you upset?"

"No," Calverly lied.

"Good, because there's no need to be. No one thinks you did anything. We just want to solve this case as quickly as possible." Gale exhaled.

"Well I don't know anything. I'm in shock right now." A tear fell from her eye and rolled down her cheek. She pulled out a tissue from the box and patted it dry.

"I understand Miss Calverly." Gale squinted at Calverly then looked at Eronie and Harlowe.

Gale slowly stood up. Eronie and Harlowe followed suit.

Calverly still sat. She wiped another tear from her cheek.

"Jon, please show Miss Calverly to the exit." Gale looked at Harlowe then down at Calverly.

"Yes, sir," Harlowe quickly replied.

Calverly got up.

Gale gently touched her hand before she turned around. "This isn't to get out. Not until we find out more information. We do not want the press to hear about this yet. All hell would break lose."

Calverly nodded.

"Right this way miss," Harlowe said as he held out his arm, waiting for Calverly to walk out first.

She opened the door. Gale caught her attention and she turned around and faced him. "Thank you Miss Calverly. We'll be in touch."

She turned back towards the door and walked out. Harlowe followed.

Gale looked at Eronie. "Dan, find out all you can about Ms. Calverly."

Eronie's head bent to the side like a dumbfounded dog. His brows lowered. "You don't think she had something to do with this now do you? Look at her size, how could she ever have killed a man like Anderson?"

"Oh no, no Dan. I don't think she had anything to do with the murder," Gale responded then took a deep breath. He exhaled slowly. "For one thing forensics says he was killed at around 7 p.m. She was probably banging her boyfriend by then."

Eronie was about to speak, but held back.

"But..." Gale paused and looked down at his desk before continuing, "I do believe there's something fishy here. She was the last person to see him alive. There's got to be a connection."

Gale looked back up at Eronie.

"Well, maybe the connection is that there is no connection, sir." Eronie thought he sounded poetic.

"There's always a connection, Dan. Always." He sat back down. "Find out what you can about Anderson's homelife, back in California. I want to know if he's got enemies. Hell, I want to know if he's got friends."

"Yes, sir." Eronie spun around towards the door.

24

The aroma of alcohol and urine still filled the apartment's air, but a new scent had been recently added.

The stench of death.

Yellowed newspapers carpeted the floor, just as it always had. On top of the torn and tattered plaid couch was a trash bag half full of clothes.

A bloodied white sleeve was draped over one side of the large, dark green bag. Blood slowly dripped down the sleeve and onto the couch. The cushion sopped up the red liquid.

On the floor lay two blood stained shoe slip-ons, the kind used by surgeons in the operating room. On the side of them were two once white gloves, now drenched in blood. They formed a puddle on the floor. The blood was quickly drying up and becoming sticky.

The bathroom was dirtier this time. The floor was still damp from whoever had showered last. Damp from whoever tried to wash their bloodstained body. A towel covered in watered-down blood was thrown to one corner. It had been used to dry off a killer. The reddened hue of the towel added color to the off-white room.

Someone had been here recently.

A murderer had been here.

The sink was still spotless and glistening, but the mirrored medicine cabinet was now slightly cracked. The room was not nearly as perfect as it had been before. It was no longer the sanctuary of cleanliness from the disgust that surrounded it. It was now solely a room of sinful sanitation, but whoever tried to wash away their sins didn't do so completely.

Sin still lurked.

A clean towel was draped over the bathroom door, waiting to be used. Waiting to be thrown into the corner with the other.

The suit that had been hanging from the doorknob was missing. Only a bent hanger was left.

The kitchen was also changed. A can of diet cola was left on the table, a half eaten ham sandwich by its side. Flies gathered around the meat. Happily they flew to and from the feast. All at once a swarm would land on the sandwich, rub their little legs together, eat what they could, fly away, then fly back for more.

It was nonstop repetition.

To and from the flies gathered.

Back and forth.

The small storage room full of tools and other objects had been invaded. The items that crowded the room were even less in order than they had been.

Someone had been searching for something.

The same newspaper clipping that had been fastened to the wooden floorboards by an arrow and an axe still remained. It was much more tattered than before. The headline was almost undecipherable. A large knife now stabbed the upper section that was once pierced by an arrow. The lower section was vacant of the sharpened axe that once befriended the spot.

In its place lay a wooden bat.

25

"Woah!" Anna looked at the long stone building before her. "It's so big."

Hank pulled out some of the luggage from the car. "Could use some help here."

Anna ran over and took her suitcase. Keith and Carol walked over to the car.

"Need a hand with that ma'am?" A red-haired man walked over to Carol as she hoisted a big black suitcase from the back.

"No, I think we're all set." Carol smiled at the freckled faced man and turned toward Hank. "I'll park the car and meet you guys in the lobby."

"Oh not necessary ma'am, I can park it for you," the man interrupted.

Carol looked at the man and then back at Hank. She gave her husband a nod then handed the keys over to the man.

He politely took them in his white-gloved hand. "Name please?"

"Garrison," Carol replied.

"Well Mrs. Garrison, the keys will be in the lobby

when you need them. I hope you have a great stay at the Vandermeer." He walked around to the driver's side and got in.

The car window rolled down.

"Ma'am," the man picked up the cellphone off the dash. "Would you like your cellphone?"

Carol turned to Hank. He smirked.

"Yes thank you." She took the phone from the man's outreached hand.

The window rolled back up and the ignition started.

The man pulled away.

"So what do you think Keith?" Hank questioned his son.

"Much better than last night's dump," Keith was quick to reply.

"I agree." Hank limped over to the door, dragging his bag behind him. "Let's check in."

Anna and Keith hurried inside.

Carol walked side by side with Hank.

Hank looked around the open lobby. It was immense. Black plush leather sofas filled the room. Solid oak tables were placed perfectly in front of each. Atop each table were a wide selection of newspapers and magazines.

Not one paper was even a day old.

Hank looked down to see the marble floor. It looked as if it were polished recently. It sparkled with the reflection of the sun's rays.

Hank looked up. The ceiling was all glass. The sun shined through the above windows and down on the Garrisons.

It was heaven.

"Wait here for a minute while I get our room number," Hank said to his family.

Anna ran to the nearest sofa and plopped herself in it. Keith threw down his bag and sat on it. Carol stayed standing.

Hank slowly hobbled over to the check-in counter.

"Hello sir," Jen said cheerily. "Welcome to the Vandermeer. How may I help you?"

"Hello. Just checking in. Hank Garrison." He smiled.

Jen looked down at the computer and began typing. "Ah yes. Garrison. A two bedroom suite, correct?"

"Yes, that's correct."

"Okay." Jen smiled again. "You will be in room 132. It's on the first floor," she pointed to her right at the elevators thirty feet away. "You can use those elevators or the stairs. Breakfast is served from 5-10 a.m. in the dining room, which is right around the corner on your left. If you would like dinner we have one of the finest restaurants in the area." She pointed behind Hank. "It's in the lounge. Checkout is before noon. Is there anything else you would like to know?"

Hank thought for a second. "No. I think that will do it."

Jen nodded. "Well okay. If you need anything just let us know." She handed Hank the keycard.

"I will. Thank you."

"Have a wonderful stay at the Vandermeer." Jen looked down at the computer screen and began typing again.

26

Barkley gently touched her left shoulder. "Oww." The tender sunburned skin ached. "Just my luck," she said aloud as she walked over the hot sands to her rental vehicle. "First full day in Florida and already I'm in pain."

She grabbed a white t-shirt from her bag and slowly put it on, stopping for a second to get her head through the hole.

She continued onward.

Arriving at her car she opened up the door and threw her towel in the backseat. Barkley placed her bag on the driver's seat, reached into it, and pulled out her shorts. Holding them in front of her she placed her left leg into them and then her right. She pulled them to her waist, buttoned them, and then pulled up the zipper.

Slowly she got into the car, removed the bag on the seat and placed it in the passenger's seat. She gently touched her shoulder again. "Ow."

She inserted the key into the ignition and turned it. The car radio blared on.

A baseball pre-season game was on.

Marty Bulworth steps up to the plate. He's batting .148 in the early going of the preseason, but he has a lot of potential to get the bat...

Barkley reached over to the volume knob and turned it lower. She glanced at the clock.

4:15 p.m.

An hour and a half later Barkley pulled into the front of the Vandermeer and waited for the quick-paced freckled man to approach her window.

"Barkley," she said with a smile then reached over and grabbed her bag.

"Yes, ma'am. The keys will be in the lobby." The man opened the car door for Barkley and helped her out.

"Thank you."

He looked in the back. "Would you like your towel ma'am?"

"Oh, no thank you." Barkley turned around and walked to the hotel's doors.

Barkley quickly walked over to the elevators, wanting to get into her room and alleviate the throbbing shoulder pain a day at the beach had caused.

She pressed the 'up' arrow, looked up, and watched as the numbers decreased.

5...

4...

3...

2...

1...

'Ding.'

Barkley got into the elevator and pressed number 4.

It started moving upward. She glanced at the top. The number 1 lit up.

'Ding.'

The doors opened.

Carol and Anna, standing in the hall, looked at Barkley.

"You going down?" Carol asked.

"Oh no," Barkley replied. "I'm going to four."
"Okay we'll wait for the next one. Sorry."
The doors closed before Barkley could say anything.
2...
3...
'Ding.'

Barkley quickly got out, turned to the left and walked down the hallway. She stopped in front of room 412.

Barkley searched her bag for the keycard.

No avail.

She rummaged through again.

Still nothing.

"Ugh," Barkley grunted. "What a day."

She spun around and started walking in the direction of the elevators.

Once in front of the elevator she pressed the down arrow and waited.

The doors opened. A man stood in the elevator. His hands held behind his back.

"Going down?" He asked in a gruff voice.

"Yes, lobby. Forgot my keycard," she answered, trying to make conversation.

The man smiled. "It happens to the best of us." He looked up at the numbers.

Barkley looked upward too.

4...
3...

The man threw out his arms and pushed Barkley hard to the side. Barkley fell to the floor of the elevator, flabbergasted.

"What's wrong," she asked, trying to get back up.

He looked at her then turned back and pressed a

large red button.
Emergency stop.
'Ding.'
The elevator came to an abrupt halt.
Barkley let out a helpless shrill scream.

27

"Four," Hank said, holding out four fingers to the hostess.

"Right this way." She led the group over to a booth.

Anna excitedly jumped in. Keith climbed in next to her, pushing her further inward. Carol and Hank sat across from their two kids.

"Your waiter will be right over," the hostess said, handing them some menus.

"Thank you," Carol replied.

The kids anxiously grabbed the menus and started looking for something delectable to calm their hungry stomachs.

Hank checked his back pocket. "Oh honey I forgot my wallet."

"Forgot it?" Carol sounded shocked.

"Just in the room. Do you think I'd be this calm if I left it back at that motel?"

Carol looked relieved. "Oh. I have my credit card."

"No. I don't want you to pay."

"You pay my credit card bills Hank." Carol smiled and grabbed Hank's hand, squeezing it tightly.

"Oh I know I do dearie," he replied sarcastically and squeezed her hand back. "But I'd still feel more comfortable if I had my wallet."

Hank quickly looked over the menu. "Get me the filet. Medium-well. Steak fries and rice pilaf as the sides. I'm going to run back to the room." He looked at the two kids. "Otherwise you two will be paying."

"Okay." Carol looked down at the menu in her hands. "What do you want to drink?"

"Lemonade." Hank got up and walked away.

Hank's knee gave out a bit and he grabbed it in pain. He stopped and then began massaging it.

"Ecks-scooze me sir," a tall, skinny man said after bumping into Hank. "You oh kay?"

Hank didn't look up at the man. He was still massaging his knee. "Yes. Sorry it's my fault. I stopped short."

"No problem." The man walked over to his booth and started to sit.

28

"What took you so long?" Kelly asked her older brother. "Your food is getting cold."

"You shore do soun' like a mother, Kel," Dunfellow said as he sat down next to Andy. "There was a line in the bathroom. Not to men-shone I almost killed someone."

"What?" Kelly asked.

Dunfellow smiled. "Well not real-lee sis.' I bumped into that guy, seems like he has a bum knee or something.'" He pointed to Hank who had finally made it outside the restaurant and into the lobby.

Andy looked. "What did you do? Hit his leg with a bat Walter?" Andy laughed.

Dunfellow smiled. "Nope. I just bumped into him. I hope I'm not the one who caused that limp of his, otherwise my first day in Fla-ree-dah will lead to an eck-spen-sif lawsuit." He stabbed a piece of cut steak and brought it into his mouth.

"Well I would be happy to be your attorney Walter. If that so happens." Andy smirked as he finished off his last piece of fish. "Who wants dessert?"

The two young boys raised their hands. "Me. Me. I do. I do."

"Okay. Okay. You can put down your hands, this

isn't school," Kelly hushed them.

The smaller boy turned toward his sister, sitting beside him. "Katie, what do you usually ask for us when we come here?"

Calverly rubbed her younger brother's head. "Mudpie," she replied with a smile.

Her father looked at Calverly. "And don't even bother asking for dessert for free Katie. You do that enough. I'd rather pay," Andy said.

"*Rather* pay?" Calverly asked with amazement in her eyes. "Who would rather pay for anything? We should get something free. I don't get paid enough to work here to not have some sort of benefit."

"You don't work at this restaurant," Andy responded.

"Same difference. The Vandermeer owns this place." Katie turned to her brothers again and nudged them as if asking for their opinion on the matter.

"Regardless. I am paying." Andy looked at Dunfellow.

Dunfellow smiled and turned to Calverly with a shrug. "Father knows best."

29

A group of six wedged into one elevator. Hank tried to limp over to it and get in, but the doors closed just before he made it. He pressed the adjacent elevator's 'up' arrow.

'*Ding.*'

The doors didn't open.

He looked up at the numbers.

Stuck on 3.

He tried again.

Still nothing.

He turned to the other elevator. Its numbers were slowly climbing upward. He turned back to the stuck one.

He pressed the button again.

Nothing.

"Sometimes it takes awhile," a man's voice said from behind the check-in counter. "Give it some time." He began walking over.

Hank turned to him. "Oh no rush."

"What floor are you on?" The man asked.

"Just up one," Hank replied.

"You could always take the stairs." He pointed to his left at a door a few feet away.

Hank looked down at his knee. "I don't think that will do."

The man looked at Hank's knee and noticed the bulging brace under the pants.

"Oh I don't suppose it would." He pressed the 'up' arrow.

'*Ding.*'

"Here we go. It's working now." The man watched the numbers slowly light up.

3...

2...

1...

'*Ding.*'

The doors glided open.

The man's eyes widened as he brought his hand to his mouth, covering it in horror.

Hank stood still.

Murder had even followed him on vacation.

30

Gale answered his cellphone after the first ring.

"Detective Gale?" The man asked.

"Yes. Who's this?" Gale sounded angered.

"It's Brian Fullmer, sir. Manager at the Vandermeer Hotel," Fullmer spoke slowly.

"Oh yes. Didn't Detective Eronie tell you I would speak with you tomorrow?" Gale asked in a harsh voice.

"Yes, it's not about that…it's…um…it's…." Fullmer stammered, unable to get the words out of his mouth.

Gale sounded fed up. "What is it?"

"It's happened again, sir. Another body was found." Fullmer finally got out what he was trying to say.

"Where is it? Has anyone seen it?" Gale sounded frustrated, as if Fullmer should have answered all his questions before he had asked them.

"It's in the elevator. No one has seen it, except me and another gentleman. He says he's FBI sir. He moved the body to the functions floor so none of the guests would have to see it."

"What? He moved the body!?" Gale was furious. "He's touching the evidence?"

"He didn't touch the body sir. He just took the elevator to the functions floor. Just so no one would be in hysterics. He said he was FBI," Fullmer repeated.

Gale started yelling, "Who gives a flying fuck who he is? As far as I'm concerned he's interfering with the crime scene. I'll be there shortly." He hung up the phone.

Hank took his final step and pushed open the door to the stairway.

He limped over to Fullmer and handed him a key. "Here's the key to the elevator." He sounded out of breath. "So much for not taking the stairs." He seemed calm, as if nothing had gone wrong.

He had seen this type of stuff many times before.

He was used to it.

"Thank you, sir. I called the police and the Detective on this case. They should be here shortly." Fullmer was still shook up.

Hank looked at Fullmer, he was a bit in shock. "What case? There isn't a case yet. This just happened."

"Well not exactly, sir. Someone...died in this hotel yesterday." Fullmer was slow to tell Hank.

"*Someone* died? *Someone* died? Do you think that woman just died in that elevator? Did you see her!? Did you see what was in that elevator!? I'm sorry, but people don't die like that. You get murdered like that." Hank, for the first time, sounded angry.

"There's more to it sir. When the police get here you can ask them if you'd like. I really shouldn't be getting into this."

Hank looked at the elevator as a family approached it.

"Out of order," he said loudly. "Use the other one or the stairs."

The family looked at Hank and Fullmer. "Hmmph," the wife huffed and pressed the 'up' arrow of the adjacent elevator.

"You should lock that elevator before someone sees the real place you're running here," Hank rudely said to Fullmer. "And maybe you should tell your precious guests some of the happenings in this place."

Fullmer remained quiet.

Hank turned toward the restaurant. "I will be back after I get my family out of this establishment of yours." He limped over to the restaurant.

Fullmer walked over to the elevator, inserted the key, and locked it.

31

"What took so long?" Carol asked Hank, sounding a bit worried.

"Long story honey." Hank was anxious. "I'll explain later." He was still standing.

"You look tired. You okay?" Carol tapped the seat next to her. "Sit down."

Hank slowly sat. "I think it's best if we leave honey."

"Now?" Carol was surprised. "We're going to get our meals soon."

Keith took a sip from his drink and grabbed a buffalo wing, ignoring his parents' conversation.

"Where we going to go dad?" Anna asked her father.

"Somewhere else sweetie." Hank was talking quickly. "Let's just go."

Carol grabbed Hank's leg and squeezed it. "You're acting crazy." She pulled up her hand and went to grab a wing.

Her fingers were covered in blood.

"Hank!" Carol screamed. "You're bleeding!"

The children looked up at their mother's fingers as soon as she spoke and their mouths opened.

She went to touch his leg again.

Hank grabbed her arm before it got to him.

He reached over the table and grabbed a napkin from a holder. He started to wipe off Carol's fingers.

She gave him a weird look. "Hank what's wrong with you? You're scaring me."

The blood still stained her fingers.

Hank didn't respond. He reached into his lemonade and grabbed a few ice cubes and began rubbing them on Carol's fingers.

The blood slowly dripped off.

"Guys," Hank began as he turned to Keith and Anna, "Me and your mother have to talk for a minute. If the food comes have the waiter wrap it."

"Why?" Keith asked.

"Just do it Keith," Hank said sternly.

"Hank please tell me what's going on," Carol pleaded for an answer.

Hank stood up. "Come with me." He offered his hand to Carol and helped her out of the booth.

"I wonder what happened?" Anna asked her brother while picking up a wing.

"They are probably going to have sex." Keith wiped his sauced up hands off on a napkin.

Anna nearly dropped the wing she held. "Ugh. You're disgusting. I'm telling mom and dad."

"Go ahead I'm sure they'll want to hear that come from your mouth." Keith sipped his cola.

Anna bit the wing.

Hank stood with Carol near the restrooms.

"Now what is it Hank? What's wrong?" Carol prodded Hank for answers.

"When I went to get my wallet." Hank paused for a second. "Promise me you won't get worried."

Carol's eyes welled up. "Hank, you're scaring me. What's the matter?"

"Just promise me," he repeated.

"I promise."

"When I went to get my wallet there was...." Hank didn't know how to tell his wife. "There was a dead body."

A chill ran down Carol's spine and she shook as if stuck in the cold. "Dead?"

Hank rubbed his wife's shoulders trying to calm her down.

"Murdered." Hank watched as a tear fell down Carol's cheek. "There's more to it than just that Carol, but right now we have to get out of here."

Carol couldn't speak.

"I'll have someone get the luggage with me and we'll go to another hotel. You get the kids and the food and wait outside. I'll get you the car keys and you can meet me at that other nice hotel just ten miles down the road. Remember? The one we passed before we got here."

Carol nodded. "Meet you?"

"Yes, meet me. I'll get a cab. I'll be there later on. I have to talk to the police. I was the first to see the body; they'll want to ask me questions."

Carol's eyes were like waterfalls now. "Do you think this has to do with you?"

Hank wiped Carol's cheeks free of the tears. "Of course not honey. This is just some freak coincidence," he reassured her.

Carol didn't look reassured. "We came here because of someone that wanted you dead Hank. It seems like more than a coincidence."

"If someone wanted me dead they wouldn't kill a helpless person. Someone that has no connection to me." Hank didn't even believe what he was saying.

Carol knew Hank was holding back something.

"The sickos you hunt down Hank, they love playing games. This is a game they're playing."

Hank didn't listen. "Honey there's no connection."

"No connection Hank?" Carol looked into Hank's green eyes. "No connection? Is this hotel not connection enough for you?"

32

Dunfellow finished his last bite of mudpie and looked at his little nephew. "Hmm...hmm...good. Thank you Mikey, for tellin' me about this dee-lish-uz dee-zert."

Mikey just smiled. His face was full of chocolate.

"Hey ree-mem-ba me?" Dunfellow asked as Carol and the kids passed by his table.

Carol looked at Dunfellow, a bit startled. "Oh yes. I'm in a rush." She walked away without saying 'goodbye.'

"She was rude," Calverly said loud enough so that Carol was able to hear her.

"I guezz so. Always in a rush too," Dunfellow replied.

"Where do you know her from Uncle Wally?" Calverly asked, more to have a conversation than out of interest.

"Gaz stay-shone I think. She waz pumpin' gaz." Dunfellow scratched his head.

"Oh, well if she's staying at this hotel I can get a hitman after her for being so rude to you," Calverly said sarcastically.

Her face drew serious after she spoke, remembering what had happened with Anderson.

"Oh that won't be nez-ah-sarie Katie. I do za-pose I could do it myself if I so chooz," Dunfellow followed with his own sarcasm.

"Okay no more killing stories," Andy said with a smile. "Let's play a guessing game."

He picked up the bill off the table.

"Oldest to youngest will guess what this meal cost." Andy looked at Dunfellow. "Wally you're first."

"Do I win somethin' if I gez correctly?" Dunfellow asked with a smirk.

"Nope," Calverly answered. "Dad, when will you ever stop with this stupid game?"

"Never, Katie." Andy turned to Dunfellow again. "Wally?"

"Um…" Dunfellow looked at everyone and tried to tally their meals in his head. "One hundred and twenty six dollars and forty-five zents."

"Okay. Kelly your turn." Andy looked at his wife.

"One hundred and fifty-two dollars and eighty-three cents," Kelly replied quickly.

"Katie?"

"Probably ninety-eight, thirty-eight." Calverly smiled.

"Oh, so Katie is going low," Kelly said.

"Mikey?"

"Five million," Mikey replied loudly.

Everyone laughed.

"I hope not," Andy said, still laughing. "Conner?"

"Forty billion hundred thousand," Conner replied happily, still eating his mudpie.

"Woah," Andy exclaimed. "I didn't think you could have beaten Mikey's, but I guess I was wrong. The correct price was one hundred seventy-four, sixty-two. You were all wrong."

Kelly looked at her husband. "I was closest." She turned her head to the window and noticed blue and red flashing lights.

Two police cars had just pulled up.

33

Gale walked up to Fullmer with a smug look on his face. "Well, well, well, what do we have here Mr. Fuller?"

"It's Fullmer, sir," Fullmer answered.

"Whatever the hell it is it seems like a lot of people are being found dead by you." Gale's forehead creased.

Fullmer remained quiet, not knowing how to respond.

"Where's the body?" Gale questioned.

"It's on the functions floor. Just down these steps." Fullmer waved Gale over to the door.

Gale remained where he was and looked at the other officers that had just arrived. He called them over. "Do you know what floor this elevator came from before you found the body?" He asked Fullmer.

"Yes. It was stuck on floor three for a short time," Fullmer responded quickly.

Gale turned to a well-built officer. "Pete, go to floor three and see if you can find anything. Maybe the killer didn't cover up so well this time. Maybe he left bloody tracks or something." He looked at another officer on Pete's side. "You go with him."

The two officers followed Gale's order.

Gale turned his attention back on Fullmer. "Now what the fuck is a functions floor?" Gale was upset.

Fullmer stopped just before the stairwell door. "It's used for business parties, sir. You can't get to the floor without the elevator key. So this way none of the guests will..." Fullmer was interrupted by Gale.

"Yeah...yeah...yeah...you told me all that before."

"Follow me." Fullmer opened the door and began walking down the steps.

Gale kept an eye on Fullmer. Two dead bodies. Same live man who found them. Gale was suspicious.

Fullmer, Gale, and three other officers finally reached the bottom.

Fullmer inserted the key into the lock and opened the door.

The room was full of long reception tables and hundreds of chairs. Fullmer walked up to the stainless steel elevator door. The others followed.

He took a deep breath and paused.

"What are you waiting for?" Gale asked, infuriated.

Fullmer exhaled. He inserted the long, pen-like elevator key into the hole and turned it slowly.

'*Ding.*'

The doors slid open.

Fullmer backed up.

Gale just looked at the battered body without the slightest bit of disgust.

He bent down and leaned in closer to the murdered corpse. Barkley's right cheekbone protruded through the skin. Blood dripped out of the back of her head. The elevator was covered with it. Handprints filled its sides. Barkley had no chance.

She put up a fight, but had no chance.

A few teeth were scattered on the ground and her jaw was broken. It was completely misaligned with her upper mouth. Barkley's eyes almost popped out of their sockets. Her face was swollen and flush.

Barkley's white t-shirt was completely drenched in blood. It had been ripped from the neckline diagonally to the mid ribcage. Her right breast had been sliced up numerous times and not much held it to her body.

Her stomach had been cut open. Blood and guts continuously dripped out as if running from whatever evil had been in the elevator before.

Two large gashes covered her right leg where she had been cut. Another gash covered the width of her neck. It had been slit open.

A bloodied, stainless steel knife was found firmly stuck in her side. Its final resting place once the damage had been done.

Gale noticed Barkley's body looked like it was propped up by something.

He pulled a latex glove from his suit pocket and put it on. Slowly he reached behind Barkley and grabbed a blood-covered stick. He pulled at the stick, with some force, to remove it from underneath Barkley's body.

Gale stood up.

In his hand he held the item.

A blood-laden, wooden bat.

34

The Garrisons stood right outside their car in the hotel parking lot. Luckily the police cars were not in sight. Anna and Keith would have questioned such a sight.

"This is dumb," Anna said under her breath.

Hank heard her. "The other place is better, Anna," Hank replied, trying to reason with her.

"I don't think so." Anna bent down to tie her sneaker.

She looked up at her father. "Why are we leaving? I like this place."

Hank tried to think of a good excuse. "The manager told me there was an exterminator coming tomorrow." Hank realized it wasn't a good reason, but he had to continue. "I know how much you hate bugs; you don't want to have bugs crawling on you at night." He bent over, grabbed Anna, and began tickling her.

She started to chuckle.

Did she buy it? Hank questioned himself.

Keith stared at his father, a bit suspicious. "Bugs dad? *Bugs*? Who leaves a hotel like this because of bugs? Did we not sleep in that dump last night? I'm sure there were more than just bugs crawling on Anna at night there."

Anna shivered at the image.

"Trust me Keith; the other place is just as nice as this one." Hank stood up. "I think it's even owned by the Vandermeer."

"That's not my point dad." Keith knew something was up. "Leaving the restaurant to go to another hotel before we even get our meals. That's a bit odd."

Hank looked back at his son, trying to think of something. Anna was only six, smart for her age, but nonetheless only six. Bugs to a six-year-old were believable.

Not to a teenager.

Hank put on a serious face, trying out his best acting skills. "Well Keith," he started, "I didn't want to tell you this in front of Anna." He turned to his daughter who was still trying to tie her show. "But the other hotel is closer to a hospital."

"So?" Keith questioned.

Anna stopped tying her shoe and stood up. She grabbed her father's hand. "You hurt dad?"

"No honey, but you know those exercises I do back at home?"

Anna nodded.

"Well the hospital has those exercises there so I can go whenever I want." Hank may have killed two birds with one stone.

"Oh," Anna responded. She was convinced.

Hank looked at Keith.

Keith was quiet. He hopped into the car.

Hank picked up Anna and put her in the car. He locked in her seatbelt.

"I'll see you guys in a little while. You'll like the new hotel, I swear." Hank shut the car door.

He walked over to Carol who was standing beside the driver's side.

He kissed her cheek. "I'll see you soon. Right after I talk to the detective."

Carol looked at Hank without blinking and tightly pursed her lips together. "Hank if it's you they want," Carol started, referring to whoever was responsible for the murder, "Going ten minutes down the road won't help."

"They don't want me." Hank leaned in to kiss his wife.

She remained still. She was not responsive to his sign of affection.

Hank kissed her regardless.

Carol got into the car and closed the door.

The ignition started and she drove off.

Anna looked out the back window and waved at her father.

Hank waved back.

35

Gale dropped the bat to the floor. The handle bounced up and hit Barkley's ankle before settling in a puddle of blood.

"Where's the guy who brought the body here?" Gale looked at Fullmer. "Where's this FBI man?"

"He went to get his family. He said he'd be right back." Fullmer was still in shock.

"Be right back, huh? Sounds a bit odd. Who is this mystery FBI man?" Gale smirked at Fullmer, but it didn't hide his cold, blank stare.

"I didn't get his name." Fullmer didn't know how to respond to the deep penetrating eyes of Gale. "He just said he was FBI."

Gale was now overly suspicious. "So let me get this straight." He turned to the other officers, looking at them one by one. "This man was the first to see the body. He said he was FBI. He moved the body to this area as to not scare guests. He doesn't have a name. And to top it all off he is no longer here."

Fullmer knew what Gale was getting at. "Yes, sir."

Before Gale got a chance to respond he turned towards the stairwell door.

It opened up slowly.

Harlowe entered. "Detective Gale, a man is here.

Says he was the other man to see the body."

Gale smiled at Harlowe. "Let him in Jon." He motioned Harlowe over.

Harlowe turned and looked up at the stairs. "Come on down. The Detective would like to speak with you."

Hank slowly hobbled down the steps.

One step.

Pause.

Two steps.

Pause.

Finally he reached the bottom and entered the functions room.

Gale began pulling off his bloody latex glove.

He looked up at the opening door and stopped.

His mouth dropped more than it had for either of the murdered bodies.

Hank stared back.

Surprise was in his eyes.

36

"Probably nothing serious," Calverly said as she looked out at the police cars.

"I hope not," Kelly responded.

They all watched as an ambulance pulled into the front of the building.

Calverly thought about what she had heard about Anderson and her face got a bit white. "Sometimes this happens. A lot of older people come here on vacation and have strokes or heart attacks or what not."

"You workin' on a killin' field Katie?" Dunfellow asked with a laugh.

Katie swallowed. "It's not unusual. Nothing serious." She hoped.

"Well if it is we'll read about it in the morning," Kelly answered.

Calverly remembered what Gale had told her. "Maybe," she responded.

"Well let's get out of here." Andy shot up.

One by one the others stood up and moved out of the booth.

"Katie, you gonna go to yaw boyfren's house or back home becuz if yaw gonna go back home I could drive with ya." Dunfellow turned towards Andy. "Yaw dad's car is a bit cramped."

Calverly thought for a moment. "I was gonna go see Tom, but I can drop you off."

Dunfellow looked back at Calverly. "No. That's oh-kay, I'll just wedge between Conner and Mikey again."

"No Uncle Walter," Calverly reluctantly answered. "It's on the way anyhow."

"Oh thank you Katie. We can ee-van catch up on some things," Dunfellow said.

Calverly didn't look too happy. She forced a smile. "Sure."

Andy kissed his daughter on the forehead. "Take care of your uncle." He walked towards the exit.

Kelly looked at Dunfellow and Calverly. "I'll see you tomorrow Katie."

"Yes, mom." Calverly rubbed her little brothers' heads. They ran over to their father.

Kelly picked up the sleeping baby from its high chair. She smiled at Dunfellow and Calverly. "Bye for now."

"Bye," Calverly answered with a smile as she watched her mother make her way to the exit.

"What's with awl these byes?" Dunfellow asked Calverly as the rest made their way out the door. "You're gonna see your fam-ee-lee in the mornin'. And why ee-van say 'bye' inside the rest-or-runt, why not outside? We're awl goin' outside."

Calverly looked out the window and saw her family. She waved.

Dunfellow was wrong. They all weren't outside.

He and Calverly still remained inside.

37

"Hello Hank," Gale said. "What a surprise."

"Ditto Charlie." Hank limped closer to Gale. "Long time no see."

Gale smiled. "Indeed it is. Too bad we have to meet like this. Why you down in Florida?"

The other officers were taken aback by the small talk between the old acquaintances. A woman had just been murdered.

Brutally murdered.

"On vacation." Hank looked down at his knee. "Hurt my knee pursuing a suspect." Hank didn't go into detail.

"Seems like crime followed you to Florida." Gale let out an eerie snicker.

"I guess so." Hank flipped the conversation around. "So I hear this is the second death in as many days at this hotel."

Gale listened to Hank then glared at Fullmer.

Hank continued. "Any leads, Charlie?"

"I don't believe that's any of your concern Hank. This is my crime. This is my jurisdiction. FBI has no say in this." Gale was angered.

"Oh I never said it did. Not yet anyway. You're one dead body from a serialist on your hands. That would be fair game for the FBI."

"Don't get your hopes up Hank. We're on this one. You said it yourself, you're *on* vacation. You're not *on* this investigation." Gale bent back over and picked up Barkley's bag.

It was the only thing free of blood.

Gale began unzipping it. He looked up at Hank. "More than anything you are a suspect at the moment."

He pulled out a wallet.

Slowly he tried to pull it open. The snap was stuck. He tried harder.

Cards and papers flew everywhere.

"Oops," Gale said without much remorse.

He picked up some of the items and placed them back into the wallet. He reached back into the bag and pulled out a book.

The Assault.

He turned to the page that was bookmarked and pulled out the old newspaper that kept the place.

He opened up the folded up paper and read the bold printed headline.

FBI Agent Shot, Murder Suspect Flees.

38

"So how long have you bin seein' this guy of yaws?" Dunfellow asked.

"About two years," Calverly responded. She felt funny talking to her uncle. She hadn't seen him in over five years.

She knew strangers better than him.

"You like him?"

Calverly looked at Dunfellow. "Of course I do. Why else would I be with him?" She was a little cocky.

Dunfellow realized her uneasiness. "You goin' to school?"

Calverly was happy the subject was changed. "Part time at UCF."

"What faw?" Dunfellow tried to catch up on all their lost time in a half hour drive.

Impossible.

"Because I think going to school is best right now." Calverly didn't understand the question.

"No, I mean what faw? Like what are you majorin' en?" Dunfellow rephrased the question.

"Oh," Calverly smiled. "Criminal Justice."

"Nice. You want ta be a cop?"

"Don't really know yet. Something to do with solving crimes I guess," Calverly answered.

"It's a dane-ja-ris job."

"Oh I know," Calverly replied.

Dunfellow got back on the boyfriend subject. "What does yaw boyfren do?"

Calverly shied away from the question at first. After a moment of silence she spoke. "He's a writer."

"Is that right? A pub-leeshed rider?" Dunfellow asked, interested in the topic.

"Yeah actually," Calverly answered. "Well one book was published." She paused for a moment. "Well he actually published it himself, but he did sell a few thousand copies. Not many have heard of it though."

"Oh yeah, what's the name?" Dunfellow asked.

"You wouldn't know it," Calverly answered, looking at Dunfellow.

"Try me. I like to read when I get da time," Dunfellow responded.

Calverly smiled at the thought. It seemed unlikely. She looked at Dunfellow. *"The Assault."*

39

Gale's eyes got big. He folded up the paper and put it back in the book.

He stood up and looked at Hank, then at Harlowe.

"Jon, get forensics and homicide on this. Have them do what they do. See if they find anything. Have everything checked out. You know the drill. I don't need to tell everyone twice." Gale looked over at Fullmer. "I'll speak with you tomorrow. You can go now."

Fullmer walked to the stairway door, opened it, and was out of sight.

Gale turned to Hank, who was bent over examining Barkley's body. "And you, Agent Garrison," Gale said, more business-like. "You and your family staying here?"

"No. We were, but I thought it'd be best to leave. I don't want my family involved." Hank reached over and picked up one of the cards that had fallen out of Barkley's wallet.

"So where are you staying now?" Gale asked.

"The Newman Hotel, I think. The one across from the hospital. Just ten miles down the road."

Hank flipped over the card.

Mama's Place- Belhaven's Finest Diner!

Hank dropped the card.

Was someone after me? He thought. *Did someone follow me here?*

Gale bent down and looked at Hank. He knew something was wrong.

"Go see your family. I'll get a hold of you tomorrow." Gale pulled his business card from his pocket and handed it to Hank.

Hank took it and slowly got up, grabbing his knee.

Gale helped him to his feet. "You okay Hank? You don't look so great."

"I'm fine," Hank lied.

Gale turned to Harlowe. "Jon, help Agent Garrison up the steps. Make sure he gets into a cab okay. Better yet, drive him to his destination."

"Yes, sir." Harlowe grabbed Hank's right arm and helped him over to the steps.

The stairway door shut behind them.

Forensics and homicide arrived soon after and started examining the body. Cameras flashed. Samples were taken. Fingerprints looked for.

Eronie opened the door and walked over to Gale. "I came as soon as I could Detective," Eronie said. He was out of breath.

"Where the hell were you?" Gale asked.

Eronie ignored the question. "What do we have here?" He looked at the body and gasped. "Another one?"

"That's right," Gale replied. "I'm going back to the station. Going to try and put two and two together. Find out all you can about this woman." Gale looked down at the body.

"Okay," Eronie said, looking down too. "Anything else?"

"Yes. Before you leave get me a list of all the people staying here." Gale knew he was onto something. "I'm sure my friend Fullmer would be happy to help you out with that."

"Who's Fullmer?" Eronie asked.

"The manager. The same guy who found Anderson dead."

Eronie's mind was on overload. "I see," was all he could utter.

Gale started walking to the stairway. He turned back to Eronie. "And Dan?"

"Yes, sir."

"The press is going to have to be notified. I don't want them to have a field day with this. Don't tell them anything in detail. The world doesn't have to know details. Not ones that have to do with my jurisdiction. Just tell them that we found two bodies."

"They'll want to know more," Eronie responded.

"We don't have more," Gale said. He turned back to the door. "But we will," he said under his breath.

40

"So do you know about the other murder?" Hank questioned Harlowe.

"I'm on the case sir." Harlowe veered away from the real answer.

"I understand that, but do you know about the other murder. Name, age, and the such?" Hank didn't let up.

Harlowe kept his eyes on the road. "I'm not at liberty to tell you."

Hank looked at Harlowe. "I can easily find out all the information. You know that all the reports you fill out immediately gets sent to the FBI. It's procedure."

Harlowe bit his lip. "Yes. I do know that, but I don't believe Detective Gale would want me to be spreading out the details of this case so quickly."

"Jon. That's your name right?"

Harlowe nodded.

Hank continued, "You seem like an intelligent man. We both know all this has to get to the press. It's not like Gale can keep stuff like this hidden. This will be tomorrow's news. I can just as easily read the paper and find out the facts."

Harlowe would not budge. "Then why not just do that?"

Hank liked Harlowe's fussiness. It showed strong

character.

"I'm not asking for much here. I just want names, ages, weapons used. Any suspects?" Hank wanted to break Harlowe.

Harlowe briefly looked at Hank. "*You*. I suppose you're a suspect sir."

"Well considering I wasn't here when the first murder occurred that may be pretty much impossible."

"We don't know if the two murders are connected. They may be two isolated cases."

Hank realized he was getting somewhere. Harlowe was finally letting out information.

"It would be pretty ironic for two isolated cases to happen in the same hotel, two days straight," Hank responded. "Any signatures?"

Harlowe looked confused.

"Signatures?" Hank repeated his question, realizing he may have an interested Harlowe in his grasp. Information flows easily when someone has interest. "You know, like a commonality among the two victims? Maybe the way they were killed. Maybe a note. Serialists do that, not all, but the sick shits that like to play games with the police. They think they're clever, but if they're so damn clever why the hell do they always get caught? Sooner or later they always do. You know why Jon?"

"Why, sir?"

"Because we're smarter than they are. That's why." Hank smiled. "So any signatures?"

"I guess not. None that I know of." Harlowe looked as if he were thinking. "I really don't know much about this murder. I get the briefing from Detective Gale."

"What about the first?"

Harlowe looked at Hank. "I'm sorry, but I can't tell

you that sir. I don't have that right." Harlowe pulled into a hotel about a quarter the size of the Vandermeer. "This is you, right?"

"Yes," Hank answered. He opened the door and got out. "I guess I'll have to read the morning paper," he said as he shut the door.

41

It was 9:17 p.m. when Eronie walked into Gale's office.

Gale was sitting at his desk writing in a manila folder. He closed the folder and looked up at Eronie.

"Dan, come on in. Have a seat. Jon should be in any minute now. He went to get some coffee. This may be a long night."

Eronie sat down. "Well here's what I have."

Eronie handed Gale a stack of papers.

"What's this?" Gale asked, taking the documents.

"That's the list of people staying at the Vandermeer. I highlighted Anderson's name as well as Barkley's…" He didn't get to finish.

"Barkley?" Gale asked. "I assume that's the murdered woman?"

"Yes, sir." Eronie cleared his throat. "I would also like to point out that Hank Garrison is on the list too." Eronie felt like he was ahead of the game.

"Yes, I know that."

Eronie looked disappointed. "You did, sir?"

"Yes. He was one of the men that found the body."

Eronie went quiet. He had another idea. "Don't you think that's odd? I mean we have a connection between the two murders." He paused for a moment before continuing, "It's Agent Garrison."

Harlowe walked into the office with three coffees and sat down beside Eronie. "Did I miss anything?"

Gale looked at him. "Not anything we didn't know." He wedged a coffee from the tray.

Eronie looked upset at Gale's statement.

"Well there's more too, Detective," Eronie said. "At the scene was a book with another newspaper clipping in it. It was about Agent Garrison, just like the others."

Harlowe nearly burnt his throat after sipping his coffee. "That's a big deal." He then remembered what Hank had told him as he was driving. "Oh, no wait," Harlowe said. "Agent Garrison told me he wasn't even in Florida when the first murder took place. He could be lying, but we can check that out tomorrow."

Gale looked at Harlowe then at Eronie. "I don't think Garrison had anything to do with these murders. It goes deeper then that." He leaned back in his chair and sipped the hot contents of his cup.

"How so sir?" Eronie asked.

"Garrison has been capturing criminals, murderers, and all that scum for over twenty-five years. I have a feeling someone is out to get him, not the other way around." He fell back to the desk and placed his coffee on the manila folder. "He told me that he hurt his leg pursuing a suspect. I looked into that myself. He was shot in the leg, the suspect got away."

"Who was the suspect?" Harlowe asked.

"They never identified the man. He was also never found. It would seem like a stretch to say he followed him all the way from Massachusetts to here, but who knows?" Gale rubbed his forehead. "But anyway, like I said, that's a stretch. Let's deal with what we have here first." He looked at Eronie. "Tell me what forensics and homicide found."

"Well besides the newspaper clipping, not much sir." Eronie finally grabbed his coffee, still stuck in the tray. "The only fingerprints they found were police officers', yours, Garrison's, their own. This guy," Eronie started, "Or girl, knows what they are doing."

"Thinks they know, but no one ever really does," Harlowe added.

Gale ran his hand over his cheek and down to his chin as if he had just shaved and was checking the smoothness. "What else do we have?"

"Well the officers that surveyed the hotel, floor three I believe, found nothing. No blood or anything. They also checked the other floors. Nothing." Eronie opened up his notepad.

"So who is this woman, this Berkley?" Gale asked.

"Barkley sir," Eronie corrected. "Tracy Barkley. She was forty-seven years old, divorced, no children. Owns a restaurant in her home town of Belhaven, North Carolina."

"What did forensics say about her death?" Gale questioned.

Eronie turned a page on his notepad. "Um, they said she suffered serious head trauma, both back and front. That knocked her out. Then her throat was cut and the rest of her body slashed and stabbed multiple times. They said she was unconscious, but still alive when she was being cut."

Harlowe's face squished tight.

"The only weapons were the bat and knife?" Gale continued with his questioning.

"That is correct. The bat gave the blows to her head. Front then back. Then came the knife. A large butcher knife. To top it all off the killer gave a couple more blows to her cheek with the bat."

Gale thought for a moment before speaking. "I moved the bat from underneath her body. There's no way the killer hit her after she was already down."

"I'm just telling you what they said," Eronie replied, almost apologetic.

"I would assume she was hit in the back of the head first. That would have her fall forward," he said, still thinking. "Hmmmm...no, that wouldn't work. Somehow the bat got underneath her. If it was under her she must have fallen on it, but how could she be hit with the bat after she was on top of it?"

Harlowe tried to work it out in his own mind. "Maybe the killer placed it under her body after he hit her in the face."

"Maybe, but it seems like too much work. And why would he do such a thing?"

"To confuse you, sir. It seems to have worked." Harlowe raised his eyebrows up, forming a few creased rows on his forehead.

"Is he really that smart?" Gale asked under his breath. "Okay, so what did you get on Anderson?"

Eronie fumbled through his notes. "Called his home. He lives with a roommate. Not married, no kids, no girlfriend, no family. Was put up for adoption at a young age, had foster parents, they died in a tragic car accident when he was twenty. That would be eight years ago."

Gale shook his head. "Any enemies?"

"His roommate said he was a quick-tempered man, yet very well-intentioned. No enemies that he could think of," Eronie answered.

"I see," Gale replied, taking another sip from his coffee and setting it back down on the manila folder.

"I did call up his agent and asked about the show he was set to film soon," Eronie said as he looked at Gale.

"*And?*" Gale asked, wanting to know more.

"And they said it was a crime drama as I told you before, but it just so happens the character he was set to play was loosely based on Agent Garrison."

Gale seemed surprised.

"So maybe the articles that were found in his bag were just to help him get into character," Harlowe said.

"Maybe," Gale answered. "Maybe someone is toying with Garrison."

"That's a lot of articles to shove in a bag, Jon," Eronie said turning to Harlowe. "And most were just headlines."

"Dan, I don't think Hank Garrison is the killer here. I do believe there is a connection, but not one as strong as that. We'll understand better when we talk with him tomorrow." Gale put his hands on top his head.

"Well other than the Agent Garrison clippings we don't have much else of a connection," Eronie responded.

Harlowe looked at Eronie and spoke, "Yes we do. We have the hotel. Both were killed at the hotel. Plus we have the neck and abdomen wounds. Both had that. And we have the weapons. Aside from the bat, they were all blade-like weapons." Harlowe took a deep breath.

Eronie knew Harlowe had a good point. "Yes, but look what else there is. Anderson is a young male, Barkley a middle-aged woman. Anderson is a white actor, Barkley a black cook."

"A cook that owns her own restaurant," Gale added.

"So?" Eronie was confused.

"We may all be on to something," Gale replied. "Anderson was an out-of-town, one day may strike it rich, actor. Barkley an out-of-town, probably already rich, woman."

"I see where you're going," Harlowe said. "Both rich, both staying at the Vandermeer."

Gale looked at Harlowe. "Well there's more to it than just that. To stay at the Vandermeer you would have to be at least slightly well off. The thing is, they are two well off people, without a family, staying at the Vandermeer, with some sort of admiration for Agent Garrison."

"Admiration?" Harlowe asked.

"Yes, Anderson was basically going to play him on television and Barkley was basically reading a book that probably has something to do with him," Gale answered.

"*Probably* is not the best word to use when solving crimes Detective," Eronie said.

"*The Assault,* the book she was reading, I read it too. Some Tim, or Tom, or Ted Zucker wrote it. Regardless of his name, it was about a former baseball player that went on a killing spree. Anyway, not very good, but the point of the matter is when I was going to college in Maine I remember hearing stories about a crazed ex-football player who went on a rampage, killing five of his teammates. Garrison was one of the teammates that wasn't killed. It was a long time ago."

Harlowe was amazed. "I remember hearing something about that too."

"Me too," Eronie chimed. "I heard they were brutally murdered."

"Yeah the stories you probably heard were exaggerated. The murders weren't gory at all. Just gunshots to the head or what not. When I worked with Garrison he told me that was what made him want to become a cop."

"Interesting," Eronie replied. "So we may have something here. Should we do something about all the people staying at the Vandermeer that fit the profile of the victims?"

"It may take a while, but yes. First thing tomorrow. Not just the single, family-less ones. Everyone. The other stuff I mentioned were just ideas. We're dealing with lives here, we can't take a chance like that," Gale answered.

"Do you think he'll strike again?" Harlowe asked.

"Let's hope not," Gale replied.

42

Tom was hunched over his computer keyboard. The only light in the darkened room was that of the monitor.

Calverly walked over and began rubbing his shoulders. "How's the writing going?"

"Writer's block," he replied as he pulled off his thin-rimmed glasses and rubbed between his eyes. "I have nothing to work with."

He took his hand and patted it over his shoulder onto Calverly's.

"Well what do you have so far?" She asked.

"Absolutely nothing. I don't even know where to begin," he sighed.

"Maybe a little time off would help," Calverly replied as she ran her hands down Tom's chest.

Tom turned on the desk lamp and looked up at Calverly.

"I don't really know. You teased me this morning." He smiled.

"And maybe I should tease you again." Calverly began slowly unbuttoning her shirt as Tom watched, his eyes wide open.

The last button was pushed through its hole.

Tom happily looked at her leopard print bra.

Tanned cleavage showed.

Calverly reached behind her back and unclasped her bra. Tom remained still.

She squeezed her breasts together and pressed her shoulders inward. The bra dropped to the floor.

She started to move her hands to her belt.

"Stop!" Tom shouted.

Calverly jumped, surprised.

"You gave me an idea. Thank you hun," Tom said as he kissed Calverly's bare stomach and turned back to the computer monitor.

"And what idea was that?" Calverly asked, a bit upset.

Tom looked down at his pants. Calverly looked down at them too.

Not a very big idea, she thought.

"A man who only kills when sexually aroused." He knew that sounded foolish and continued, "Well the basic premise. There's more to it than that, but that's the general idea. It's never been done before."

"Oh I wouldn't think it has," Calverly said as she bent over to pick up her bra.

Tom smacked her buttocks. "Thank you Katie."

Calverly jumped as Tom's hand hit her. "Oh you're welcome, Tom," she answered angrily.

Calverly put her bra and shirt back on and let Tom continue his writing, as crazy an idea as she thought it was. She walked over to the bed and grabbed the television remote that was on the pillow. Calverly pressed the red 'power' button and starting flipping through channels.

Cartoons.

Click.

An old western.

Click.

The ten o'clock news.
Click.
She stopped for a second. She thought she recognized the man talking on the news. It was one of the men that questioned her at the station.

She turned back to the news channel.

It was Eronie.

She turned up the volume.

'There isn't much else we can tell you right now. Just that we're hard on the case.'

Calverly missed the beginning of the news report. She looked at the clock.

It was 10:12 p.m.

It flashed over to a reporter. *'So all we have is confirmation that there have been two people brutally murdered inside one of the most well-known hotels in America...'*

"Two?" Calverly muttered.

'The twenty-eight- year- old, Robert Anderson and the forty-seven-year-old, Tracy Barkley, just a day later. The details to this case are being withheld until more information can be found. As of right now there are no suspects. This is certainly a scary situation and we will be the first to bring you the updated information as soon as we get it.'

'Certainly is scary, Mallory,' another newscaster responded.

'Yes it is,' Mallory said. *'Terrible, terrible thing to hear about in this area. Terrible in any area. Just two people on vacation.'* She squinted her eyes, bit her lip, and shook her head. *'This world is made up of some sick people. There are some scary people out there, Greg.'*

Greg looked at Mallory. *'Let's just hope they find whoever did this. And soon.'*

Calverly turned off the television. She had heard enough.

"What you watching honey?" Tom asked, still typing.

"Just the news," she answered as she fell back onto the bed.

"Anything interesting?"

"Yeah," she started, "A good book idea."

43

It was a new day. The warm Florida breeze gently caressed the leaves of the Palm trees planted outside the Newman Hotel. It was early, only 6:30 a.m., but the morning sun was just starting to cover all with its fiery breath.

Anyone who would have looked out the window would have thought it was a beautiful day.

Hank didn't think so.

He had woken up early again. Too much on his mind. The murders. His children. His wife. He was the protector of his family and he had the inclination someone was out to get him. On one hand he wanted to just get away, leave this place, and take his family somewhere safe. On the other hand he realized that as long as he was around nowhere was truly safe.

He was both the protector and the curse.

Hank watched as the others slept peacefully. He wished he, too, could do the same. It was a rare occurrence when he did. He didn't last night. Didn't plan to any time soon.

Hank limped over to the window and sat down in a chair pushed against the wall. He pulled out a few pieces of paper and a pen that were in a plastic standee on the adjacent table. *The Newman Hotel* was imprinted on both.

Hank thought about what he had heard on the news last night. He recounted every detail he could. He had watched every news station there was in order to find out more information on the murders. Just enough light shone through the blinds and he slowly wrote down the information.

Robert Anderson.
28.
Actor.
Los Angeles.

He looked down at what he had written. Nothing seemed to catch his attention. He had no connection with Anderson. If someone were after him, why would they kill Anderson? He knew he was missing valuable information.

How was he killed? With what? Was it like Barkley? The questions filled his head.

He scribbled out what he had written, ran his hand through his salt and peppered hair, and began again.

Robert Anderson.
White.
Male.
28.
Single.
Actor.
Los Angeles.
??Wounds??
??Weapon(s)??
Still nothing.
He continued.
Tracy Barkley.
Black.
Female.
47.

Divorced.
Restaurant owner.
Belhaven.
Head trauma.
Multiple lacerations.
Bat.
Knife.
Nothing.

He began to think more, pulling at his hair. *There's got to be a connection. I went to her restaurant. Did I see a movie he was in?*

He couldn't answer the question his mind posed to him. He was unfamiliar with actors and actresses. Not very interested in movies. Not realistic enough.

Although Hank's own life seemed pretty unrealistic to others.

He jutted down another word.

Connection!

He looked down at the notes he had written.

Just a bunch of words and letters. Nothing jumped out at him.

He needed more.

44

"Look at this," Dunfellow said as he motioned Kelly over.

"What is it?" She asked.

He held out the front page of the newspaper for her to see.

Two Murdered at Vandermeer.

Kelly ran over to Dunfellow and grabbed the paper from his hands. "That's awful. We were just there last night. That must have been why there were police there when we left."

Kelly read the article over quickly.

"Call up Katie, see if she knows en-nee-thang," Dunfellow said calmly.

Kelly gave her brother a cold stare. "This is awful. I hope they close down the hotel until they find whoever did this. I don't want Katie working there."

From another room the baby could be heard crying.

"Wally, can you get him? I'll call Katie up now."

"No prob-lum." Dunfellow walked over to the other room and picked the baby up from his playpen. "What's da mat-ta lit-tul one?" He cradled the baby in his arms and swayed back and forth.

Kelly started dialing up Calverly's number, but

stopped as a large yellow bus pulled in front of the house and beeped. "Ugh," Kelly grunted as she looked out the window. "Mikey! Conner! The bus is here. Hurry up I am not bringing you to school again," she shouted.

The two boys quickly emerged from the poolroom; their shoeless feet were all wet.

Kelly looked back out the window.

The bus still remained.

She walked over to the door and held up her index finger at the driver. She needed a minute.

"Put on your shoes and get out there. I told you never to dip your feet in the pool when you're waiting for the bus. Ugh. You guys are driving me insane."

The boys hurriedly slipped their socks on and pried their feet into their sneakers. Mikey didn't get his all the way on; the backs of the white sneakers compressed and his heel could be seen.

Conner ran over to the bus and hopped on. "Bye mom," he said.

Mikey, followed, trying not to fall down. His shoes wobbled as he walked.

"Bye guys. See you later," Kelly said waving.

The bus driver's face could be seen, it was contorted in anger.

Kelly closed the front door and walked back over to her phone.

She dialed up Calverly's number.

'Ring.'

'Ring.'

Kelly put her hand on her hip and started tapping her foot, a bit worried.

'Ring.'

'Ring.'

Calverly's voicemail picked up.

Kelly hung up the phone.

She tried again.

Still no answer.

This time Kelly left a message. "Katie I hope everything is all right. Call me when you get this."

She hung up the phone.

Dunfellow walked out of the room holding the baby. "You get a hold of her?" He asked.

"No," Kelly answered, irritated.

"Maybe she's at work," Dunfellow suggested, without thinking.

"That's what I'm worried about," she replied.

She picked up the phone and dialed Tom's number.

45

Eronie threw some papers down on Gale's desk. "Here's the people at the Vandermeer we spoke to so far."

Gale looked over the papers. "There's only about fifty names here. The list of people staying at the hotel had over five hundred names. You guys have your work cut out for you."

"There's seventy-two names there Detective. Most of the people have either left the hotel because of the news or they are at a park or a beach or somewhere else," Eronie answered.

"Four hundred people?" Gale asked skeptically. "Four hundred people checked out of the Vandermeer this morning?"

"I guess so, sir. Either this morning or last night. The updated guest list had about one hundred and fifty people on it. That includes everyone, not just the people who paid for the rooms, but everyone staying in the rooms as well."

Gale didn't know how to respond. "Did you find anything?"

"Not a single person interviewed, according to those of us who spoke with them, knew anything about Agent Garrison."

"None whatsoever?" Gale questioned.

"Not one, sir. Those I interviewed I even asked if they

read that book you told me and Jon about. They had no clue." Eronie sat down. "No one staying there knew of the victims either. A couple said the names sounded vaguely familiar, but they believed that was because they heard them on the news."

Gale took a deep breath and exhaled slowly. "So not a soul?"

"Well, not entirely true, sir," Eronie answered. "None of the people staying there, but a young lady did know Agent Garrison. She checked him in. Her name's on that paper," he answered, pointing to the sheet Gale was holding. "Jen something."

Gale looked at the paper. "Elkind," he said. "Jennifer Elkind."

"Yes, that's her," Eronie replied. "She only knew of him because she checked him in. And she only said she recognized the name, nothing more."

"So that's all we have? Seventy-two people and not one with a connection to Garrison," Gale said.

"Well they are still talking to people. They should be there all day."

"They'll be there a lot longer than that. I had eight officers posted to watch that place until we apprehend this son of a bitch," Gale shouted as he pounded his fist on the desk.

Eronie jumped. "Well one more thing," he said.

"Yes?"

"When I was talking to that Jen girl...the other girl we spoke with...um...Katie...she was shocked when I mentioned that book."

"Why?" Gale asked.

"Because her boyfriend wrote it."

Gale leaned back and looked up at the ceiling. "We may have something here, Dan. We may have something."

46

Tom was rapidly typing at the keyboard. His writer's block had long since subsided and now the words just seemed to flow onto the pages with relative ease. Nothing would be able to hinder his focus.

'Ring.'
'Ring.'
'Ring.'

Almost nothing.

Tom lost his train of thought as the phone rang incessantly.

Even though he did not want to answer it he feared it was Calverly's mother again and he did not want to get on her bad side. Not many men would. Tom had seen her temper on various occasions and he was in no mood to witness it again.

He picked up the phone. "Hello."

The voice on the other end responded. "Yes, hello. Is this Tom Zucker?"

It wasn't Calverly's mother.

"Yes, this is he," Tom answered, relieved it wasn't Mrs. Calverly.

"Sorry to bother you Mr. Zucker, but this is Detective Daniel Eronie of the Orlando Police Department. Would you mind coming to the station and answering a few questions?"

Tom's thoughts went wild.

Is Katie okay? What happened? Who died now?

"Why, what's wrong?" He asked in a worried whisper.

"Oh nothing is wrong Mr. Zucker. We would just like to speak with you. It will only take a moment."

"Only a moment?" Tom asked.

"Yes. Just a moment of your time. Can you be here in forty-five minutes or so?"

Tom thought for a second. "I guess I can, but why not just ask me questions over the phone?"

"Because right now Detective Gale is at lunch and he's the one that would like to do the questioning."

"Can you call me back when he's in?" Tom fussed.

"No," the voice answered sternly. "Be here in forty-five minutes. The station across from Keller's Garage."

Tom didn't get to respond before the other line went busy.

"Strange police," he said to himself as he hung up the phone.

He walked over to his computer and looked at the screen. The words glared back at him.

Just my luck. I get in the groove and this happens, he thought.

Stubbornly he grabbed his car keys off the computer desk, pressed save, and walked out the door.

47

"So big day today, huh?" Harlowe asked as he walked into Gale's office.

"How so?" Gale asked.

Harlowe moved closer to Gale's desk. "Dan tells me you may have something. He said that book author is the boyfriend of the Vandermeer worker. He wrote the book that Barkley had been reading. Could he be the prime suspect?"

"It would be premature to jump to that conclusion, but we may be headed in the right direction. That guy certainly has a connection with Garrison, as well as Barkley, even if it may only be a coincidence. That girl works at the Vandermeer, is dating him, and we are where we are."

"We'll take a coincidence at this point," Harlowe said as he sat down.

"Where is Dan?" Gale asked, looking at Harlowe.

"I just saw him in the hall. Nature called I guess," Harlowe laughingly replied.

"We have a few people coming in here in just a bit."

"Who?" Harlowe asked.

"The author, Garrison, and the Vandermeer manager."

"Ah...I see. Loaded schedule."

Gale opened up his desk drawer and pulled out a manila folder. "Unfortunately we got nothing out of the people staying at the Vandermeer. Not a shred of information that could possibly lead us even in the general direction of the culprit."

"Well you did end up with something. I mean the author could now be considered a suspect," Harlowe said.

"Seems too easy." Gale opened up the folder and pulled out some photographs.

Harlowe looked over at Gale as he thumbed through the pictures. "Well sometimes it's those you least expect. The ones right under your nose."

Harlowe turned to the door as Eronie walked in.

"What you guys talking about?" Eronie asked with a smile.

"Just about the loaded schedule we have today," Harlowe replied.

Gale looked up at Eronie. "When will they be here?"

"Agent Garrison just arrived, sir," Eronie answered. "He's out in the hall."

Gale put the pictures back in the folder and closed it. "Let him in."

Eronie peeked his head outside the office door then pulled it back in and looked at Gale. "Well now the manager is here too, and I think I may see Zucker right behind him. At least I think it may be Zucker, never saw the man before."

"Three suspects all at once," Harlowe said softly. "Who should we let in first? We could do it alphabetically, or by prestige, or first come first serve."

"As valiant as the alphabetical option may be I believe first come first serve would be our best bet," Gale said. He looked at Eronie. "Let Garrison in."

Eronie went into the hallway and looked at Hank. "Agent Garrison, Detective Gale is ready to see you."

Hank got up and hobbled over to the office door.

Eronie turned to the other two men. "I'll call for you in a moment. Help yourself to coffee and donuts." He walked back into Gale's office and shut the door.

Gale stood up and offered his hand to Hank.

Hank shook it.

"Have a seat Hank," Gale said, pointing to a chair. He slowly sat back into his own.

"Thank you," Hank replied as he sat.

"You've met Detective Jon Harlowe," Gale said, pointing to Harlowe.

"Yes I have." Hank looked at Harlowe who was sitting on his left. "Nice to see you again," he said as he shook Harlowe's hand.

"And I don't think you met Detective Eronie yet." Hank turned around and looked at Eronie. "Sort of. In the hall. Nice to see you." He shook Eronie's hand.

"I want to make this as quick as I possibly can. I have enough shit on my hands right now." Gale paused. "But, I think there may be a connection to you in these murders."

Hank nodded. "I believe so too, Charlie. That's why I would like to know more about this case."

Gale crossed his arms. "Well until I hear from your superiors, unfortunately I am not at liberty to reveal to you any more than what you already know."

Hank was not pleased with Gale's answer. "Charlie, c'mon, we know each other. We've solved crimes like this before. Ten times worse than this. I don't want my family to be in the middle of this. It would be best if you just told me what's going on. Just some things about Anderson's murder."

Gale didn't budge. "I'm sorry Hank. Once again you're turning the tables on this conversation. *I* should be questioning *you*. Like I said, you are still a viable suspect. You are the sole person the two murders have some sort of connection with."

"And what connection is that?" Hank asked.

"There you go again with the questions. I know it's difficult to be on the other side of the law, but just deal with it Hank," Gale replied as he uncrossed his arms.

"I know how the law works Charlie and I know that if there is a connection with these murders and myself it is *your* lawful responsibility to tell me what the connection is so that I am protected. The police motto is still 'to protect and serve,' is it not?" Hank asked.

"True," Gale answered. "But until we know for sure you are not a suspect in these crimes you do not have a civilian's rights."

"I saw Barkley's body. So did the manager. I was the first to see her dead. That doesn't give you enough evidence to conclude I killed her," Hank said calmly. He knew he had a point.

"That is also true, but it also doesn't give me enough evidence to say you *didn't* kill her," Gale responded. "Your fingerprints were found at the crime scene."

"As I am sure yours were too. For that matter a whole bunch were probably at the scene. We all know how useless fingerprints are with stuff like this. Crime scenes are contaminated all the time. I had to move the elevator. A dead woman lying inside of it, in a soon to be crowded lobby, is not a great sight to see." Hank was becoming less calm.

"So why were you there Hank? What were you doing by that elevator?" Gale questioned.

Hank was a bit amused at the question. "I was going to use it. Why else would I be there? The fact of the matter is it would have been impossible for me to kill that woman. I was downstairs at the restaurant with my family. I went to get my wallet, which I had left inside my room."

Gale was listening intently. "Continue."

"I pressed the button and the elevator was stuck. On floor three. Have you seen my leg? Have you seen me walk, or at least try to walk? A snail may be quicker. I have the hardest time climbing up a flight of stairs, nevermind having to kill a woman, running downstairs because the elevator is stuck, meeting my family, and then running back to the elevator. Extraordinary task for many. Impossible for me," Hank said, pleased at his monologue.

Harlowe looked at Gale. "It does make sense."

Gale wasn't satisfied. "Even if that does check out there's still Anderson."

"Well tell me Charlie," Hank started, ignoring Gale's statement, "You would agree that the two murders are connected, correct?"

"I would certainly say so, yes."

"And you agree that it would have been pretty much impossible for me," Hank said, pointing to his knee before continuing, "To have killed Barkley, and still manage to have dinner with my family, without breaking a sweat?"

Gale knew what Hank was getting at. "Okay, make your point."

"Well if I didn't kill her I couldn't have killed him. If they are indeed connected, me not being able to kill one directly leads to me not killing the other. And my alibi about him is even tighter than mine is for her."

"Do tell," Gale said.

"When Anderson was found dead I was probably in

North or South Carolina. I wasn't even in the state yet. Face it Charlie you know I didn't kill either of those people. Why are you making this about me?"

"Because it *is* about you. We both know there's a connection. You said it yourself," Gale answered.

"I could just as easily be working by your side on this case Charlie. I'm asking you to give me a little bit of information as a favor because I need it to protect my family. If someone is out there to get me I need to be at least a step ahead of them. Or I could just as easily call my superior and have myself put on this case. Is that what you want? We've worked together before, why not again?"

Gale finally gave in. "What is it you'd like to know?"

"Good," Hank exclaimed. "First off tell me what the connection is between me and the murders."

"Anderson was an actor."

"Yes I heard that," Hank replied.

"Well he was going to begin taping a pilot for some crime show. Apparently it was loosely based on you," Gale said.

"Oh really?" Hank asked.

"Yes. And Barkley had a book, *The Assault*, which was basically based on the Johnson football murders, but with baseball."

So no one knew that I was at Mama's Place, he thought.

"I see. Funny how I didn't know about either and both were based on me," Hank said, still thinking. "Can you tell me about the Anderson murder? Weapons used, crime scene, stuff like that?"

Gale opened up the folder. "I can do better than that," he answered, throwing the folder over to Hank. "Here's the pictures. Now get out of here. I don't want to see you, unless I need to, from now on."

"Thank you Charlie," Hank said as he slowly got up from his seat. "You solve this one before another person gets killed and you won't ever have to." He limped to the door.

Eronie followed Hank out the door and called for Fullmer, who was reading a magazine.

"About time. Quick, huh? I have a hotel to run," Fullmer said as he looked at his watch.

"I'm sure an assistant manager can take care of the four hundred people still staying there today," Eronie replied.

Fullmer looked angered. "I don't understand. You spoke with me yesterday. You spoke with me this morning. Do you really have to speak with me again?" He asked as he got up and walked to the door.

Tom was jotting down his thoughts on a napkin. A word here. A word there.

Fullmer entered Gale's office as Eronie peeked over at Tom. "The Detective will be with you next. Thank you for being patient," he said.

Tom stopped writing and looked at Eronie. "Okay," was all he could muster. He returned back to his napkin.

Eronie closed the office door.

"So Mr. Fullmer, we meet again," Gale said without standing up. "Have a seat."

Fullmer sat down.

"I'm sure by now you've met Detectives Harlowe and Eronie."

"Yes I have," Fullmer responded.

"Well thank you for waiting. Agent Garrison took longer than I had expected."

"So he is with the FBI then?" Fullmer asked.

"Yes, but you can't just assume what people say as being the truth. Did he show you a badge before he tampered with the body and moved the elevator for you?" Gale asked in a powerful tone.

Fullmer looked a little nervous. "No, sir."

"Then why did you allow him to move the body? Was it perhaps so you could have an alibi?"

"No, not at all, sir. He told me he should move the body. It seemed like a good suggestion. He did that as I called the police."

"Where did he go after he moved the body?"

"Like I told you before, when you questioned me, he went to talk with his family in the restaurant. Do you believe he killed that woman? Those two people?"

"No he's cleared of that. No evidence," Gale responded. He looked at Harlowe and Eronie and smiled. "Once again I'm the one being asked questions." He turned back to Fullmer. "Mr. Fullmer *you* are here to answer questions, not the other way around."

"I understand," Fullmer replied.

"Okay. Now that we've settled that. As far as we know you are the only person to have seen both dead bodies, other than the police. That seems a bit odd to me. Does it seem odd to you?" Gale leaned in closer to Fullmer, trying to scare him.

Fullmer jumped back a bit. "I can see how you would think it was odd, but if you're trying to imply that I killed those people you're wrong."

"Okay. I can deal with that. So tell me, what were you doing the day Anderson checked in?" Gale asked.

"That depends," Fullmer answered. "I do a lot of different things depending on the time."

"Between six and 7 p.m., Mr. Fullmer. What were you doing between those times?"

Fullmer understood that those times were when

Anderson must have been killed. "From six to seven, sir, I do computer work and cash people out."

"Cash them out?" Harlowe asked.

"Yeah that's when the new shift desk teller comes in and I have to take any money we have in the registers out. Basically I close a register down until the new staff person comes in."

Eronie looked confused and spoke from behind Fullmer's chair. "People actually use cash at that place? They carry that much on them?"

Fullmer turned to answer Eronie. "Well most use credit cards, but there are some who use cash or traveler's checks."

Gale nodded. "So from six to seven you were cashing people out?"

"Yes."

"Do you remember what people?" Gale asked.

"I know there were three people on." Fullmer stopped and thought. "Mike was at six, Katie at 6:30, and then Jen at seven," he said to himself.

"Last names?" Gale asked.

"Mike Turner, Katie Calverly, and Jen Elkind. Does that help you out at all?"

"Not really, except for the fact they couldn't have killed Anderson," Gale answered. "So why did you go to Anderson's room?"

"He scheduled a wake up call the night before. It was for 6:30 a.m. I believe. He didn't answer the call and it is the hotel's rightful duty to see that he wakes up…"

Harlowe interrupted, "You failed that duty, huh?"

Eronie smirked. Fullmer ignored Harlowe's dark humor. "I knocked on his door a few times and he didn't answer. So I opened the door with my key."

"If he didn't answer why didn't you just assume

that he was in the shower?"

"At first I did, sir, but it is not uncommon to walk into the room after knocking if there is no answer. I walked in and called out his name. There was no answer, so I walked further into the room and saw his body."

"It's not uncommon to walk into people's rooms?" Eronie asked.

"Yes. I'm sure you know that maids do it all the time. We also do so to leave breakfast."

"Oh yeah," Eronie replied.

"You called us as soon as you noticed the body?" Gale asked.

"Yes, sir. I was in terrible shock, but I called the police right away."

"From the room's phone or another?" Gale questioned.

"Oh not the room's, sir. I had my cellphone on me. I used that."

"The night before you saw the body, did anyone suspicious arrive at the hotel? Anyone that may have caught your attention?"

"No, sir. If there had been I would surely have mentioned it before."

"So is it easy to bring in arrows and axes into your hotel?" Gale asked as he rubbed his chin.

Fullmer didn't know how to respond. "We see people walk in with bags everyday. Anything could fit in them. We don't have the right, at least not yet, to check every bag we see."

Gale intertwined his fingers together and placed them on his desk. "So would it be easy?" He asked again.

"If it got there then I suppose it would be," Fullmer answered.

"How about a bat and a knife? A large knife? Would those two items be easy to get in?"

"Detective, I do not know exactly where you are going with this. Somehow they got in without anyone seeing them. And if someone saw them then they are either dead or not telling," Fullmer answered.

"Are *you* not telling Mr. Fullmer?"

"I told you all I know," Fullmer answered anxiously. "Now may I go?"

"Are you not telling?"

"I didn't see any bat, or knife, or arrow, or axe. I didn't see any of those things."

"You may go," Gale said.

Eronie opened the door. Fullmer quickly got up and walked out it.

Eronie looked out at Tom, who was now drinking a cup of coffee. "Just a minute Mr. Zucker." He walked back into the office and closed the door.

"So what do you think about Fullmer?" Harlowe asked.

"Nothing. He didn't kill anyone," Gale responded.

"He did seem nervous though, towards the end," Eronie said.

"I tried to drill him hard. He did as any innocent man would," Gale replied. "He was telling the truth. He knows nothing. We'll keep him on a tight leash, but it's not him. I assure you of that."

"Suspects keep dropping like flies, sir," Harlowe said.

"At least they're not dropping like dead bodies," Gale replied. "Let Mr. Zucker in. I'd like to meet the man who wrote that book."

Eronie walked over to the door, opened it, and peeked out at Tom.

"You can come in now," Eronie said.

Tom got up, placed his napkin full of scribble in his pocket, and walked over to Eronie.

"I'm Detective Eronie," he said as he shook Tom's hand. He pointed to Harlowe. "That's Detective Harlowe." He looked at Gale. "And that's Detective Gale."

Tom looked at the other two. "Nice to meet you all," he said politely.

"Have a seat Mr. Zucker," Gale said. "I happened to have read your book. *The Assault.* Great story."

"Oh thank you, Detective," Tom responded graciously. "Speaking of which, can I ask you a question? I'm writing a new book and it would be helpful."

Gale looked at Harlowe and Eronie and smiled. "More questions guys. More questions." He looked back at Tom. "Go ahead."

"Well you were sort of interrogating those two people that came in here, right?"

"Yes, I suppose you could say that," Gale replied.

"Don't you have one of those two-way mirrored, interrogation booths?"

"We do."

"Why don't you use it then?" Tom asked.

"Well, unlike the movies or books or crimes shows, sometimes we prefer to just speak with people in offices. I think television and books blow the interrogation process out of proportion," Gale responded.

"So you don't ever use it?"

"We do, but not for stuff like this. We need to have some hard evidence on a guy. Or the guy needs to be a proven guilty man. We don't have enough on the guys that came in here."

"Okay. Thank you," Tom replied. "So why am I in here?"

"I'm sure you've heard of the two murders at the Vandermeer," Gale stated.

"Yes, my girlfriend works there. She told me about it after she watched the news last night. But what does this have to do with me?"

"Well your girlfriend was the last to see the first victim alive. And you are her boyfriend. Every connection we see, whether it be small or smaller, we check up on it. You can use that for your next book. That's what we do," Gale said.

"So because I'm dating Katie, who happens to work at the hotel that two people were killed at, you believe you may have something on me?"

"Let me just ask you the questions," Gale said, all of a sudden serious.

"Okay," Tom nervously responded. "What is it you'd like to know?"

"Another question." Gale looked at the other detectives. "Where were you two nights ago, between six and seven o'clock?"

Tom thought for a minute. "Oh I was with Katie from around seven onward, we went to see a movie."

"What about around six?" Gale asked.

"I was at home."

"Did you go out at all during that day?"

"No my car didn't work. I just had it fixed yesterday."

"So you were at home? What were you doing?" Gale questioned.

"Writing."

"You don't have another job?"

"Not currently. I was laid off. I just write now," Tom replied.

"So basically, for all we know, you may not have been writing. You don't have anyone who could say that's true. At least not any time before your girlfriend saw you."

"She knows I was writing. What are you getting at?"

Gale was onto something. "Okay so you were writing. I'll give you that. How did you get to the movies if your car wasn't working?"

"Katie picked me up," Tom answered, trying to understand what was happening.

"Okay. What time did you get your car fixed yesterday?"

"Around five o'clock."

Gale looked at Harlowe and Eronie. They both looked back. They knew what Gale was getting to.

"How did you get to the garage to have it fixed?" Gale asked.

"Well it wasn't broken down yet. But it seemed like any second it could have. The garage was five minutes from my house. I drove there."

"So technically you could have driven to, say the Vandermeer, with your car and it may not have broken down. I mean, you were able to drive to the garage. So it couldn't have been that bad."

Tom looked worried. "I could have driven, I guess. But I didn't."

"So coincidently enough, at the time the first victim was said to have been killed, you claim you were at home writing. But no one can actually say they saw you at home writing. And to add to that, around the time the second victim was found dead, you claim to have been at a garage." Gale leaned back. "Something seems fishy to me. And where was your girlfriend when you were at the garage? Was she with you? It certainly would help your cause if someone were."

Tom was completely bewildered. "No, she wasn't with me."

"Oh. I see," Gale said. "Where was she?"

"She was with her family at a restaurant."

"So you really don't have an alibi, do you?" Gale asked.

"I really don't believe this," Tom said, sounding scared. "You came to all this just because one of the people who were killed had a book I wrote?"

"Yes. But, like I said, that's how we do things around here."

"You can call the garage up. They can vouch for me being there," Tom hurriedly replied.

"You have the number?"

Tom fumbled through his pockets.

Nothing.

His napkin fell to the floor. Eronie bent over to pick it up. He caught a glimpse of some of the scribbles.

Manager. Detective. Pretty Girl. Hotel.

"The garage's name is Bart's Tire and Service. You can call them up. They'll tell you I was there," Tom said.

"What's this?" Eronie asked, holding up the napkin.

"Just some notes I jotted down for my next book," Tom replied.

"Eerily familiar notes," Eronie replied as he handed the napkin over to Gale.

Gale looked at the words on the small, square piece of paper. "Certainly are."

"What are you talking about? I just wrote that while I was waiting. There's like five words on it," Tom said.

"I think I'm going to keep this for now, Mr. Zucker," Gale said with authority.

Tom was shaking. "Are you going to arrest me?"

Gale glared back at Tom, squinting his eyes to look more demeaning. "No, Mr. Zucker. I don't have quite enough evidence on you. No warrant. No nothing. But I'm going to keep an eye on you. You better be careful."

Tom took a deep breath. "Can I go?"

"We'll keep in touch."

Tom stood up, still shaking, and walked over to the door. Eronie opened it for him. Tom walked out.

"Seems awfully suspicious if you ask me Detective. I don't know why he's walking out of this place," Eronie said as he sat down.

"As suspicious as it may be we do not have enough on him. If we're going to do things around here we better do them right. We'll keep a close eye on him," Gale replied.

"Just think," Eronie started, "You have the garage incident, you have no alibi, you have that napkin, you have a connection to Agent Garrison because of that book he wrote, *and* you have a Vandermeer connection with his girlfriend. What more could you possibly want?"

"This napkin is worthless. Killers don't jot notes down about possible people to kill. We don't have enough. Not yet," Gale replied.

"Well what about that book of his, was it full of sick shit?" Eronie asked.

"It was very sick. Very descriptive," Gale replied, thinking.

"So he has the mind of a killer, wouldn't you agree?"

"If every writer who wrote books about murder were murderers themselves, we'd be in a very bad situation right about now. Intelligence is not a sure sign of evil. Don't get me wrong, it's certainly a useful weapon, but it is not always a sign of evil," Gale answered as he leaned back.

Gale rolled his chair closer to his desk and picked up the phone. As soon as a voice picked up he said, "Yes, can you connect me to Bart's Garage."

"What location, sir?" The operator asked.

Gale looked at Eronie. "Where did Zucker say he was from?"

"He lives in Clermont," Eronie answered.

"Clermont, please," Gale said into the phone.

"No listing for Bart's Garage in Clermont, sir."

Gale bit his lip. "Thank you."

"*But*," the operator said before Gale hung up. "We do have a Bart's Tire and Service."

"Connect me, please."

"Being connected, sir. Thank you for calling."

'*Ring.*'

'*Ring.*'

'*Ring.*'

Gale waited for someone to pick up.

'*Ring.*'

'*Ring.*'

No answer.

He hung up.

"Nothing?" Harlowe asked.

"Nope," Gale answered.

"Strange, it's early and not a holiday." Harlowe scratched his head.

"So what if that garage doesn't even exist? Or what if they say he was never there? Then what?" Eronie asked.

Gale thought. "Then we have more than we ever had."

"What are you thinking Detective?" Harlowe questioned.

Gale looked at the two men. "I asked Mr. Fullmer if it would be easy to bring in those weapons. Regardless of what he said, it certainly would not be easy. I highly doubt the killer is shoving those weapons in his back pocket or carrying them in his shirt. And I don't believe he's toting around a big bag either. Whoever brought those weapons in was not seen by anyone that works there *because* someone that works there is in on this."

Eronie was shocked at Gale's conclusion. "Are you serious?"

"It's just a thought, but if Mr. Zucker is the killer, then his girlfriend may very well be his accomplice."

48

It was nighttime and the sun's brightness had long since given way to the moonless sky. The chirping of crickets kept Hank up. Even without the constant noise he'd find it hard to sleep.

He had a feeling someone was after him. No one could be trusted. Everyone was suspect.

As much as he wanted to keep his promise with his wife about having the perfect vacation he knew it would be safest if his family had left. In the morning he would tell them.

Tonight he let them sleep.

He turned on the lamp by the table and sat down. He placed the manila folder down and pulled out a paper and pen.

Hank dropped his head and softly slammed it down on the table.

Up and down.

Up and down.

Up and down.

All he could think about was his wife and children. *Why does my life have to be so complicated?*

For the longest time he'd been chasing criminals, now he caught a glimpse of what it felt like to be chased.

But why?
Why now? Why here? Why me?
The questions invaded his head. They tore him up inside.

Hank was a strong-willed man. Emotionally he was as cold as ice. For years he covered up his emotions with his sarcasm, but his thoughts were beating him. They were slowly getting to him.

Why? Why? Who? Not now. Not my family.

A single tear trickled down Hank's stubbled cheek.

They had broken him. Hank's thoughts had torn down his defensive wall.

His family meant too much that even he was unable to control the emotions that beat down upon him.

His thoughts never ceased.

When will this end? Who are you?

Hank stopped pounding his head against the table and wiped away his tears. He looked down at the blank sheet of paper. A few teardrops had wet it.

Hank picked up the pen and began writing.

Robert Anderson.
28.
White.
Male.
Single.
Actor.
Los Angeles.
Detective show.
Hotel room.
Arrow.
Axe.
Vertical chest lacerations.
Newspapers.
Tracy Barkley.
47.

Black.
Female.
Divorced.
Restaurant owner.
Belhaven.
Detective book.
Bat.
Knife.
Numerous lacerations.
Newspaper.

Hank stared at what he had written. Still nothing popped into his head.

It was still just a jumble of letters and words. Nothing that grabbed his attention.

"Is there a signature?" He asked himself.

He thought about what he had written. He tried to analyze the details.

They couldn't be more different. Maybe there are no signatures. Weapons are all different. Different sexes. Different races. Different ages. Different marital situations. They were complete opposites. Was that the signature? Was being completely different the signature? Those thoughts ran through his head as he strained his eyes looking at the notes.

Hank saw the word 'newspaper' and thought. "Am I the signature?' He asked aloud.

"No," he answered himself. *I can't be,* he thought. *That's what he wants me to believe. That's the ploy signature. There's still a game he's playing. That signature is so that I know it's for me to figure out. He wants me to play his game.*

"I'll play," Hank said loudly.

"Play what?" Carol asked in a tired voice as she turned on the nightstand light.

Hank looked at her. "Nothing honey. I was just

talking to myself. Sorry I woke you. Go back to sleep."

"Hank you get to sleep. You haven't slept in three days."

"I can't sleep Carol, not with this looming over my shoulder. I need to figure this out."

"Hank, you cannot go your whole life doing what you're doing. It's not safe. Let's leave and go back home tomorrow. This is too much for all of us to worry about. We came here to spend a great vacation together. We took the kids out of school and we came here to forget about everything that has happened back home." Carol looked sad. "But it hasn't worked. Instead we are in the same situation. Scared for our lives. Scared for our children's lives. We haven't escaped anything. We ran right back into it."

"I was thinking the same thing Carol," Hank replied. "I was just thinking it may be best to go back home. I know I promised you a great vacation, but I think that has gone down the drain. I'm sorry."

"I understand that dear. Sometimes you need to break a promise. This time is one of them. It's for the best. We should leave tomorrow morning. First thing. The kids will be upset, but they'll get over it," Carol said with a yawn.

Hank looked back down at his notes then back up at Carol. "It would be best if you and the kids took a flight tomorrow."

"Me and the kids? What about you?" Carol asked in an angered tone.

"I have to figure this out Carol. I have to stay here and figure this all out. If not, then what am I going back to? A life of fear? I have to solve this, Carol. You know that."

Carol looked at Hank and shook her head in disgust.

"I don't believe you Hank. I really don't believe you. Do you hear what you're saying? What are *you* going back to? How about your family. Do you know when to give up on work, Hank? Because it sure as hell seems like you know how to give up on all else. You spend all your time trying to solve others' problems when maybe you should be trying to solve your own."

Hank was upset at Carol's comments and didn't know what to say. He sat at the table with a blank stare.

Carol reached over and turned off the light.

A tear fell from Hank's chin and splashed onto the paper.

PART II
A WEEK LATER

1

It would be hard to say that life around Orlando had returned back to normal, but it seemed as if things were headed in the right direction. Every day was a new beginning for anyone who had been a part of the two murders. A chance to start again. Although the world stopped for Anderson and Barkley, it still moved forward for everyone else. Everyone had to move on. The sun still came up every morning and the moon still lit the sky each night.

Gale sat in his office fumbling through the complete list of guests staying at the Vandermeer. Each morning Eronie delivered an updated list to him. Fewer and fewer people who had been at the Vandermeer a week ago still remained.

Only twenty-six were left.

It had been over a week since Barkley had been murdered and Gale had no more leads or new suspects. Tom's alibi checked out, he had been at the garage. Gale was still suspicious of the young writer, but he had no solid evidence against him. He had no solid evidence against anyone.

Could the murders really have been perfect?

Hank sat alone in his hotel room, his family had

long since left for their home in Massachusetts. All he did was scribble anything that popped into his head down on his paper. He had looked at the pictures in the manila folder hundreds of times, read his notes hundreds more, but nothing seemed to give him anything useful. It had been a week and he was still lost.

Lost and alone.

Back at the Vandermeer, Fullmer tried his hardest to bring back the good name to his hotel. Business was certainly not booming, but it had grown slightly from the one hundred and fifty people that graced its five levels a week ago. Having police on every floor made it difficult, but at least guests would know it was safe.

Safe or a hot spot for crime.

Calverly had returned to work even against the urging of her parents. She needed the extra money. She was never afraid to work at the hotel to begin with. The crimes were heinous, but Calverly knew she was safe. There was a police officer in the lobby and numerous others throughout the hotel. Eventually they would have to leave, but not yet. Until then she felt secure. She was always behind the check-in counter with others, in the middle of an open lobby. No one would be able to get to her.

No one.

Tom was hard at work writing his second novel. He had learned a lot from his interrogation, and being a suspect in a crime gave him a different outlook on things. It was good for his writer's block. It was even better for his book. Since he had been in Gale's office a week ago he had written over one hundred pages.

Over one hundred murderous pages.

Kelly and Andy occasionally brought up the horrific crimes when there was an update on television.

The updates just rehashed what had been known for the past week, which was nothing at all. Until someone was caught they still constantly worried about their daughter's well being. It was scary to think that she worked at the hotel that housed the victims of two awful murders. Until the murderer was found not many felt safe.

Certainly not the Calverlys.

Dunfellow was in the guest room packing his suitcase. Tomorrow night he would be leaving vacationland and heading back to his own home. He thought it would be good to get a head start on his packing, that way he could leave whenever he wanted without having to worry about forgetting something. He didn't consider his time in Florida well spent, but he didn't blame any of that on a lack of hospitality from his sister and brother-in-law.

He blamed that on death.

2

There's only so much a man can take. Sometimes the weight of the world seems to be thrown on one's shoulders and there's nothing they can do to relieve it. It crushes them. It destroys them. It eats them up inside.

Gale was that man. The two crimes had taken their toll on him. Not finding the killer, or even a suspect, made it worse. He needed to find the murderer, even if no one else fell victim. Even if life eventually returned to normal Gale would have this weight on his conscious. Its power was immense. Gale sought justice. He would not rest until he had found it.

"Detective Gale," Eronie said as he entered Gale's office. "It's been over a week since the last victim was found and we still don't have any new leads. Nothing at all. No suspects. Nothing."

Gale was at a loss for words. "We may have to wait this one out."

"What do you mean?" Eronie asked, shocked at Gale's statement. "Wait it out, as in wait for another body to turn up?"

Gale's eyes were lifeless as he looked up at Eronie. "Sometimes as hard as we try we find ourselves lost. Sometimes we don't know what we're looking for.

Sometimes, Dan, we're stuck. Trapped in a hole with nowhere to go. Sometimes we reach a dead end. This may be one of those times."

Eronie was shocked. The once powerful Gale had seemingly given up. "You cannot believe that it's over. Not like this. The killer hasn't struck again. There's still time. You can't really think it's best to just wait until he strikes. How can you think backing ourselves into a corner is the right thing to do?"

Gale looked troubled. "I never said it was the right thing to do. But at this point it may be the only thing." Gale had never encountered such a state of depression. He had always known how to handle a situation.

This time was different.

This time he was lost.

"Whoever is doing this is playing a game. They're playing a deadly game. And someone isn't cooperating correctly. *Someone* isn't playing along."

3

It had been over a week since someone had last entered the apartment. It was no cleaner. The room still smelled of rot, more so than ever before. Each time it got worse. Each time more papers seemed to litter the floor, more blood seemed to stain the couch, and more horror seemed to pile inside. If the rancid smell of death didn't frighten anyone who opened its door, then the shocking sights within it would assuredly do so.

A second, large green trash bag full of bloodied clothes had been sitting on the couch, nestled against the last. Dried, sticky blood painted the wooden floorboards. Looking at the room was torturous in itself. Death resided here, not life. Evil's footsteps could be heard here, not good's.

The bathroom was messier than ever. Blood adorned its tiled floor and splattered its walls. A second bloodied towel lay atop the first, signifying the latest victim. The mirrored medicine cabinet was cracked further, a sign of frustration. The suit that had once been missing from its hanger gracefully hung from the doorknob again. It was the only thing in the place without a drop of blood on it.

The only thing vacant of death.

The kitchen was left as it had been. The same

sandwich remained on the table. Younger flies still picked at it. The ones who feasted on it last were now dead, flipped over and hardened amongst the room.

The room full of weapons remained the same, barring the missing bat and knife. The Garrison article was still on the floor, more torn and tattered than it had been. The headline was unrecognizable. The only thing that could be made out was the smudged image of Garrison's face, a jagged dagger piercing his left eye.

A long piece of nylon rope dangled from the ceiling, wrapped securely around the fan. It spun slowly around, as if circling what was underneath. Circling the picture of Garrison.

This room had more evil in it than the rest of the house did combined.

It was the room of pure evil. It was the sign of death.

The only bit of good that seemed to ever shine on the room came from the window looking outside. Even when the dark night took over there could still be a sign of light in the distance.

A sign of life.

Three blocks from the darkened apartment building were the lights of the city. Like stars, sleepless buildings, would light the sky. One building was the most powerful. The most bright. One building just never seemed to sleep. Whether it was due to fear or fun it always lay awake. The light from its eyes glared back at the darkened apartment building.

The light of the Vandermeer.

4

Tom sat by his desk typing away. He hadn't moved from the area in over four hours. Writer's block no longer stalled his thoughts, but he may have fallen victim to something far worse. His thoughts were too quick for his fingers to keep up with them. Thoughts and ideas filled his head, but they spewed out too quickly.

He had a dilemma: if he allowed his rampant thoughts to take over he would have a book that made little sense. It would be a stream of consciousness no one, other than himself, would understand. Books don't sell if the author has to explain every word written in them. On the other hand, if Tom blocked out the images his mind bestowed upon him his book would lack realism. He needed a mix of the two.

Tom stopped typing and looked at his watch.

10:23 p.m.

His thoughts were flooding his head. He fought them back.

Tom got up and walked over to his bed, leaving the solace of his computer. He lay down and waited for his thoughts to settle. He didn't want them to subside completely, but he needed them to calm down. Too much all at once was not good.

He starred at the ceiling tiles. More thoughts penetrated his head. Now thoughts that didn't have anything to do with his book bombarded him. Thoughts of life and death. He shook his head, trying to dislodge them, but to no avail. More and more thoughts overflowed inside.

Everything seemed to spin. He felt weightless, almost ill. The tiles started to get wavy. Tom blinked his eyes, trying to restore his vision. The wavy, incongruent images only worsened. Everything was askew. Tom's world seemed to be slowing down.

What's happening? He thought. *Why am I dizzy? Is it because I have too much on my mind?*

Tom couldn't answer his own questions. The ceiling continued to spin out of control. His eyes got heavy and everything suddenly went dim.

It was 10:30 p.m. when Calverly pulled into Tom's driveway. She had had a long day at the Vandermeer and was ready for bed. She got out of her car, locked the door, and quickly walked to the front door. Ever since the murders Calverly never liked returning home after dark because she believed that the darkness was where the killer lurked. Only at night did she get the strange feeling that someone was following her.

Tonight was no different.

Calverly fumbled through her keychain in search of the house key. She always had trouble finding it, and the darkened sky didn't help her cause. She held up one key towards the house's spotlight and squinted to see if it was the right one.

It was the Vandermeer's register key.

She tried another.

Her parents' house.

Her chain was overcrowded with keys. They all looked the same. At night everything looked the same.

Calverly continued her search, but then stopped as she heard a rustling in the bushes.

Her heart sank. Her eyes widened.

She spun around quickly to see the two beady eyes staring back at her.

5

Dunfellow was sitting on the sofa, his eyes focused on the television. Some old gameshow filled the thirty-two inch screen. He reached into a bag at his side and pulled out a few potato chips, popping them into his mouth. Andy walked over to the couch and sat down beside his brother-in-law.

"So Wally, you ready for your trek back home tomorrow?" Andy asked.

Dunfellow finished chewing the chips and then swallowed. "I gez I am. I'd like to stay lawn-ger, but I have to get back home and back to workin.'"

Andy looked puzzled. "I thought you didn't work. I thought you were retired. Back troubles and the such."

"Well I don't work in the same senz az you do. I'm no big shot loy-ya, but after retirin' from con-struc-shone I decided to start a lan-scapin' biz-nez. My back ain't like it use-ta be, but I manage. It's far less tirin' than my ol' job was." Dunfellow turned to Andy. "I thought I had told you that befaw?"

"No, I don't believe you mentioned it, but it certainly would explain the giant lettering of 'Dunfellow Landscaping' that fills up the back of your truck. Maybe you told it to Kelly. I was probably working."

Andy smiled and continued, "You know me, the big shot lawyer, has to make a living. But anyway, how is that business going for you?"

"Not too bad, I gez. The con-struc-shone com-pen-nee gave me a lot of their ol' tools. So that is helpful. I have a lot in my truck," Dunfellow answered.

"Yeah I noticed that too. Lots of stuff."

"Too bad most of it is a lit-tul rusty, but it gets the job done," Dunfellow said.

"Well whatever gets the job done, Wally." Andy stood up, patting Dunfellow on the knee. "I'm headed to bed. Have a goodnight. I'll see you in the morning. Maybe you could help with my lawn."

"I think your lawn is jus' fine. You have people betta than myself takin' care of it," Dunfellow responded.

"You'd be surprised." Andy walked towards his room. "Goodnight."

"Goodnight," Dunfellow answered back.

Dunfellow turned off the television and returned to the guest bedroom. His suitcase was set on the bed. He rummaged inside to retrieve the clothes he would wear in the morning so that he could place the suitcase in his truck tonight.

He pulled out a dark black shirt and some worn out blue jeans and placed them on the bed. He closed the top of the suitcase, but the mess inside wouldn't allow him to get it completely shut. He pushed hard on the top flap, sleeves and pant legs draped over the side. Dunfellow poked them back in with his hand. Squeezing the bag shut he began to zip it up.

The zipper was halfway to the other side when it broke.

"Damn!" Dunfellow exclaimed. "Good for nothin' old bag."

He walked out of the bedroom and into the living room then took a left over to the front door. He unlocked the door and walked outside to his truck. He looked in the bed of the truck for something. "This will do jus' fine," he said softly to himself.

He reached into the back and pulled out a nylon rope.

6

Calverly glared back at the eyes in terror, but let out a nervous laugh as the light shone on the body of the beady-eyed creature.

An opossum.

Calverly took a few more steps towards the front door as it scurried away. She had finally found the right key. As she approached the door she tightly gripped the key in her right hand, not wanting to lose it. Calverly grabbed the doorknob and inserted the key. She turned it inside the hole.

No clicking sound.

"Are you serious?" Calverly asked herself. "All that trouble to find a key and he left the door open?"

Calverly walked into the house and locked the door behind her. She turned the knob to make sure.

Locked.

Calverly walked into the kitchen and placed her keys on the counter. "Tom."

No answer.

"Tom," Calverly called out again.

"Katie?" Tom's voice sounded different. "Katie, I'm in the bedroom."

Calverly walked into the bedroom. She saw Tom lying on the bed. "Tom, I told you before to lock the door when you get here. Why don't you listen?"

Tom ignored Calverly's question. "What time is it?" He asked in a tired voice.

"Tom what the hell is wrong with you? Have you been sleeping all day?"

"No." Tom glanced down at his watch. "Wow. I just had the weirdest experience of my life."

Calverly sat down on the bed and starting taking off her shoes. "What are you talking about?"

"Last time I checked my watch it was 10:23," Tom replied, still in a daze.

"So?"

"Well it's 10:33 now and it seems like not a second has passed."

"Tom you're making no sense. All that writing has corrupted your mind," Calverly said.

"No. I stopped writing and came to lie on the bed just to straighten out my thoughts. Then the room seemed to be spinning and now you're here. It was such a strange feeling. I don't think I can even describe it. Nothing like that has ever happened to me before." Tom paused and the started again, "I think I fainted."

Calverly kissed Tom's forehead. "People faint all the time. No big deal."

"Katie, I think it may be a big deal. Why would I just faint? I've never fainted before in my life. Why now?"

"Maybe all the stress," Calverly answered.

Tom wasn't buying Calverly's reasoning, but he humored her. "Hmmm. Maybe you're right. All this stuff going on has probably gotten to me."

Calverly kissed him again. "Get something to drink. Orange juice or something. Maybe you just need a little something in your stomach. A little late night snack would do you good."

Tom slowly got up from the bed. The spinning sensation had departed. "I think I'm going to take a nice, long shower."

Calverly looked a little worried. "If you just fainted, do you really think that would be a good idea? What if you pass out in the shower? You could split your head open or something."

"I feel fine now. A little tired, but I need to keep writing. A shower will wake me up. I'll eat a little something first though," Tom answereds.

"Well I will not help you up if you do pass out," Calverly said with a smile.

"I don't expect that you would," Tom joked back. "Hey, by the way, did you end up getting me that list I asked you for?"

"Yes I did. I left it in the car. I still don't know why you would want that list. Can't you just look in a phonebook for names to use? That's what you did last time."

Tom massaged the back of his neck. "Yeah I know I did, but I like to do things differently for each book I write."

Calverly snickered. "Thomas Dale Zucker you are officially the dorkiest guy I know."

"Well hopefully my dorkiness will pay off," Tom replied as he left the room and walked to the kitchen.

He picked up Calverly's keys and grabbed a few chocolate chip cookies from the cabinet. Tom placed a whole cookie in his mouth and munched on it as he opened the front door and walked out to the car to retrieve the list of names. He found the list underneath the visor. Happily he grabbed it, locked Calverly's car, and walked back inside his house. Tom shut the door behind him.

It remained unlocked.

"Katie," Tom called out. "I'm going to take a shower. You want to join me?"

"No, I'm very tired. It was a long day at work," Calverly shouted from the bedroom, her voice muffled by the distance. "And remember, I'm not going to be here if you pass out."

"Don't worry about it," Tom shouted back.

Tom walked into the bathroom and shut the door. He took of his t-shirt and reached into the shower, turning the knob to 'hot.' He unbuckled his belt and removed his pants and then his boxers. His socks soon followed. Tom tested the water's temperature with his hand.

"Just right," he said as he slowly stepped into the shower.

Calverly was putting on her pajamas when she heard a muffled sound in the distance.

"Tom?" She asked quietly.

No response.

She hurriedly put on her pajama pants and walked over to the half-shut bedroom door. "Tom?" She asked louder.

She inched closer to the door.

Bam!

The door swung open hard, hitting Calverly in the face. She instinctually reached up to grab her nose, holding her hands up against it as if in prayer.

Blood started to drip.

"Tom that fucking hur..." Calverly couldn't finish as a masked stranger emerged
from behind the door and quickly wrapped a rope around her neck.

She didn't even get a chance to completely remove her hands from her face. The taut rope securely held them against her neck.

She was choking herself.

Calverly struggled against the stranger's tightening of the rope. She tried to scream, but nothing came out.

The rope got tighter.

She tried to kick the stranger, but her legs didn't seem to work.

Tighter.

Calverly's fingers snapped as the nylon rope, pressed so forcefully against them, bent them backwards.

The pain was excruciating, but she fell silent.

Tighter.

Her palm was directly pressed against her trachea. Harder and harder her hands pushed against her throat with the tightening of the rope.

Calverly's face started turning red. The blood vessels in her eyes began to burst.

She fell to the floor in pain.

Tighter.

She struggled for one last breath. No air came in.

Tighter.

Calverly's body went limp. Her eyes glossed over. Her struggle ended.

7

Although it was almost 11 p.m. Hank figured his wife would still be up and decided to call her. He desperately needed someone to talk to and for the past twenty years she was the only one he truly trusted.

Hank picked up his cellphone and quickly dialed his home number. On the third ring Carol answered.

"Hello," she said, sounding awake.

"Hi honey, it's me. Did I wake you?"

"No, not at all. I was just reading," Carol answered.

"Good. I know I called you earlier, but I just needed to talk to you again. I needed to hear your voice. I miss you and the kids so much."

"I know Hank. We all miss you too. I've had to deal with this part of you for so long, but it never gets easier. I know it's your job. I know it's what you have to do, but a big part of me hates that you do it. Sometimes I wish it would all stop. I wish you and I and the kids could live a normal life, one where you're at home instead of handcuffing criminals, or analyzing profiles, or getting shot at. I wish everything were just easy. But I also know life's not easy, if it was then it wouldn't be worth living."

"I know how you feel. I know I've been selfish with work for so long and I'm sorry. I wish I had realized sooner all the pain I've put you guys through. I have been thinking a lot this past week, since you've been gone, and I think it might be best to just give up what I'm doing here and just come back home," Hank sincerely said.

"Hank that's not like you. We miss you. *I* miss you. But I also know how you are. You want to find whoever did this, and as great as it would be to have you here, I know that one day you'll regret not trying your hardest. I know you'll regret not staying there. At least that's the Hank Garrison I know."

Hank fell silent for a moment.

"I know that's the Hank Garrison you know, but I also know that's the same guy you wish I wasn't. I should be home. I stayed here to protect all of you. I stayed to protect all of us. But in the end I realized that I also stayed because I was selfish. Because I wanted to catch the guy that is playing games with me. I wanted to beat him at his own game. I now know that protecting you all would be easier if I was with you. And in the same breath I need you all to protect me."

Carol let out a long sigh. "You've got to do what you think is right."

"I know," Hank replied.

"So if you leave there and come back home you won't regret that decision?"

Hank changed the topic. "Carol for the first time in my life I feel lost. Lost with what to do with everything. Two people have been murdered. Both have a sick connection to me. I have tried so hard this past week to figure out a deeper connection than that and I cannot."

Hank's eyes welled up.

"I look at the same photographs every night. The same sick shit, every single night. I write down the same words on a piece of paper every night. The thoughts of what has happened haunt my dreams. I can't sleep. I hardly eat. The more I stare at the pictures and my scribbles, the more I seem to be lost. I have no idea what to think about this psycho. I have no idea where to start. I look at the pictures and they mean nothing anymore. The gruesome images have no effect on me. I stare at the words I write and they quickly blend into one another. They become unreadable. The only thing I end up seeing are the wet droplets on the bottom of the pages. Tears, Carol. Tears are all I see now. Nothing but tears. There's nothing more I can do," Hank said, finishing his rant.

A tear slowly left the corner of his eye and began rolling down his cheek.

Carol sensed Hank's depression. "Then come home."

Hank didn't hear her. "I wish there were more I could do here. I wish I could help. I have dedicated over a week of my life, my precious time that could have been spent with you, to a case I'm not even on."

The tear stopped at Hank's chin.

"And sadly I have not found a single thing more than I had the day I began. I have given all I could have to this case. It wasn't good enough. It never will be."

"Come home," Carol repeated.

Hank dipped his head and watched as the tear fell from his chin and splattered onto the floor. Its journey had ended.

So had Hank's.

"I'll leave tomorrow," he said.

8

Tom rinsed off the last bit of soap that rested on his body and twisted the shower nozzle. It had been a refreshing time for him. The water seemed to erase away both his dirtiness and his overplayed thoughts. He grabbed a towel from the rack and began drying himself off, then wrapped it around his waist.

Tom nearly slipped on the puddles of water he made, but caught his balance. He let out a little laugh as he thought about what Calverly had said if he did happen to crack his head open.

She wouldn't be there to help.

Tom grabbed the doorknob and walked into the kitchen. He was about to get more cookies from the cabinet, but thought he'd better wait until dressed because the crumbs had a tendency to stick to his wet skin. He opened the refrigerator door and pulled out some orange juice, then rinsed out a used glass that was placed in the sink and poured the juice into it. As he brought the glass towards his mouth an idea came to his head. He put the glass back down on the counter and reached into one of the drawers for a pen and paper. He wrote down his thought.

A killer passes out after he kills.

He smiled and then picked up the juice again and began drinking it. He finished in two gulps.

"Ahh...that hit the spot."

Tom placed the empty glass into the sink and then picked up the list of names he had set on the counter before taking a shower. He tucked the idea he had just written into the list's pages and walked to his bedroom.

He slowly opened the door.

The lights were still on so he figured Calverly was still awake. "Katie?"

He pushed the door even further, but it was blocked by something. He noticed Calverly's legs and squeezed through the door's opening in a hurry.

Tom looked down in horror at Calverly's corpse. He fell to his knees, dropping the papers.

They fluttered about every which way.

Out of pure shock he started to scream. "Katie! Katie! What happened? Get up! Please get up!"

No response.

The pained face of Calverly was still apparent. Tom placed her head gently on his lap, as if not to hurt her.

Too late.

He tried to quickly unravel the rope that was so tight around her neck. It was of no use. She had taken her final breath a while ago. Tom kept chanting her name. "Katie. Katie. Katie. Please don't do this to me. Katie. Please."

He kept rocking her head in his lap. The blood from her nose dripped onto his towel. "Please, Katie. Please."

Tom's eyes got blurry. He shook his head to fight back the blur.

No use.

The thoughts invaded him again. He tried to shake

them, but they still endured.

The walls got wavy. The floor looked as if it were spinning.

Tom looked at Calverly's face. It, too, was spinning quickly.

All of a sudden the room started to slow down. Tom's eyes grew heavy. Everything went dim.

3

At least ten minutes had gone by since Tom passed out. He awoke in a state of confusion. He wanted it all to be just a dream. He wanted Calverly to just wake up.

Neither was about to happen.

Tom was sick to his stomach. Sick that he wasn't in the bedroom to protect her. Sick that he forgot to lock the door, even though she had told him many times before to do so. Sick that it was her instead of him. Tom was also afraid that they'd think it was him who had done this. That it was he who strangled Calverly. All signs pointed to it. If they thought he was a killer with nothing but a book he wrote, then, most assuredly, they would believe so now.

He wanted to clean up, but that would only make him look guiltier. He wanted to pick up the list, get dressed, and call the police, but what good would that do? He knew how the police worked. They would assume he was ridding the evidence. He was lost.

Why her? He thought. *What did she do?*

Tom reached for the phone, Calverly's head still on his lap, and dialed the police.

Within minutes Clermont's police and medics ran into the house and into Tom's room. He still held Calverly's head. He still wished he awoke from the nightmare.

It still would not happen.

"Sir?" An officer asked, shaking Tom's shoulder.

Tom didn't respond. Too much was happening in his head.

"Sir?" The officer repeated, shaking Tom more violently.

"Huh?" Tom uttered.

"Sir, are you okay?"

"No. What's happened to Katie? Why? Who did this?" Tom was in hysterics and he didn't make much sense.

The officer helped Tom up off the ground. "Sir, come with me. I know this is hard, but I need to ask you some questions. Do you think you can answer some questions?"

The officer walked Tom into the living room and sat him on the couch.

"Do you think you can answer some questions?" The officer asked again.

Tom blankly stared at the officer. His eyes were lifeless.

"Can you hear me, sir?"

"Huh?" Tom was still unable to speak.

The officer left Tom alone and walked back over to the bedroom.

"Detective Calloway," a large, bald police officer said. "Look what we have here." He held up the list of names.

"What is that?" Calloway asked.

The other officer handed the papers to Calloway. "It's the list of people staying at the Vandermeer. That guy just may be the 'Vandermeer Slasher.'"

Calloway looked at the papers. "Is that what they

are calling him?"

"I think so. It was a headline in the paper not too long ago," he answered.

"Who's on that case? Someone in Orlando?" Calloway asked.

"Yeah. Charlie Gale."

"Get him down here to look at this. But if you ask me," Calloway started while looking down at Calverly's body, "She doesn't look slashed.

Tom was rocking back and forth on the couch, still with only a towel on. A few officers guarded him.

Calloway walked back over to Tom.

"Sir, what happened here? Can you tell me what happened?"

Tom stopped rocking. "She died. Katie was killed. Someone killed Katie. I didn't help. I couldn't help."

"What's your name, sir."

"Someone killed Katie," Tom continued to mutter. "I couldn't help. I didn't help."

"Sir, who killed Katie? Did you see the man who killed Katie?"

Tom grabbed Calloway's hands. Calloway pulled away.

"Someone killed Katie. I didn't see him. I couldn't help. I didn't see him. I couldn't help," Tom chanted.

"Sir, please slow down. What is your name?"

Tom took a deep breath, trying to calm himself. "Tom."

"Okay good," Calloway said. "Now can you tell me what happened?"

"I was in the shower. I came out and Katie was dead. I tried to help, but she was dead. Katie was dead. Someone killed her. I didn't help."

"What do you mean you didn't help? Did you see

who did it? Did you see the guy?"

"No. I should have been with her. I didn't help."

"Tom, slow down. Take deep breaths. Listen to me. What happened to Katie?" Calloway asked.

Tom breathed heavily in and exhaled back out. He put his head in his hands and started to cry. "I don't know what happened. She died. Katie's dead."

Calloway patted Tom's back and turned to a nearby officer. "Alex, go into the bedroom and get a shirt and pants for this guy."

Alex walked away.

"Tom, we're here to help. We want to find who did this just as much as you do. We need you to tell us all you can. Can you do that?" Calloway asked, still patting Tom's back.

Alex returned with a t-shirt and sweatpants.

Calloway took the clothes and put them on Tom's lap. "Would you feel more comfortable with these?"

Tom nodded. He grabbed the sweatpants and stood up. He put them on slowly, not taking off his towel until they reached his waist, then he put on the shirt and sat back down.

"Tom," Calloway started, "Tell me what you know."

"She was fine when I went to take a shower, but when I finished and came into the room she was on the floor. I tried to help her, but it was no use."

"Was she dead yet, Tom?"

"I don't know. I think so. I tried to get the rope off her neck. I wanted her to breathe, but it was too late," Tom answered.

Calloway was about to ask another question, but stopped as Gale walked into the room.

Calloway stood up and looked down at Tom. "I'll be right back. Would you like some water?"

"Yes please," Tom replied.

Calloway turned to Alex. "Get him a glass of water."

Gale walked into the bedroom. Calloway followed.

"Detective Gale, I'm Detective Calloway of the Clermont Police." Calloway shook Gale's hand. "Sorry if we disturbed you, calling you this late." He looked at his watch.

11:37 p.m.

"I know you must have a lot of work with the Vandermeer case on your hands, but I figured you should see this." Calloway held out the list as Gale looked over Calverly's body.

"I know this girl. I know that man you were talking to. I spoke with him no more than a week ago. I spoke with her too. You think this is another victim of the Vandermeer killer?" Gale took the papers.

"Yes, Detective Gale. I think it may be," Calloway answered.

"The crime scene looks different, what makes you suspect it?" Gale asked.

"Just a hunch I guess."

The bald officer interrupted. "Well I know the crime scene isn't nearly as violent and grotesque as the ones you've seen, but that list you have in your hand is of the people staying at the Vandermeer."

Gale looked over the list. "I see that it is. What's your name officer?"

"Raymond Freestone, Detective," he replied.

"Well, Officer Freestone, I like the way you think. You may be on to something," Gale replied with a smile.

Gale turned back to Calloway. "What did you find out? Did he see who did this?"

"No, sir. He claims to have been in the shower

when it happened. He was in a state of shock when I was speaking with him. Seemed to have just come out of it."

"I see. That's certainly understandable. His girlfriend dies in his house while he was showering. When did he call the police?" Gale asked as he walked out of the bedroom.

Calloway followed. "We got the alert just about fifteen minutes ago."

Gale's eyebrows rose. "And you say he was in the shower?"

"That's what he said." Calloway had an idea why Gale was asking that. "He just changed into those clothes. When we arrived here he was still in a towel."

"Oh I understand that he has clothes on, Detective Calloway. That's normal. What's not normal is that his hair is not wet at all."

Calloway looked at Tom, who was still sitting on the couch.

"Was it wet when you arrived?" Gale asked.

"I don't remember," Calloway answered. "Are you suggesting that he killed that girl?"

"Not at all. Not yet anyway. I just find it weird. He says he was in the shower. How long did he wait before he found her body? Or worse, how long before he called the cops?"

Freestone came out of the bedroom and tapped Calloway's shoulder.

Calloway spun around and faced the chubby officer. "Yes," he replied.

"I just thought you two would like to see this." Freestone held up a newspaper article. "I found it under the bed. It was next to a few more pages of that hotel list."

Gale and Calloway read the article headline.

Garrison Makes No Mistakes.

They immediately turned towards Tom.

10

It was 1:03 a.m. when Kelly woke up to the knocking at her door. She turned to Andy. "Who could that be? Can you get it?"

"Honey it's so late. It's probably just your imagination," Andy responded in a tired voice.

The knocking continued.

"Honey, I'm scared. Can you get it?"

Andy threw the covers off his body. "I swear Kelly if there's not a person out there I will kill you. You always wake me up during the best dreams and it's never anything. Always a stupid opossum or skunk."

Andy walked out of the bedroom and over to the front door. He looked out the window and noticed the police car. His heart began beating rapidly.

Andy opened the door. A police officer stood before him.

"Is there a problem?" Andy asked.

The police officer took off his hat. "Is this the Calverly residence?"

"Yes," Andy answered. "What's the problem?"

"I'm sorry Mr. Calverly, but I've got some terrible news."

So many terrible thoughts ran through Andy's head. He didn't know what to expect. "What is it?" His heart was pounding against his chest.

"Your daughter, Katherine, was found dead..." The officer didn't continue as Andy started shouting.

"No! Not Katie! Not my little girl! Not Katie!"

Kelly walked into the room and saw Andy in hysterics. She only looked in his eyes before she, too, started crying.

"No. No. No. No. Not Katie! Why? Why?" Kelly kept chanting the same thing over and over.

Andy ran over to Kelly, who was now collapsed on the floor, and held her. The officer walked inside.

The raucous awoke Dunfellow. He got up and walked over to his sister and brother-in-law. "What's happened?"

Andy and Kelly didn't answer. They remained holding each other on the floor.

Dunfellow walked over to the officer. "What happened?"

The officer looked at Dunfellow. "Are you related to them?"

"Yes. Of course I am. She's my sis-ta," Dunfellow replied as he looked down at Kelly. "What happened?"

The officer looked at Dunfellow. "Your niece was killed," he answered, almost emotionless.

"What!? What the hell happened? How'd she die? A car axe-ee-dent?" Dunfellow asked.

"I was just sent to tell you this. I have no details," the officer answered.

"So yaw the fuckin' bear-ah of bad news? Is that yaw fuckin' job? How does it feel to ruin people's lives?" Dunfellow didn't mean to berate the officer, but the emotions were bringing him to do it. He was full of emotions. He tried not to break. He tried to be strong for the others who were in hysterics. He tried to be strong for his sister who lost her oldest child.

"You come hea and you tell uz this news and you have no details. Yaw goin' to go home awl happy to yaw wife and kids. This means nothin' to you. How does it feel to make othaws cry when you have nothin' to cry about?"

The officer glared back at Dunfellow, obviously having done this many times before. "It's true, sir, I have no clue what it feels like to lose someone. I don't like doing this. How could anyone? But it's my job. I have to do it. If not me then someone else. I'm sorry for your loss. I truly am."

"Yaw not sorry at awl," Dunfellow said. "I know exact-lay what yaw goin' through. I'm not stupid. Sorry doesn't mean a damn thing comin' from you. Yaw just fuckin' glad it wasn't someone ya know. Yaw just fuckin' glad some otha man isn't knockin' on yaw door at night tellin' you someone died. Tellin' you that you lost someone you loved. Yaw just fuckin' glad there's no emo-shone-less person wakin' you up to de-liva bad news. That's what yaw thinkin.'"

The officer still kept his composure. Dunfellow made a lot of sense, the officer knew that. It was certainly true. He wouldn't want to be the one on the floor crying because someone he loved died. As much as he didn't want to be the man to deliver bad news, he didn't want to be the man having bad news delivered to him even more.

Dunfellow was now rubbing his sister's back. Andy and Kelly were like zombies. They didn't speak at all. Lost in memories. Lost in emotion. Lost in pain.

Lost in a world of their own.

Dunfellow walked up to the police officer. "I would like to see Katie. I would like to I-den-ta-fie her body," he said.

"You can come with me. I can bring you there,"

the officer responded.

"Oh...ka..." Dunfellow stopped as he heard the baby crying. "I better stay hea faw now. I have to make shore everythang is okay. I'll be there early to-ma-rah."

The officer took out a pen and wrote out the directions on the back of a business card.

"Come whenever you can," he said, handing the card to Dunfellow. "Once again, sir. I am sorry." He had nothing left to say. 'Goodnight' wouldn't seem appropriate, as nothing would be good any longer. He backed out of the doorway and left.

Dunfellow walked into the baby's room. He knew how to stop the baby's cries, but the others would be hard to fix.

11

The holding cells were small, dark, and filthy. They only contained a thin, wooden bench, much too uncomfortable to sleep on, and a small, dirtied toilet. The walls were covered with obscenities and scratches. The obscenities were written with the soles of boots and sneakers. They were unclear writings, but the scuffing did the job well enough. The scratches that adorned the walls were made by fingernails, teeth, and whatever else was sharp enough to engrave an everlasting image within the cell. They were the lasting memories of the others who were kept there.

The floor was disgusting, full of dirt, grime, and the remnants of vomit and spit. It looked as if it was hardly cleaned, and when that time came it was only quickly mopped. Criminals don't need comfort. They do not need cleanliness.

Criminals need nothing.

There were a few cells, each directly beside one another, all housing someone who had done something wrong.

In one cell an old bearded man laid, face first, in his own vomit. He moaned and groaned every so often, but he was passed out. His dirty clothes were only made dirtier by the scum that amassed on the floor. His ripped gray sweatpants were pissed and yellowed in front. The old man was drunk. Yet as disgusting as his cell was, it must have been a better haven to him than the streets and alleys he was used to.

Another cell contained a sickly looking thin man. The veins in his arms protruded. You could actually watch the blood being slowly pumped into them, although it was obvious that more Heroin than blood thrust its way through the veins. He had no shirt on and his ribs were easily visible, as his stomach seemed to cave in. His legs looked as if they were twigs stuck in a pair of shorts. The man's face was sunken in and he had dark circles under his eyes. The circles only made his eyes seem more protrusive. The skinny man was drugged out, stuck in a small cell, but it was the drug that traveled through his veins that was stuck in a far worse spot.

Another cell contained a young Hispanic man. He was dressed well in comparison to the other prisoners. He had on a button-down blue shirt and baggy blue jeans. The man lay asleep on the thin wooden bench, tired from his late night job selling drugs to people who need to fulfill their cravings, like the other prisoner. He would be sentenced to a while behind bars. His youth would be wasted.

The final cell held Tom. He quietly sat on the hard bench, contemplating what had happened earlier in the night. He was too afraid to go to sleep, too afraid to become accustom to his cell. He just sat, staring at the etchings on the walls and watching the dust swirl around the floor. Occasionally he would glance over at the other cells and the scum that was caged inside, but then it would dawn upon him that he was just as caged as they were.

That he was just as much scum too.

No matter what Tom had told the police at his house, it wasn't enough to keep him out of jail. They had too much. All the evidence pointed to Tom, regardless of whether he did it or not. He knew that if he were in their shoes he'd think it were him too. Tom was most definitely the prime suspect. He had no solid alibi. Even the garage attendant didn't know when Tom had arrived the day Barkley died, just that he did arrive around 5 p.m. At the time, 'around' was good enough, now Tom doubted it would be. He was found with the dead Calverly in his hands. The list of names were strewn everywhere. They probably had found his book idea note among the wreck, so to say he passed out would be preposterous. They wouldn't believe it anyhow, he was never prone to passing out before. He never had problems before the day Calverly was murdered. No doctor could testify that he had fainting spells. All signs pointed to Tom. Even he couldn't deny that.

But Tom was sure he didn't kill Calverly. He was sure he had nothing to do with it. Thoughts raided his mind. *I never keep rope in the house. I would never hurt her. I never lifted a finger to her in the past. Why would I have done it now?*

He was sure it was someone else. But being sure didn't change where he was. Being sure had no bearing on his situation.

And was he actually sure?

Tom's mind retraced his memory. *I remembered talking to Katie, taking a shower, seeing her dead, passing out, calling the police, and then waiting. I did have awful thoughts all day about death. Were the thoughts because of my book, or were they something more? Am I sick? Did I think of the passing out after killing someone idea for my book or from a hidden memory?*

So many thoughts ran through Tom's head that he didn't even know what to believe any longer. Everything was so puzzling that he wasn't as sure as he thought he'd been.

Could I have killed her? He thought.

12

Once again Gale was sitting in his office. It had been a while since there was any new information of the Vandermeer murders, and he was still unsure that Tom had any part in it. He was uncertain of the connection between Calverly's death and the two others. They were too different, except for the newspaper article.

It was true that all the signs pointed to Tom. And even if he wasn't responsible for Anderson and Barkley, he still could have been Calverly's killer. The article could just have been a coincidence; it didn't necessarily mean Tom was the 'Vandermeer Slasher.'

Eronie and Harlowe arrived at Gale's door. Gale invited them in.

"So we found the killer," Eronie said. "No need for the FBI now. Too bad we didn't lock him up a week ago."

Gale rubbed his forehead. "Dan, I know you have this complex with trying to find out who killed Anderson and Barkley, but you have basically suggested everyone we interrogated since day one. Tom may very well have killed that young girl, but we still do not have enough on him to hold him responsible for the other two murders."

Eronie didn't understand. "Detective, you told me what you had on him. The hotel list, the bad alibi, the delay with calling the police, the newspaper. If he isn't the killer then who the hell is?"

"I'd like it to be Tom, I really would. It would make my job easier. But my job isn't supposed to be easy. That's not how it works. If he did kill that girl, why was he still at the crime scene? Why did he call the police instead of fleeing? And why didn't he cut her at all?" Gale asked.

Eronie thought about Gale's questions. "I don't know what you're trying to get at Detective. Sure this would seem too easy if it were a movie. It's never the one that seems too obvious. It's never the one you find that all the evidence points to. But this isn't a movie. The guy got caught. Plain and simple. He got caught."

"Dan has a point," Harlowe chimed in.

"Whether Dan has a point or not, I'm still not convinced. Why would he want to get caught? He played us so well the last two times. Why get caught now? And why so easily?"

"He's a smart man. Maybe this is what he wants you to think," Eronie replied.

"He's not *that* smart. I think Tom is in a cell in Clermont, while the real killer is still running around here, in Orlando. Think about the first two murders. Both at the Vandermeer, both tourists, both horribly cut. That girl's death doesn't fit any of the criteria. Yes, she works at the hotel, but she's not a tourist. She was killed in her house, not in the hotel. And she was strangled, not cut," Gale stated firmly.

"Well how could she be killed at the hotel? There are too many police posted inside, it would be impossible," Eronie answered.

"Nothing is impossible. Not for a cold-blooded killer."

"So you think the killer is still out here somewhere?" Harlowe asked.

"I think so. I think this is just what he wanted. He got lucky. Tom killed that girl, or maybe he didn't kill her, but everyone thinks he did. The killer got lucky because now people aren't afraid any longer. They'd never suspect a knock on their door to be a murderer, or a man in an elevator. They think they're safe again."

"So just say Tom didn't kill the other two. Even say he didn't kill that girl. Where does that put us?" Harlowe asked.

Gale leaned in. "I'd say we're very close to being helped by the FBI. But more importantly it would mean that the killer had his time off to prepare for what's next on his agenda. Time off to plan his next victim."

13

Hank had just got out of the shower when his cellphone rang. He picked it up and looked at the caller ID. He didn't recognize the number. It was the first time since he'd been in Florida that someone other than his wife had called.

He pressed in a green button. "Hank Garrison," Hank answered.

"Hello Hank. It's Victor."

"Hey Victor. I didn't recognize the number."

"Yeah I'm using my wife's phone. My battery is dying," Victor replied. "So how are you doing?"

"Well to be quite honest, not so great."

"Oh you're not enjoying your vacation?" Victor asked as a means of conversation, not even thinking about the happenings that had occurred where Hank was.

"I wouldn't call what I've been through a vacation. So how's work without me?"

"Well actually Hank that's why I called. I wasn't sure if you were back home…"

"No. I'm still in Florida, leaving in an hour or so actually," Hank replied.

"Oh I see. I just wanted you to know that Jeffrey Gunderson of the Florida Bureau gave me a call about an hour ago. Apparently a Detective Gale from the Orlando P.D. had contacted him. Last night a young girl was found strangled in her boyfriend's house. The police from her jurisdiction, Clermont I believe, have locked up a man they believe to have enough evidence against..."

Hank interrupted, "Victor what are you getting at?"

"Clermont thinks the guy who strangled his girlfriend also killed the two people from the Vandermeer. I'm sure you've been hearing lots about that case."

"They think they found the person who murdered the two people at the Vandermeer?" Hank asked.

"Well Clermont seems to think so. They found another newspaper article with your name on it at the scene. There was also a list of names from the Vandermeer. But it gets better. That Gale guy thinks they locked up the wrong man. Or he thinks they may have locked up the wrong man. He thinks the Vandermeer murderer is still on the loose. He thinks that either the killer had nothing to do with the girl's death or her boyfriend was falsely suspected."

Hank had just heard too much information. "So who did they lock up?"

"Hold on, I have the name written down here somewhere... A man by the name of Thomas Zucker. The victim was a Katherine Calverly."

Hank was shocked by what Victor had just told him. *That's the guy Charlie must have interrogated after me.* "And Gale thinks Zucker wasn't the killer?"

"Well there's more to it than just that. He's unsure. But he doesn't want the Vandermeer case just to close because they assume this Zucker guy killed his girlfriend and had some Vandermeer stuff at his place."

"What does Gale want then?" Hank asked.

"Help from the FBI. He doesn't want the case to

close until they are one hundred percent certain Zucker was the killer. He needs FBI to help him with that."

"Then why are you calling me? Can't they just get Florida's Bureau to deal with it?" Hank asked.

"Well they don't want to put that many of the Florida Bureau on this case because they pretty much think the case is closed already. At least from what they've been told. So they are putting just a few on the case. I figured you'd like to get your feet wet. It's been awhile since you last had a case. You know, since your accident."

Hank thought about what he had told his wife. "I don't know Victor. I promised my wife I'd head home today. I think I'm getting tired of all this bullshit."

"Oh, well that's up to you Hank. Do what you want. I just called to tell you all this. I know you're great with solving crimes. Hell, I think the whole world knows that."

Hank deliberated. "What information have you got?"

"The basics that Gunderson told me are..." he paused. "Um...he said that the victim, Calverly, was found strangled with a rope. She also had hand marks around her neck though. Broken nose. Five of her fingers were broken, bent backwards."

"No cuts?"

"No," Victor answered.

"How old was she?"

"Only nineteen. I could fax the hotel you're staying at what I have," Victor said.

"No. I think I'm just going to get the information from Gale."

"So you are going to be on the case then?"

Hank thought for a moment. "I guess."

Victor could be heard laughing. "You don't sound

too sure. You don't have to if you don't want to."

"No. I do want to," Hank said.

"Okay, well I'll let you do what you have to do. I'll call you if I have anything more."

"Okay. Thanks for calling Victor," Hank replied.

"You're welcome Hank. Take care."

As soon as he got off the phone with Victor, Hank called his wife.

The phone immediately was picked up.

"Hello," Carol answered.

"Hi honey."

"Have you left yet?" She asked.

"No. That's why I'm calling. Victor Perrelli called me from the Bureau. Another victim was found. He wants me to join the case."

"You told him you would?"

"I'm going to see what I can do, just for a little while. No longer than a week. I just want to see what I can figure out. I need at least that much. I hate not being able to figure things out, you know that," Hank answered.

"I know," Carol replied.

"Are you upset?"

"Well I won't lie and tell you I'm happy. But I'll get over it," she replied.

"Will the kids be disappointed?"

"I didn't tell them you were coming home soon anyway. The one thing I learned about you in my time spent with you is that I know you're never too sure about the decisions you make," Carol answered.

"I can still come home if you really want me to," Hank said.

"No, Hank. I know this is what you have to do. I just want to know when it will all end."

"Soon," was all Hank could reply.

"I hope so Hank. Because if you keep it up, *soon* will never come."

"I know. Trust me I know." He stopped. "I love you honey. I'll call you later tonight. Tell the kids I send my love."

"I will. Goodbye for now."

"Goodbye."

14

Hank arrived at the Orlando Police Station at 1:23 p.m. He approached the counter.

"Hi, I'm Agent Hank Garrison, FBI. I'm here to see Detective Gale."

"Oh Detective Gale actually just left about an hour ago. I suppose he will be back soon," the officer behind the desk replied.

"Do you know where he went? Lunch?"

"I think he headed out to Clermont," the man replied.

"Is anyone from the Vandermeer case here now?"

"Actually Detective Harlowe is in his office," the man said, pointing behind Hank. "First door on the right."

"Oh thank you," Hank replied as he walked away.

Hank knocked on Harlowe's half shut door.

"Come in," Harlowe answered. He looked at Hank. "Hello Agent Garrison. Detective Gale isn't in right now."

"I know. I came here to talk to you," Hank said.

"Oh, well how can I help you then?"

"I've been officially put on the Vandermeer case. I would like to know any information you have."

"I haven't gotten word of you being put on the case.

I know Detective Gale is with some of Florida's Bureau right now in Clermont. I think they went to speak with Mr. Zucker."

"I see. Well you can call up Jeffrey Gunderson and ask him about me right now. I'm sure he knows," Hank said.

"Jeffrey Gunderson?"

"Yes. Have you not heard of him? He heads the Florida Bureau."

Harlowe thought. "Name doesn't ring a bell, but then again I don't know much about the FBI," he replied.

"Well that's beside the point. Call Gale up and ask him," Hank ordered.

"I can't do that sir, he is doing an investigation."

"I see. What about your partner in crime, where's he?

"Who? Detective Eronie?" Harlowe asked.

"Yeah. If that's the guy that I saw the last time I was here."

"Yeah. I suppose I could get a hold of him. I doubt he'd know anything about whether or not you're on the case," Harlowe responded.

"Where is he?"

"Probably with Detective Gale."

"Then I'm sure he'd know. Give him a call. Why would I lie about being on this case anyhow? I haven't even spoken with you or Gale in over a week. Why would I lie now?" Hank asked.

"Sometimes people do crazy things. Things that just don't make sense. I don't know how your mind works. You don't know how mine does either."

"I have a pretty good idea." Hank was angered. "What exactly *do* you do? Do you follow around Gale? Do his dirty work? Do you taxi people around? Report to him when he needs it? Buy him coffee?"

"I do what I have to, just as you would."

"Are you even part of the case?" Hank asked.

"Of course I am."

"Then why are you never around? What do you do? Shouldn't you be with him investigating right now?" Hank continued to question Harlowe.

"I don't have to hear this shit from you."

"That's right you don't have to. Just call someone and I'll be on my way with the information I need."

"And what information would that be?"

"The information you have on the murder that occurred last night."

Harlowe was perplexed that Hank knew of the death. It hadn't reached the papers or the news yet. He picked up the phone atop his desk and dialed a number.

"Dan, hey this is Jon. You guys still in Clermont?"

Eronie's voice could be heard on the other end. "I'm not any longer. I'm headed back now. I think Detective Gale and some of the FBI men are still there."

"What did you guys do? Did you find out anything?" Harlowe asked.

"I didn't do anything. Detective Gale didn't do anything either. The FBI was interrogating Zucker. We weren't allowed to do so. That's why Detective Gale is staying; he's going to ask questions of his own afterwards. I don't know why he even wanted help from these guys. He always talks so badly about them. Now we're shut out of anything good."

"Yeah. Well Agent Garrison is standing in my office. He wants to know if you heard anything about him being on the case," Harlowe responded.

"Yeah I heard Detective Gale talking about him. He's on the case. Probably won't be much of a help though."

"Well I just wanted to know. I'll see you in a bit I guess."

"Yep. See you in twenty minutes or so," Eronie replied.

Harlowe turned his attention back on Hank. "Well Agent Garrison I guess you were right. I do apologize. I just have a job to do and that job description involves not giving out details unless told to do so."

"Oh I understand Jon. I like that about you."

"So what is it you actually need?" Harlowe was a completely changed person.

"Anything you have on last night's murder. Pictures, files, notes, whatever."

Harlowe opened up his desk drawer and fumbled through numerous folders. He picked out the one labeled 'Vandermeer' and pulled it out. "You can have my copy of all we have so far." He handed the folder to Hank.

Hank reluctantly took it. "You sure? I could always have them photocopy this for me."

"Yeah don't worry, I'll just get another one later. It's pretty pointless anyhow. We usually all just look on with Detective Gale."

"Okay. Well I will keep in touch," Hank said.

"I'm sure you will."

Hank walked out of the office.

Harlowe let out a sigh as Hank shut the door.

15

"So Tom, is this room more like the kind you pictured being in when being interrogated?" Gale asked as he sat across from Tom at a small table.

Tom didn't find the humor very amusing. "Yeah."

"Tom, I want to make this quick and easy for you. I don't think you killed the two people at the Vandermeer. I cannot say the same about your girlfriend. But I want to know about the night she died. I want to know everything that happened."

Tom remained silent and then turned to his black-suited lawyer at his side.

The lawyer nodded.

"I don't know what more I can tell you that I haven't already told the ten other people that have asked me the same questions," Tom replied.

"There's a difference between me and them. They don't believe you. They would love to just end the drama and handcuff anyone who seems to have a connection with the other murders. They want to end the whole search, blame it all on you, and let people go on with their lives. I *do* believe you."

"Is this about Katie or about the other murders?" Tom asked.

Gale ignored the question. "Did you kill Katie?

Did you kill your girlfriend?"

Tom bowed his head then slowly picked it up and looked directly at Gale. "No."

"Who did?"

"I wish I knew. Whoever it was deserves to die. Die a slow death."

Gale did not like Tom's tone. "Tell me what happened. Every detail."

Tom took a deep breath. "Katie came home around 10:30 last night. I was in my room when she arrived. I was writing about ten minutes before she came, but all of a sudden I felt dizzy so I went to lie down on my bed. The next thing I knew several minutes had passed and Katie was there. I must have passed out."

"Has that ever happened to you before?" Gale asked.

"No, it was strange. I don't know why it happened. Katie said maybe from stress. She told me to eat something so I got some juice and cookies."

"What about the hotel list?"

"Oh yeah. I had asked Katie to bring me the hotel list because I wanted to use some of the names in my book, not the whole name, just the last names. I used a phonebook the last time, but I wanted to do something different. It made sense to me at the time," Tom answered.

"So you were using the list for the book?"

"Yes."

"Okay so continue from the time you were in the kitchen," Gale urged.

"I ate and right afterwards I went outside to grab the list from Katie's car."

"So Katie didn't bring it in to you?"

"No. She left it in her car. So I went outside to get it." Tom slowed down. He thought about how he forgot to lock the door. "When I came back inside I must have forgotten to lock the door."

"You forgot to lock the door?"

"I always forget to do it. My house isn't residential. There's like five other people who live on my block year round. The other houses are vacation homes bought by Europeans. I never thought it was necessary before."

"So did you see anyone while you were outside? Anything suspicious?" Gale questioned.

"It was pretty quick. I didn't notice anything unusual. No cars. No people."

"Then what did you do? Did you see Katie after you came back inside?"

"I didn't see her, but I did speak with her. She was getting ready for bed and I was about to take a shower. I asked her to join me and she said 'no.'"

"So you didn't actually *see* her after you came inside?"

"No. I came inside, spoke with her from the bathroom, and then took a shower."

"How long were you in the shower?"

"No more than twenty-five or thirty minutes. I thought it would help me with my fainting spells. I didn't want them to occur again," Tom replied.

"About what time was it when you got in the shower?"

"I'm not exactly sure, but I remember that it was 11:19 when I saw Katie. So I guess I went in at around 10:45 or so."

"When you saw Katie what did she look like?"

Tom didn't like the question; it brought back the awful image. "She had a rope around her neck, but it was even worse than that. The rope was tied around her hands too, and her hands were fastened to her neck because of the rope. Her nose was bleeding. She looked awful. She wouldn't wake up. I didn't want her to be dead, but I knew she was. I couldn't help her. That's what pains me more than anything else, is that I wasn't there to help her." Tom started to cry.

"I understand Tom. I understand. Why did it take you so long to call the police then? I know they arrived just before 11:40, but you said you found her dead at around 11:20. It wouldn't take twenty minutes for the police to arrive at your house," Gale said.

"When I saw her laying there I tried to help her, but then I started getting dizzy. I passed out like before. It must have been about ten minutes later when I came to and that's when I called the police."

"So you passed out a second time? Twice in about an hour span?" Gale sounded curious.

"Yes."

"But before that night you had never passed out before in your life?"

Tom nodded. "Yes, I had never passed out before."

"And what about the paper that had a line about passing out and killing someone on it? What was that about?"

"I wrote that after I got out of the shower. I thought it would be a clever plot for a story. I placed it in the list's pages and I dropped the pile of papers when I saw Katie."

"What about the newspaper article I found under your bed?" Gale questioned.

Tom looked at Gale quizzically. "What newspaper article?"

16

It was just after 2 pm. when Hank arrived at his hotel. He hadn't yet glanced at the folder Harlowe gave him, although he was certainly curious to find out what new information was inside. He opened up his room and walked over to the desk by the window. The room seemed so empty without his family in it. It was too big for just himself, but he didn't feel like asking for a smaller one.

In a way the larger room reminded him of all he was missing. It made him think of back home. It made him want to solve as much of the case as he could so that he could get back to his family. Get back to the ones who would make his life more comfortable. The room symbolized Hank's heart.

It was almost completely empty without them.

He placed the folder on the desk and sat down. Slowly he opened it up to reveal all the stuff he had already known about Anderson and Barkley. The same images he'd seen hundreds of times. He flipped through the pages of notes and photographs and finally came across some new things. The packet now contained several pictures of Calverly and a few pages of notes pertaining to the investigation.

Hank meticulously looked at each picture. He

stopped when he saw the close-up of Calverly's strangulation wound. There were bruises all over her neck that looked like hand marks. It was as if she was both choked by hands and by the rope. He looked at her broken fingers and nose. Nothing immediately came to him. It seemed like just a regular murder. Unrelated to the Vandermeer deaths. No slash wounds. No blood or guts. Just a simple strangulation. The only thing that made Hank a bit weary was that Calverly was from the Vandermeer herself. Although not a guest, she did work there.

He wanted to think that this was an unrelated murder, just a coincidence. Whoever they found was certainly not the same man who killed the others. He was only the culprit of this one crime. But he didn't know the complete details about the suspect and his alibi, or lack thereof. He had to give this crime the same credence as he did the other two. That was why he was asked on the case in the first place.

He grabbed the sheet of paper that contained his old notes and began to write some newer ones underneath the others.

Katherine Calverly.
White.
19.
Single.
College Student/Check-in Cashier at Vandermeer.
Clermont.
Strangulation.
Broken nose and fingers.
Rope.
Newspaper.

Once again nothing immediately popped into Hank's mind. It was still just a bunch of letters. Nothing more. Nothing had changed since the last two. Calverly didn't fit the puzzle any more than any other strangled victim would. She just wasn't the missing piece. She wasn't part of the killer's game.

Hank stared at all he had written once more.

Nothing, he thought. *Nothing, but letters. Letters. A bunch of letters. She is not part of the game. Calverly is not part of his game.*

Something quickly dawned upon Hank as he stared at the notes. "Letters," he uttered. "Game."

Hank thought about the games he played on his way down to Florida. All the games to make the ride go by quicker. One was the alphabet game. He looked at the notes again.

Robert Anderson.
28.
White.
Male.
Single.
Actor.
Los Angeles.
Detective show.
Hotel room.
Arrow.
Axe.
Vertical chest lacerations.
Newspapers.

Tracy Barkley.
47.
Black.
Female.
Divorced.
Restaurant owner.
Belhaven.

Detective book.
Bat.
Knife.
Numerous lacerations.
Newspaper.

Katherine Calverly.
White.
19.
Single.
College Student/Check-in Cashier at Vandermeer.
Clermont.
Strangulation.
Broken nose and fingers.
Rope.
Newspaper.

Their names were in alphabetical order. First Anderson, then Barkley, and now Calverly.
Was this the game? Was it really that simple?
The alphabetical order of the victims' demise alone wasn't a good enough lead. It could just have been coincidental. He needed something more.

Hank looked at where they were all from. Calverly from Clermont and Barkley from Belhaven. Anderson was from Los Angeles. He didn't fit the criteria.

Hank fumbled through the pages within the folder and pulled out Anderson's information.
Born in Anaheim, CA
Resided in Los Angeles, CA
Now he *did* fit. Their names matched their locations. Hank was on to something big.

"My name is Anderson, my wife's name is blank, I live in Anaheim and I sell…" Hank said aloud, looking at the notes he made. "Arrows and axes."

Hank was amazed. It had been in front of his eyes all along, yet he didn't see it.

He glanced at his notes again and noticed all the 'A' words.

Actor. Anaheim. Anderson. Arrow. Axe.

He looked at Barkley's information and read it out. "Barkley. Belhaven. Bat…" Hank stopped. "Knife doesn't fit."

He fumbled through the photographs and stared at the picture of the knife. "Butcher knife," he exclaimed.

"Barkley. Belhaven. Bat. Butcher knife…restaurant owner doesn't fit either. Is he trying for the whole one letter theme or just some?" Hank asked himself. "Tell me you son of a bitch! What game are you playing?"

Hank thought for a moment. "Bistro!" He said loudly. "Another name for restaurant is bistro."

Now she fit the criteria exactly. Both Barkley and Anderson had their jobs, places of birth, and weapons used to kill them start with the same letter as what their last names did.

Hank looked at his Calverly notes. "Calverly. Clermont. College student. Cashier." Hank pulled out the picture of the rope found wrapped around her neck and stared at it for a minute.

Suddenly it all became clear.

17

Gale had just returned from his interrogation with Tom. He had a feeling Tom had nothing to do with Calverly's murder and now he was almost certain he was not involved with the other two.

Gale was known for his skill at reading people, and he knew Tom was sincere when he asked about the newspaper. Tom was definitely oblivious to the fact that the police found the article. Gale's gut instinct was that Tom didn't put the article under the bed, someone else had.

A killer had.

Gale could only think of the three people who had already died. He knew that as long as people suspected Tom was the murderer there could be a few more. The killer was smart.

Almost too smart.

Three people dead in a span of ten days. Three people would signify a serial murderer. If Tom wasn't the real killer, and Gale believed that he wasn't, that meant a serial murderer could very well go uncaught. Three would certainly not be enough. Whoever it was would want more.

They may never stop.

Gale's thoughts were interrupted as his phone rang

loudly. He jumped as the unexpected noise jarred him from his thoughts.

He picked up the phone. "Detective Gale speaking," he answered.

"Charlie, this is Hank. I have to tell you something."

Gale was bothered. "Listen Hank, if you're not going to tell me that you are the Vandermeer murderer I don't have the time to talk right now."

"I think you'll want to hear this," Hank said on the other end.

"What is it?"

"I think I have a lead. I found a connection with the three murders. If they have nothing strong on Zucker then there's still a killer out there. And if there is then I think I may have a way to catch the guy."

Gale was curious. "I hope it's more than just a hunch."

"I believe it is," Hank said. "I would rather have gone there to show you what I found, but I didn't want to wait."

"Well go on, what is it?"

"I was looking at the information on the case and taking some notes of my own and I found out the killer's signature. It's not the newspapers that are left or the slashing. It's the alphabet."

"What do you mean?" Gale asked, completely interested.

"Anderson. Barkley. Calverly."

"I hope you have more than just that. It could be coincidence," Gale barked.

"I know. I thought the same, but I looked into it further. Anderson was from Anaheim, he was an actor, and he was killed with an arrow and an axe. Barkley was from Belhaven, North Carolina, she owned a bistro and she was killed with a bat and a..."

Gale didn't let Hank finish. "It sounds childish. It sounds like a childish game."

"I know Charlie, but as childish as it may sound they all fit. It's more of a deadly game than a childish one in his eyes."

Gale opened up his own folder. "I have that Calverly was from Clermont, a college student, strangled with a rope. I do see a lot of 'C's, but rope is not one of them. I know that Barkley was slashed numerous times by a large knife as well. A knife, Hank, doesn't begin with 'B.'"

"Look at the picture of the knife Charlie. It's not just a regular knife. It's not a steak knife or a dinner knife. It's a *butcher* knife."

Gale looked at the picture of the weapon. Indeed it was. The blade was rectangular and it even had the small hole on the upper right hand corner.

"Okay," Gale said.

"And now look at the rope that was used to strangle Calverly. That isn't an ordinary rope. You wouldn't use that rope to tie your boat to the dock. You wouldn't use it in a game of tug of war. Do you know what you'd use it for Charlie?"

Gale looked at the rope. It was thin and made of fine fiber. "I'm not sure."

"You'd hang your clothes on that rope, Charlie. That's what you'd do. It's a fucking clothesline. It all fits. The alphabet *is* his signature."

Gale was amazed. "So what do you suggest?"

"I suggest someone goes down to the Vandermeer and finds anyone who is staying there whose last name begins with a 'D' and to get them the hell out of there."

"Why the Vandermeer?"

"All the victims have something to do with the

Vandermeer. Anderson and Barkley were guests. Calverly worked there."

"So you want us to evacuate everyone whose name starts with 'D' at the Vandermeer?"

"Exactly. If the killer is out there he'll go after his next victim soon. The first two were back to back. I'm sure whoever he wants to kill has already been targeted. It would take too long to look for anyone with a last name starting with a 'D,' who was born in a place that also starts with a 'D,' and who has a job that begins with 'D.' We're better off being safe and getting everyone out of there that has a 'D' last name."

"And you think this will do what?"

"Well if we keep an eye on the people that fit the criteria then the killer can't strike," Hank answered.

"How can we keep an eye on that many people?"

Hank hadn't thought about that. He was stumped by the question. "I don't know," he admitted. "But I would think they'd all want to leave if they knew about this."

"We couldn't just tell them all about this hunch of yours. No matter how great it seems. It would cause mass hysteria. And what if your hunch isn't even correct?"

Hank once again had no quick response. He thought for a few seconds and then spoke, "What if it is?"

18

Eronie arrived at the Vandermeer at 4:12 p.m. at Gale's request. He was told to speak with the police posted there about the hunch Hank had come up with. Since Tom's arrest there were only about half as many police inside the Vandermeer. Eight had dwindled to five.

The police would have to be on the lookout at all times and suspect anyone who seemed even the least bit suspicious.

Eronie approached the check-in desk and Jen immediately put on a happy face and walked over.

She wasn't aware of her friend's death yet. It hadn't made the morning news.

It would undoubtedly make the evening news.

"Hello Detective," she said. "How can I help you?"

"I'm just looking for your manager, Mr. Fullmer, I believe it is."

"Oh yes, Mr. Fullmer. He's actually not working today. It's his day off. Would you like to talk to the manager that is on?"

"Yes, that would be fine," Eronie replied with a smile.

Jen picked up the phone and pressed a button.

The manager's office.

"Hello Mr. Donnelly, a detective would like to see you. He's waiting in the lobby." She hung up the phone and looked at Eronie. "He'll be right out."

"Okay. Thank you."

Jen decided to make small talk while Eronie waited. "Any new leads on the case?"

Eronie was surprised at her question. "Uh…sadly no," he lied. "But we're working night and day on it."

"That's good. I'm glad we have police here or else I'd be afraid to come to work."

"Well you know that's why we do it. For everyone's protection," Eronie replied.

"You don't think we'd have another incident here do you?"

"Let's hope not…" Eronie paused for a moment. "But like I said, I think everyone is safe as long as we're here."

A tall, skinny, blonde man walked over to Eronie. "Hello. I'm Edward Donnelly, the manager."

"Oh hello Mr. Donnelly. I'm Detective Daniel Eronie." Eronie shook Donnelly's hand. "I'm here on behalf of Detective Gale. Have you met him?"

"Yes I have. Recently actually. He asked me a few questions," Donnelly answered.

"Okay, well he would like it if you would have someone card the guests that come in here. Make sure no one comes in unless they are staying here."

"Why is that?" Donnelly asked.

"He just figured it would be the safest thing to do," Eronie answered.

"Do the police know of something? Because we haven't had the slightest bit of a problem recently, why tighten the security already set in place?"

"It's nothing Mr. Donnelly. Detective Gale would

just like you to do this until further notice. I will tell the police that are here to do the same. I'll also have them check each room in order to see that anyone who is not staying here leaves."

"So you want me to check everyone that walks into this hotel and see if they are on the guest list? That will take a long time."

"You have plenty of man power. I'll have a few officers help you out. And it wouldn't have to be you doing it. Just someone. Maybe you should make a posting somewhere or something."

"What about the restaurant?" Donnelly asked. "People from all over go there."

"Detective Gale gave me orders to have no one enter the hotel without proper ID. I suppose as long as the diners don't use the stairs or elevators everything should be okay."

"Tomorrow we have a business function on the functions floor. Most of the people attending are not guests here."

"We'll worry about that tomorrow. For now don't let anyone in here unless they are staying here," Eronie said.

"Okay, no one except guests," Donnelly repeated.

"That's correct," Eronie said. He realized it wasn't exactly correct. "Actually if they aren't a guest, an employee, or a police officer, then they should be somewhere else."

19

It was Fullmer's first day off in quite some time and he was very much thrilled with it. He even had planned a nice dinner with his wife. He had not spent a full day at home since he was hired as a manager of the Vandermeer, over a year and a half ago. Having the murders take place during his schedule was difficult, especially since he hadn't made the greatest impression in his short tenure there. He was on thin ice and he knew it. The day off would help him a lot. It was a chance to get back to normal.

Fullmer's wife was in the shower, getting a head start on being ready for their 7:30 p.m. restaurant reservation. It was a fancy restaurant and she was excited to be able to dress up. It was something she rarely got to do.

Fullmer was in the living room channel surfing. He was partially dressed for dinner, wearing a white button-down shirt and blue slacks. His tie and sports coat were neatly placed on the arm of a nearby sofa. He would put them on when heading out the door. It was too early, and much too hot, to do it yet.

Just before six o'clock Fullmer flipped to the evening news channel. He realized he hadn't watched the news in a long time, and it was something he once religiously did. He liked to keep up with the world.

As soon as the clock under Fullmer's television flashed 6:00 p.m. the news' theme song started playing.

'Breaking news in the Vandermeer murder case,' Mallory said. *'A possible third victim was found late last night in Clermont. The police are saying that the victim was a nineteen-year-old girl. Her name cannot be given out at the moment. She was found strangled to death. Police believe she is the latest victim of the 'Vandermeer Slasher,' but nothing is definite yet. The awful death comes only a week after the two deaths that occurred at the Vandermeer Hotel. The girl's boyfriend, twenty-five-year-old writer, Thomas Zucker, is believed to be the only suspect. He was found at the crime scene with what police are saying to have been 'sufficient evidence against him to warrant an arrest.' We will keep you updated, just as we have all week, on this tragic story.'*

Mallory turned to her co-host, Greg. *'If they do convict Zucker then he would be considered one of the worst serial killers Florida has ever seen.'*

'Absolutely awful. Just when you thought maybe it was all over, maybe it had ended, this happens,' Greg responded. *'A young girl with her whole life ahead...'*

Fullmer had heard enough. He turned off the television and sat back on the couch in shock.

Ten minutes after he awoke from his dazed state he walked into the kitchen. Fullmer's day off had turned from great to absolutely terrible. His wife saw the blank look on his face.

"What's wrong Brian?" She asked.

"Nothing," he said, unconvincingly.

Fullmer walked over to the kitchen phone and dialed the Calverly residence.

20

Hank hadn't left his hotel room since he returned with the case's folder. Although he was excited to have something about the murders to work with, he realized he wasn't out of the woods yet. Many questions still lingered, unanswered, in his head.

He asked himself, *Was it really Zucker?*

I doubt it. No criminal would stay at the crime scene. Not one who's playing this kind of game. Where does he fit?

Hank picked up an apple that lay among the rubbish on the table. The desk was full of his room service orders. He had not eaten out since his family left. Everyday was just more room service. Bacon and eggs in the morning, a ham or turkey sandwich for lunch, and pizza or meatloaf for dinner. The food wasn't good, but it saved him time. Time to ask himself questions.

Time to figure out the murders.

Hank didn't answer his last question. He had no idea what Zucker had to do with the crime, if anything at all. He had to answer a more important question first.

"Where do I fit? What do I have to do with this?" He asked aloud, as he bit into the apple.

Nothing. Absolutely nothing.

He began to think again. Thoughts and questions flooded his head. They seemed to be never-ending.

How does he know all this information about the victims? How does he have that access? Hank continued to chew the apple piece in his mouth. *Who has that kind of access? He would have to know them all.*

He's smart for using the biggest hotel in Orlando. Among all the guests he's bound to find letters 'A' through 'Z.' A hotel like the Vandermeer sleeps hundreds of people. Hundreds of vacationers. Hundreds of people from all around. It sleeps the whole alphabet a hundred times over. He picked the right spot.

The earlier question still loomed.

But how does he know the information he needs to target them?

Hank put down the apple.

Who has access to the guest names and other information?

"An employee," Hank answered himself.

He thought further before speaking.

"A manager."

Hank had another lead. *Could it really have been an employee? Could it have been the manager who found Barkley's body? He has access to the list.*

"The list," Hank repeated his mind's thought. He flipped through some of the pages within the folder and pulled out a statement pertaining to Calverly's death.

"Zucker had a list too," he said aloud.

A list from 'A' to 'Z.'

"'Z' for Zucker."

It was all too much for him to register. He had two possibilities.

"The manager or Zucker." He thought of the options. *The manager has complete access. He was the first person to see Anderson and Barkley dead. He would have access to Calverly's address.*

"No. That isn't right," Hank said to himself. "Calverly died in Zucker's house, not her own."

Now Hank turned his attention towards Zucker.

Zucker had a list. His book was based on me. That would give him a reason to leave the newspapers.

"The newspapers are the key," Hank said loudly.

He turned to the folder and thumbed through its pages, pulling out a copy of two of the newspaper articles. He placed them side by side and looked down at them.

FBI Agent Shot, Murder Suspect Flees.
Garrison Makes No Mistakes.

"He's telling me something. This is his way of communication." Hank shook his head.

"What do they mean?" He asked aloud.

Hank looked again at the article headline that was found last; *Garrison Makes No Mistakes.*

His eyes widened and he looked up from the desk. "He wants me to fail. He wants me to make a mistake. I fit because he knows what I'm good at. And he wants me to fail at it. He wants to finish what he started before I catch him."

Hank closed the folder.

The manager or Zucker, he thought.

"I won't let him finish."

21

Fullmer just finished putting on his tie when he heard the doorbell ring. He was surprised by the unexpected guest and hurriedly walked over to answer it.

He quickly turned the knob and pulled open the door, completely stunned by Hank standing outside.

"Hello. Can I help you?" Fullmer asked.

"Actually you can. Remember me?"

"Yes." The image of that wretched evening flashed in his head. "I'm sorry, but I don't remember your name."

"It's Hank."

"Well Hank, I don't quite know why you're here or even how you got my address, but my wife and I were just headed out." Fullmer glanced at his watch.

6:49 p.m.

Hank ignored the apparent rush Fullmer was in. "I'm here because I have to ask you some questions pertaining to the murders. And as for how I got your address, I called up your hotel and spoke with Edward Donnelly. I told him I needed to urgently speak with you, that this was FBI business, and he gave me it without any further questions. You see I guess police can just about do anything, especially the FBI," Hank said in a harsh tone. He was toying with Fullmer, trying to get a reading on him. If he were the murderer he would give away a sign or two.

Fullmer was uneasy with Hank's tone. He nervously looked at his watch again. "Come on in. I have a few minutes to spare."

Fullmer's wife came into the room. "Honey we have to head out." She looked at Hank. "Hello. I'm Brian's wife, Amy. Are you a friend of Brian's?"

Hank smiled. "We're just acquaintances. I'm Hank, from the FBI. I'm sorry to bother either of you, especially because it seems like you're in a rush, but I have some important questions to ask your husband. It won't take too long."

"I understand," she said. "Take your time. Would you like anything to drink?"

"No thank you," Hank answered.

Amy touched Fullmer's shoulder. "I'll be in the T.V. room, just get me when you're finished here."

"Okay honey."

"Nice to meet you Hank," Amy said as she slowly left the room.

"Same here."

Hank turned his attention back to Fullmer. "You were the first person to see Anderson dead, correct?"

"Yes. I already answered all these questions. Can't you just get all this information from the police?"

"I suppose I could, but I would rather get it from you," Hank answered. "I figure you know that your employee, Katherine Calverly, was found dead last night?"

"Yes. I just saw it on the news. I was in shock. Still am. So terrible. I still can't believe it happened. And her boyfriend...it's just sad. I never liked that guy. I should have sensed he was a murderer."

Hank was suspicious of Fullmer's answer. "You

didn't like the guy?"

"No. He just seemed a bit odd. Almost manipulative. Every time he came in to visit Katie I felt uncomfortable. And that book of his. That pretty much tells enough right there."

"What do you mean *manipulative?*"

Fullmer thought for a moment. "Just that he seemed scheming. It's tough to describe. It's just a feeling you get I guess."

"Uh huh. Did he show up at the Vandermeer often?"

"Not really. On a rare occasion, but it was often enough for me."

"Do you know if he showed up the days of the murders?" Hank asked.

"I don't really remember. I don't think I've seen him in awhile, but he must have been there."

"Why is that?"

"Because he's the killer," Fullmer replied.

"Well that hasn't been proven yet. It's too early to tell. Right now anyone could be."

"Are you saying he's not the guy who murdered those people?" Fullmer asked.

"I'm not saying anything. Just that you can't jump to conclusions."

Fullmer looked at his watch again.

6:54 p.m.

"I really got to get going. I have a 7:30 reservation at Gior's. Do you know how long it takes to get a reservation there?"

"I haven't the slightest idea. I don't even know where it is. In fact I haven't even heard of it," Hank answered, not caring about Fullmer's reservation.

"It's an expensive place. And at least twenty-five minutes from here. If I miss the reservation my wife will kill me."

Hank scratched his head. "Well that wouldn't be very good, now would it? We don't want any more bloodshed around here."

Fullmer didn't realize how badly what he said had sounded. "Yeah. So can I talk with you another time?"

"I just have one more question," Hank said.

"What is it?"

"How much information about the guests do you and your employees have access to?"

Fullmer didn't like the question; it meant he was suspicious about him. "Names, dates of birth, addresses, phone numbers, how they paid, what they owe, stuff like that," he answered.

"What about their occupations?"

"No. That would have no relevance to us. Why do you ask?"

"Oh no reason. I was just wondering. So do all of the employees have access to that information?"

"Well not all. Just the managers and the ones behind the desk," Fullmer responded.

"I see. Well okay, I'll let you catch your reservation. Thank you for your answers," Hank said as he walked towards the door.

"You're welcome," Fullmer replied. "But can I ask you why you couldn't just have called me? I could have answered all your questions over the phone. It would have saved you the trip here."

"Let's just say I needed to get out." Hank smiled and opened up the door. "Thanks again. Have a goodnight."

Fullmer didn't understand. "Goodnight," he replied. He closed the door and looked at his watch.

6:59 p.m.

Just enough time.

22

After Hank's short chat with Fullmer he couldn't help but think that he was taking the alphabet too seriously. Hank knew that it would be impossible for anyone, employee or not, to find out all that information about the victims. The killer couldn't be using the alphabet as a stepping-stone in every possible aspect of his murders. It would be much too difficult a task.

Maybe Charlie was right, he thought. *Maybe it was only a coincidence.*

Hank let out a long sigh.

But it had to be more than a coincidence. There is just too much. The odds of having all the letters matching, from the victims' last names to their jobs, are just too low.

Hank shook his head. "Almost impossible," he said aloud.

On the other hand, a sleep-deprived mind, such as Hank's, could make a connection with almost anything. Maybe he was trying so hard to find some sort of connection that eventually he saw one that went unnoticed to others. It looked obvious now, but it hadn't before.

Not to him. Not to anyone else on the case.

Hank once again pulled out his page of notes and stared at it, looking at each of the victim's races.

White.
Black.
White.
They seemed connected too. They had a pattern. One race and then the other. But was he taking it too far? Maybe he was completely wrong. He wasn't sure anymore. Now everything seemed to become connected if he looked at it long enough. Everything was a possibility if he thought hard enough.

He looked down again and scribbled on the side of each one.

American.
Black.
Caucasian.

The alphabet worked there too. Anyone could take a letter and find a way to make it pertain to a certain person.

Especially a dead person.

His mind was playing games with him now. Games even more dangerous than the killer's. He saw a connection in everything. The alphabet was everywhere. Hank put his face in his hands. "I don't get it," he said. "Is this even the alphabet game?"

Hank took out the pictures of each victim.

Axe cut through the abdomen. An arrow in Anderson's neck

Hank stared at his half-finished apple from earlier. "His Adam's Apple," Hank said softly. "More 'A's."

A bat to the back of Barkley's head. Butcher knife to her breast.

"More 'B's."

Rope to Calverly's neck.

"Nothing. I'm going crazy," he said as he shook his head, trying to remove the alphabet from his thoughts. "I am overanalyzing it."

Hank tried to forget about the alphabet connection for a moment and concentrate on finding something else. He looked at each victim again.

Arrow in neck. Axe-inflicted mutilations on the body.

Bat to head. Knife lacerations on neck and body.

Rope around neck.

"Another connection," he said aloud. "The neck."

Hank didn't know what to think any longer. He closed the folder in anger. "What is the real connection? Is it the papers, the alphabet, the Vandermeer, the neck, or is it something greater?"

Hank was confused. He was lost in his own instability. Lost in his own desire to find the murderer.

Lost in the game.

Just as Hank had been completely engulfed in the car games on his way to Florida, he had found himself the same way with this killing game. The ones he played driving were used to pass the time. This one had a time limit.

A time limit until someone was killed next.

Thoughts flashed through his head. *If it's the Vandermeer and the alphabet connection everything will be okay. He wouldn't be able to get his next victim. If it's not, I made the wrong move. He'll capitalize on my incompetence. But if it's not the alphabet, then what the hell is it?*

Hank shook away the thoughts. "No," he said loudly. "It's got to be the alphabet. It's got to be."

Hank softly banged his head against the desk.

"'D' is for death."

23

"Okay Brian, so you didn't speak at all about the cop during dinner. Can you tell me what that was all about now?" Amy asked her husband as they pulled out of Gior's Restaurant.

Fullmer loosened his tie. "I really don't want to get into it Amy. I've had a long day. It was going great and then it all came to a crashing halt. Topped off by that guy tonight. Let's just forget about the whole thing. We had a great dinner and we'll have a great time at the movies. Let's just focus on that."

"Dinner was lovely. We do need more times like tonight," she said, but then noticed Fullmer's face. "Well not like earlier tonight, but like at dinner."

Fullmer remained quiet and focused his eyes on the road.

Amy didn't like the silence. She so badly wanted to ask more about Hank. She couldn't keep it all in. "You know people don't usually come knocking on someone's door to ask them questions unless there's a good reason to do so."

Fullmer's face tightened. He was mad. "Look," he started, "I don't know what the whole thing is about. I don't know why he showed up. I don't know what's happening at the hotel, with the murders, with my life.

I'm stressed Amy. Stop it with the damn questions. I don't know the answers! I am not a cop!"

Amy was frightened by her husband's response. He had never acted so angry before. "Okay. I'm sorry. I just wanted to know about what's going on in your life," she said. "Is that too much to ask?"

Fullmer was silent again. He didn't answer.

"I guess it is. Please just take me home." She turned and looked out the window.

"Are you serious?"

"Yes. I don't like this. We were supposed to have a great night and it just hasn't worked out that way. Not to you anyhow. I just want to go back home. I don't feel like a movie any longer," Amy said without turning to her husband.

Fullmer shook his head and huffed. "You always do this. You always make it about me. This isn't about *me*, Amy. I don't know what you want from me. I asked you politely not to ask me questions. Not tonight. I'm not in the mood to be interrogated by you too. It's just too much."

"Okay," she agreed. "Just take me home."

"I'm not going home. We're seeing the damn movie."

"Brian don't play this game with me. Take me home. I don't want to see the movie."

"All this because I didn't want to answer your question? You want to know what the damn cop wanted? He wanted to know about the murders. More shit about the murders."

Amy was still mad. "And you couldn't have just said that before?" She asked audibly, but under her breath.

"Ugh. There's more to it than just that. He wanted to know more about the murders because I think he suspects I did..." Fullmer didn't finish as he swerved into the left lane to avoid a broken down car. "Holy shit! That man almost got us killed!"

Amy was catching her breath, visibly nervous at how close they came to an accident. "That man almost got himself killed," she said.

"What an idiot. Ugh. Is it too much for him to put on his hazards? It's pitch black outside. He's bound to hurt someone sooner or later," Fullmer responded.

"Maybe he needs help. Should we turn around?"

24

It was 9:10 p.m. when Dunfellow finally left for the morgue. He had wanted to go much earlier, but there was so much going on. It was as if Kelly and Andy were non-existent. He had to console the children and do all else. He hadn't slept since he awoke to the awful news of his niece's death, and it didn't appear he would any time soon.

Everyone in the household, with the exception of Dunfellow, just sat and cried. They didn't talk. They didn't eat. They didn't sleep. They did nothing more than cry since they had found out of Calverly's death. What made it worse was they never turned on the television, and although Dunfellow had wanted to, he didn't out of respect. All day, not one of them knew Calverly was murdered. They all assumed it was a car accident. They never thought of suggesting otherwise.

It wasn't until around 6:30 p.m., just after the newscast, that Dunfellow found out the truth. The phone had ringed constantly, but no one seemed to notice. No one, except for him. He was the only one that found it extremely suspicious that so many people would offer their condolences for a car accident, only because no one would have read about it in the paper. Calverly had died too early in the morning to have it make the newspaper. And even if it had, why wait until the evening to call?

Eventually Dunfellow answered the phone. That's when he found out about the newscast and their report on Calverly's murder. Dunfellow didn't know how to tell Kelly or Andy, so he unplugged the phone to prevent any more calls.

It wasn't until Dunfellow thought he had done all he could with Kelly, Andy, and the children when he decided to leave for the morgue. That was a full seventeen hours later. They were still a wreck, and would be for a long time, but he was at a loss on how more to console them. There are only so many times someone can say 'I know' and 'let it all out.' There are only so many times you can rub someone's back and hug them in order to try and ease the pain. Dunfellow realized all that. He also realized that when it was all said and done there was nothing that would truly take the pain away, certainly not him, not the guy who visited every five years. There was nothing that could stop the pain.

Pain would always endure.

The roads were surprisingly empty; a few occasional headlights could be seen every so often, but for the most part the streets looked vacant. The night was once again moonless and extremely dark; the sun was not even close to lending its brightness onto the road. It had only an hour ago disappeared and wouldn't soon be peaking through the horizon.

The truck made a weird gurgling sound. Dunfellow checked the dash to see if the 'Check Gages' light was on.

No.

The sound was beginning to annoy Dunfellow so he turned on the radio to drown it out. Country music filled the air. The sad song lyrics made Dunfellow realize that he didn't want to identify the body.

Maybe it would be too hard to handle, he thought. *But if I don't do it then Kelly or Andy will, and that would be even worse. I have to do it. Even if I don't want to see her dead, I have to. I shouldn't have to read it in the paper first. I shouldn't have heard from someone else how she was murdered. I should have been the first to know.*

Dunfellow turned off the radio realizing its thought-provoking effects. The gurgling sound persisted, even getting louder. Dunfellow was not in the mood to pull over, but in order to save himself the time of having to call a tow truck because of his car overheating, he advised himself to do so.

He flipped on his hazards and slowly drove into the breakdown lane. *It's probably just the antifreeze. I have some in the back.*

Dunfellow put his truck into 'park' and opened the door. He walked around to the front and popped the hood. The car smoked a little when he opened it. It continued to gurgle. Dunfellow checked the antifreeze. "Yep, a lit-tul low," he said. He walked back to his car and opened the door and then looked in the backseat.

No antifreeze.

He closed the door and started walking to the back of the truck. He saw headlights in the distance getting closer. They seemed to be coming right at him.

They got closer. He continued to walk.

Closer.

He was now at the back of his truck.

The car came closer.

"Holy shit," he said loudly.

Just at the last second the car switched lanes.

Dunfellow took a deep breath.

"Can people not see the haz-ards on? Must be some

ol' man." Dunfellow looked at the hazard lights.

They weren't on.

"Well that's dane-ja-ruz," he said. "Must be a fuse. Don't God damn drive the car faw a week an awl hell break's loose." Talking to himself made him feel more at ease.

He peaked into the bed of his truck. No antifreeze.

"Damn."

Another car could be seen in the distance. Dunfellow moved over to the grass, fearing the worst. As the headlights got closer they slowed up. The car veered over to the breakdown lane and stopped right behind Dunfellow's truck.

A man walked out of the car. "You need any help?" He asked.

Dunfellow started walking towards the stranger. "Yeah ak-chew-ollie. You don't happen ta have any an-tie-freeze, now do ya? I seem to be runnin' low and I'm afraid my car may ova-heat."

The man looked at Dunfellow. "I just may. Hold on, let me check." The stranger started walking to his car.

"Oh I don't think I can do anythin' otha than hold awn. I can't go anywhere until this is fixed," Dunfellow responded.

The man laughed at Dunfellow's response and opened his trunk. He quickly pulled out a bottle of oil. "Think you need more oil too?" He asked, holding up the bottle to Dunfellow.

"No. I think it's jus' the an-tie-freeze. But thank you."

The man started to laugh. "Okay, but don't say I didn't ask. I seem to have a whole garage in the trunk of my car." He pulled out a bottle of antifreeze.

"Then I za-pose yaw jus' the man I needed to have

help me out," Dunfellow said.

"I guess I am."

The man walked over to the front of Dunfellow's truck with the bottle. Dunfellow followed.

"You don't need ta paw that in. You've bin maw than kind enough. I wouldn't want you ta dirty yaw nice suit," Dunfellow said as the man looked into the hood.

"I doubt my suit would get dirty from me pouring this into your car," the man replied.

"Well ya never know. I doubt ya hands will stay clean though."

"Oh don't worry about that," he put his hand in his jacket pocket. "I have gloves."

"You seem pra-pared. Almost like ya expected to help me," Dunfellow joked.

The man placed the bottle of antifreeze on the ground and put on his gloves. "You never know when you'll need gloves," the man said. He picked up the antifreeze bottle. "Did you check to see if the cap of the truck's antifreeze container is still hot? I wouldn't want it bubbling up on me."

Dunfellow leaned over the hood. "It's not gurglin,'" so it prob-…" he didn't finish as the hood bashed down against his head.

The man dropped the antifreeze bottle and reached into his jacket again and pulled out a short-pointed, jagged-edged knife.

A dagger.

He inched closer to Dunfellow.

Dunfellow was dazed from the hood's impact upon his skull. He was grabbing at the back of his head, holding together the wound. Blood oozed from the deep gash. The hood was still over his head. He pushed it upward.

The first thing he saw was the stranger. His eyes widened as the dagger cut directly across his neck. Blood sprayed everywhere, splattering the pavement. He grabbed at his neck, trying to stop the bleeding.

A few cars darted by, but they didn't stop. Just two people helping each other out.

Dunfellow thought about running to the man's car, but it would be useless. He didn't have the keys. He didn't have the strength.

The man dropped the weapon and walked away, back to his car. It started up and he pulled away.

Dunfellow fell to the ground.

25

Detective Calloway and a few other Clermont police didn't arrive on the scene
until after 11 p.m. It had almost been two hours since Dunfellow had died. His strength had allowed him to crawl a few feet closer to the back of his truck, so that a passing car might be able to see him. So that it might be able to help.

When one did it was far too late.

Dunfellow had already bled to death. The deep wound across his neck could not be held shut well enough by his trembling hands. The blood continued to pour out until he had no choice but to succumb to death's invitation.

The woman who pulled over had the urge to drive off; not knowing what horror might pursue her. Not knowing if the criminal had vacated the scene or not. She pulled in behind Dunfellow's truck and saw his dead body sprawled on the pavement, his outreached left arm signaling for help. His right arm close to the gaping hole across his neck, but no longer holding it.

The woman was horrified by the dead man's image and immediately locked her doors and called the police. She remained in her car until they arrived less than ten minutes later.

Before Calloway even looked at Dunfellow's dead body he tapped on the woman's car window. She rolled it down in a nervous, emotional wreck.

"I called as soon as I got here," she said.

"I understand that ma'am," Calloway replied. He tried to calm her down. "Would it be okay if an officer just got in the car with you and asked you some questions?"

"I don't know anything. I just got here. I saw that man on the ground and called you guys," she answered in a trembling voice.

"We know that, but we just have to ask you some questions. Would that be alright?"

She couldn't say anything other than 'yes' because she knew Calloway would continue to ask her. "Yes," she finally responded.

"Okay," Calloway replied. He called Alex over. "This is Detective Alex Kershner. He'll be asking you a few questions, okay ma'am?"

"Okay," she answered.

"What's your name, ma'am?" Calloway asked.

"Cindy Pyle."

"You from the area?"

"Yes."

"Okay," Calloway said to her. He turned to Alex and spoke softly, "Just try and calm her down. She doesn't know much about this. Don't interrogate her; just ask her questions to calm her down."

"Yes, sir," Alex answered.

Calloway walked over to Dunfellow's body. The other police were already taking pictures and examining the site.

"What have you guys got so far?" He asked.

An officer looked up from Dunfellow's body. "Large gash on the back of his head. Probably from some sharp object. But it's obvious the lethal wound was this." He pointed to Dunfellow's neck. "Deep horizontal slice from right to left across his neck."

"Any weapon?"

"Yes. A small, pointed knife was found just a few feet from the body. Kasey's got it over there," he said, pointing to a short, bearded man near the hood of Dunfellow's truck.

Calloway looked at the open hood and licked his lips, forming a dimple on his cheek. "Must have been stopped to check his oil or something. Someone must have surprised him."

The man nodded in agreement. "Do you believe this may have something to do with the other murders?" He asked.

"I'm not so sure nowadays. If that guy Zucker is the man, then obviously not," Calloway answered.

"Yes, but this guy looks like he's been slashed. Maybe Zucker didn't have anything to do with the Vandermeer murders."

"Well as of right now there's no sign that points us to anything other than another crime. It may be unrelated. He may not even be staying at the Vandermeer. Or for that matter have anything to do with it. Get out his wallet. See who he is," Calloway ordered.

Calloway turned around and walked towards Kasey, pulling a cellphone out of his jacket pocket, he dialed a number.

"Hello, Detective Gale. This is Detective Calloway of the Clermont Police again. I'm sorry for calling you late again tonight. I hope this doesn't become a habit."

"Is there something wrong?" Gale asked.

"Well I guess you could say that. I'm at a crime scene right now. Another victim. This time he's slashed."

"Where are you located?"

Calloway gave Gale the directions and hung up the phone.

"So Kasey," Calloway started, "What have you got?"

Kasey was pulling at something from under the hood with tweezers. A few hairs. He put them in a little plastic bag. "Ah-ha," he exclaimed. "It seems as if the victim was trying to fix a problem. Someone must have pulled over to help him. These hairs look like they probably came from the back of his head. Looks like the hood was smashed down on him. He was probably being helped by the criminal in question. As the victim was pouring the..." he looked at the bottle of antifreeze a few feet in front of the truck, "...antifreeze in, the helper must have slammed the hood down." Kasey took a deep breath and then exhaled loudly. "The head trauma probably knocked him unconscious while the killer went to work." Kasey pointed to the trail of blood. "When he came to he probably crawled to try and get help. It was obviously too late when it came."

Calloway looked under the hood at the antifreeze compartment. "If he was pouring the antifreeze like you said, then why is the compartment for the antifreeze closed? It would have been left open if the antifreeze was being poured in when the hood slammed down. And the bottle would never have gotten that far away either."

"You do have a point there," Kasey agreed. He looked at the antifreeze compartment inside the truck. "The compartment is nearly empty too, so maybe no antifreeze was actually poured. Maybe he was just checking."

Calloway bit his lower lip. "If that's true, if no antifreeze was poured," he walked over to the bottle that remained untouched, on the pavement, a few feet away, "Then this bottle would be..." He bent over to pick it up. "*Empty.*" It wasn't what he intended to say, but he was shocked at the bottle's weightlessness.

"No, Detective. It would be full."

Calloway was still shocked. "I know. That's what I wanted to say, but the bottle *is* empty."

"That's odd," Kasey said. "Why would there be an empty bottle of antifreeze around if it hadn't been used to fill up the truck? Unless..."

"Unless someone *intended* to pull over and kill this man," Calloway finished. "Unless someone had no intention for anything else but that. The bottle could just have been a ploy. He needed to pretend he was going to help."

"That would imply that he knew the victim was going to stop," Kasey said. "How could he have known he was going to need help?"

"I don't know, but maybe he had something to do with the truck's troubles," Calloway answered.

Kasey took a closer look at the antifreeze compartment. His eyes lit up. "You may be right," he said. "There looks to be a small hole on the side of the compartment. But if he made the hole then it would mean he meant for this guy to be next."

Calloway nodded. "I think he means to kill each one, I don't know the reasons behind it, but I think he knows who is next. I think he plans out his targets." Calloway shook the antifreeze bottle. "This feels weird. Like there's something else inside. Empty of fluid, but full of something else." Calloway turned the cap and pulled it open. He flipped the bottle over. A few drops of syrupy liquid dripped out and splashed on the pavement. He looked inside and his eyes grew big.

A newspaper.

26

Hank was once again caught up in his thoughts. Every single thing he looked at he found some relevance to something else. All at once everything made perfect sense, and yet, no sense at all.

He tried to shut the folder, believing that, in doing so, it would shut out everything else.

It didn't work.

The alphabet played, endlessly, in his head. He was beginning to become tired of the game. Tired of playing. He didn't want to play any longer. But he couldn't stop now. He had gone too far. He had found out so much. If he gave up he'd consider himself responsible for all the others who may fall victim.

If he gave up he may *become* a victim.

Hank's cellphone vibrated on the desk, violently shaking the papers and rubbish upon it. He looked at the caller ID.

Gale.

"Hello Charlie," Hank said, happy to be removed from his thoughts. "What makes you call?"

"The Clermont Police have found another body. They called me to go check it out. Apparently the victim was slashed so they figure I should take a look at it. Maybe it's another from the Vandermeer. Maybe

Zucker was telling the truth," Gale said.

"How far are you from the scene?"

"Hmmm. Maybe fifteen minutes or so. You want to meet up with me?"

Hank was a little apprehensive. Gale hadn't seemed to care for Hank since the day he wanted to find out information. *Why was he chummy all of a sudden?* "It would take me at least a half hour to get there. Most of the dirty work will be done by then. Why didn't you call me earlier?"

"I just got the call from Clermont five minutes ago. You're the second person I called. I could just get some of the details when I get there. You could meet me in my office in a little over an hour if you want. We can discuss it there."

"Why do you want me to help all of a sudden?" Hank asked.

"I don't think I have much of a choice. It's either you or Florida's Bureau. I figure they'll get into my face more than you would. Plus you have a head start on the whole thing. If your hunch is right, anyhow. I know how you work Hank, we've done this before."

Gale was right. They had done it before. Hank looked at the clock near his bed.

11:21 p.m.

"I don't sleep anyway," he said. "I'll be at your office by 12:30."

"Good. I'll see you then."

"Yep."

The phone hung up.

Hank wondered if his hunches were right. If they were he'd know for sure what the killer wanted. Any two people may have a coincidental connection, three is a little more ironic, but four would be the key.

If the victim was somehow related to the Vandermeer, had a neck wound, had a newspaper article, and had a 'D,' it was all but certain that the alphabet was the game.

The killing game.

27

Gale got out of his car and walked over to Calloway, who was standing over the body. "So tell me all you have."

Calloway looked at him. "Oh, well hello Detective. Nice to see you again. Wish it weren't so soon though. Apparently the victim stopped because his car was doing something weird. The antifreeze was low so it was probably overheating. We found a hole in the antifreeze compartment; looks like it could have been intentionally drained. This could just be a guess, but the victim could have been planned out, maybe even followed until he pulled over. Who knows? We'd have to check to see what made the hole in the compartment to know for sure. Anyway, he must have pulled over to fix the problem. I assume the murderer pulled in later. The victim must have thought he was going to help and instead he was murdered soon thereafter. We have a gash on the back of his head that we concluded was from the impact of the truck's hood being slammed down upon it. Neck laceration was the lethal wound. Weapon was a small knife. It had jagged edges so the neck wound was extremely bad. The skin was torn every which way. Seems like the poor guy tried to get help. As you can tell the trail of blood is a good five feet long, starting at the front of the truck and ending here. He must have tried to get into the sight of oncoming traffic. It was all for naught though."

"So the weapon was a knife? Do you know what kind?"

"Yeah. My men say the weapon was a dagger. You don't see them much anymore, mostly for show. They're typically not used for cutting, more so for stabbing. The victim wasn't stabbed though.""

"Dagger," Gale muttered softly.

"That's correct," Calloway answered.

"So how do you figure this is related to the Vandermeer case? Was he staying there?" Gale asked.

"I'm not sure if he was staying there Detective, but we found another paper."

"What!?" Gale was shocked. "Where?"

"In a bottle of antifreeze. More of a reason to think the killer had planned this one. He had no intent to stop and help the victim. He only had the intent of killing him."

"Who is the victim? I would like to call the Vandermeer and ask if he's staying there. And where is the article?" Gale asked.

Calloway turned to Kasey. "Kasey go get the newspaper for Detective Gale."

Kasey walked over to some of the other officers.

Calloway looked back at Gale. "The victim is a Walter Dunfellow..."

Gale looked stunned, even before Calloway finished.

"He was a vacationer, so I suppose there's a chance he's staying at the Vandermeer. Although from the look of this beat up truck and his clothes I would doubt it," Calloway said.

Gale glanced over the red truck. "Well he owns his

own business. Says so right there," Gale said, pointing to the writing on the truck. "'Dunfellow Landscaping.' He could be successful." Gale thought of Hank's hunch about birthplace being a part of the murderer's signature. "Where is he from?"

"From Kentucky," Calloway answered.

Gale only thought of the one Kentucky place he knew of: Frankfurt.

Not a 'D.'

"Where in Kentucky?" Gale asked.

"DeWitt, Detective," Calloway answered. "I've never heard of the place, but then again I've never heard of a lot of things outside of Clermont."

Gale was amazed that Hank could have been so correct. *He was wrong about the occupation part,* he thought. *Landscaping doesn't begin with a 'D.'*

Kasey came over and handed the newspaper to Gale. "Here you go sir."

Gale took the dirtied paper. It still had some of the greenish antifreeze liquid on it, but most had been wiped clean. Not enough to smudge the headline.

Garrison Awarded FBI's Highest Honor.

Gale was on edge at all that he'd seen and heard. The victim seemed to fit Hank's criteria, other than the occupation, but he didn't know for sure that was true.

Not yet.

The victim also seemed to have been killed similarly to the first two, but not quite as brutal. But how brutal could someone be with a small knife?

Gale dug out his cellphone from his pocket and dialed the Vandermeer.

"Can I speak to the manager please?" He asked as soon as someone picked up.

"This is he. Mr. Donnelly. What can I do for you?" Donnelly asked.

"Hello, Mr. Donnelly. Nice to speak with you again. This is Detective Charles Gale."

"Yes. I remember you. I would like you to know we've kept the hotel just as you asked us to. We card everyone who enters. No one, aside from the employees, the guests, and police, are allowed inside."

"That's great. I have a question for you, Mr. Donnelly."

"Whatever it is I'm happy to answer it," Donnelly replied.

"Well I would hope so," Gale said. "I was just wondering if you could check to see if a Walter Dunfellow is staying at the hotel?"

"No problem. Hold on let me check." Donnelly typed in the name and looked at the screen.

No match.

"You sure that's the name you want?" Donnelly asked.

"I'm sure."

He typed it in again.

No match.

"I'm sorry Detective. There is no Walter Dunfellow staying at the hotel."

Gale didn't know what to say.

"Are you still there?" Donnelly asked.

"Oh yes. Sorry. Does the name ring a bell at all? Maybe he visited the hotel recently, maybe he did some landscaping there, perhaps he knows someone."

"I have not heard of the name," Donnelly replied.

"Do you have a way of checking if he did any work there?"

"I suppose I could check on that. You say he's a landscaper?"

"Yes," Gale answered.

"I guess I could check some of the recent landscaping hires the hotel has had. I can just check what companies have billed us recently for maintenance work," Donnelly replied. "Do you know the company name off the top of your head?"

"It would be Dunfellow Landscaping," Gale answered.

Donnelly typed in some words into the computer.

No *Dunfellow Landscaping*.

"No. I'm sorry once again, sir," Donnelly apologized. "Nothing showed up."

"Okay. Well thank you for your help," Gale said.

"Thank you. Have a good one."

Gale wasn't having a 'good one.' Not tonight. Not in the past two weeks. "You too."

He hung up the phone.

Calloway looked at Gale. "No?"

Gale shook his head. "Not from the Vandermeer. Who reported the crime?"

"Some woman. We asked her the basic questions. She left right before you got here. We have her number if you care to ask her some questions."

"No I don't think that would be necessary," Gale replied. "Well I better be heading back out. Can you have someone fax over the write-up for me? E-mail me the photographs once they're developed?"

"Oh yeah, sure. I'll have someone do that as soon as I can."

"Good." Gale inhaled, his chest inflated. He exhaled loudly. "And I mean it when I say I don't want to see you anytime soon."

Calloway wasn't sure how serious Gale was. "We'll keep you updated."

Gale slowly walked to his car with his hands on his hips. He stopped and looked down, thinking. He thought about Hank's hunches and how, for the most part, they fit.

Yet there was still no criminal behind bars. Or behind an officer's gun.

This guy's playing hard, he thought. *I'll play harder.*

28

"You're early," Gale said as he entered his office.

Hank spun around. "Not by much. I just got here five minutes ago. They said it would be alright if I let myself in."

"Oh yes, yes. It's quite alright. Have a seat." Gale walked around his desk and sat in his own chair. "You're not going to believe it."

Hank didn't know what that meant. "It's a related crime?"

"I would guess it was."

"Then what is it that I wouldn't believe, because I certainly believe that?" Hank asked.

"It's almost exactly what you said. A few minor things aren't the same as your ideas, but for the most part it is exactly what you said."

"Last name began with a 'D'?"

"Yes," Gale answered. "His last name was Dunfellow. He was from DeWitt. Some town in Kentucky or Kansas or some place like that."

Hank was almost frightened by how real his hunch had become. "What was the weapon?"

"Another knife. But the police said it was a dagger. I didn't get to see it, but that's what they said."

"Damn it! I wish I would have seen this sooner,"

Hank replied.

"It's not your fault. This is a big lead. We know the next guy is an 'E.' I'm not sure what sick and twisted shit he'll use for that one, but I think we can figure it out before he strikes again. I found out something myself. His first two were just a day apart and then he took a week off. These last two came back to back. He's probably going to take a week off," Gale said, as if proud that he also found something to work with.

Hank thought it made sense. *Back to back and then a week off to gain his composure and attune himself to his next two victims.* "So you're saying we have a week? A week to save whoever may be next?"

"Yes. And hopefully we'll be able to nail him before then. If not the criminal, then at least his potential victim."

"If Dunfellow was staying at the Vandermeer, or worked there, it would make our job much easier. Was he staying at the Vandermeer?" Hank asked.

"Not exactly. That's where things may get a little tricky. He had no connection, which I know of, to the Vandermeer. I called and checked. He wasn't staying there, nor was he a worker."

"Well, then my Vandermeer hunch isn't entirely correct. He would have to have something to do with the Vandermeer. It would only make sense." Hank thought about all the various connections he was able to come up with. Maybe it wasn't as complicated as he saw it. *Maybe the victims don't have to be connected to the Vandermeer.* "Actually I may have thought too much into it. Not everyone has to be connected in every way possible." He stopped talking, but couldn't help but see all of the connections he had found. The neck was one. "What about a neck wound?"

"Is that a new hunch of yours? When did you come up with that?"

"Did he have a neck wound?" Hank asked again.

"Yes, actually. His neck was cut. It was his only wound, besides a gash on the back of his head. His hood was slammed against it. Must have dazed him before he was cut."

"That's four people with something to do with their necks. Anderson had the arrow. Barkley's throat was cut. Calverly was strangled. And now this guy."

"So you think that's another sign?"

Hank squeezed his eyes shut, trying to shut out the images. "I don't know what to think anymore. It seems as if lately everything is a sign to me."

"Speaking of which, they also found another newspaper."

"They did? What did this one say?" Hank questioned.

"Another thing about you. Something about you winning an award," Gale answered.

"What does he want from me? It's like he's taunting me."

"Maybe he is. But then again you seem to know a lot about him. Maybe you're taunting him. You were the one to find out about the alphabetical things he does. And his latest victim fits that so far," Gale said.

Hank was upset. "I don't know if 'so far' is good enough. What about his occupation?"

"Landscaper," Gale replied.

Hank closed his eyes and shook his head. "That doesn't fit either."

"Not everything has to fit Hank. Not everything is going to fit the design you came up with. Maybe he's changing. Maybe he knows you know and wants to screw with your head," Gale said.

"Nobody knows what I know. Hell, I don't even know what I know. I'm the only person screwing with my head. It just doesn't make sense right now. There's got to be something we're missing."

"Not everything has to make sense," Gale replied.

"What? Of course everything has to make sense. If nothing made sense we'd be at square one right now. It has to make sense. This isn't a fantasy, Charlie. You know that just as well as I do. A killer cannot just pop in and out of people's lives at his free will. He cannot just kill the ones he wants and spare the ones he doesn't. This guy is not omnipotent. This guy is not God. How the hell does he know what he knows? Everything has to make sense. If it doesn't then it's not real. And I assure you, unless I'm completely insane, this is real. This is *very* real."

"All I'm saying is he doesn't have to do everything as perfectly as you intend him to. He doesn't have to find someone to fit every part of this script you drew up in your head. How would that work? No one is that creative. What happens when he gets to 'X,' huh? What then? I don't recall anyone ever being killed by an xylophone. I mean come on Hank, how many people do you know whose last name starts with an 'X' or whose profession does? How many?"

"I don't know. But I do know that I am hoping he doesn't have a chance to get that far. I also know that people can be creative. And whoever this sick fuck may be, I know he's creative."

"What makes you so sure?" Gale asked.

"Because he thinks like I do."

29

It was a new day and just like usual the sun smiled down on all of Florida, oblivious to the darkness that happened the night before. Ignorant of Dunfellow's death. Each time someone was murdered it only seemed to make the sun shine more brightly. Maybe it was trying to blind the evil. Maybe it was trying to make everyone forget what happened.

No one would forget. Especially not the ones living through it. As powerful as
the sun seemed each morning, it could not fight the evil that had been lurking the past two weeks.

It almost seemed wrong, to anyone involved in the deaths, that the next day was always so beautiful. The birds didn't show their respect and offer sad songs; instead they were just as happy as ever. They sang just as wonderfully as any other day. The sky didn't offer its condolences and cry. It didn't drop a single tear on the dying grass below that begged for refreshment.

For most the day had gone on as if nothing had ever happened.

But *most* didn't include those caught up in the game.

Gale had invited Hank to join him, Eronie, and Harlowe for a cup of coffee and some sandwiches at a diner nearby the station. Hank was thankful just to get out of his hotel to eat for a change. Anything other than room service would seem like a five-star restaurant to him by now.

"I'm sorry I'm late guys," Harlowe said as he pushed into the booth alongside Hank.

"Oh don't worry we just got here ourselves," Gale replied. "Why aren't you in your normal suit? What's with the uniform?"

"I was doing evictions. Extra pay from the county and I get to wear the uniform like the olden days," Harlowe answered.

"How's that going for you?" Eronie asked.

"Ah it pays some of the smaller bills, not that bad of a side job. I think I'll need a little extra money soon anyhow."

Gale smiled. "Why do you say that? Going to get something special?"

"I guess you could say that. But let me keep you in suspense as I tell my dramatic story," Harlowe said.

"Do it," Eronie replied.

Harlowe smiled. "My wife called me when I was putting an eviction notice on some estranged man's house. Another welfare case I'm sure. But anyway, Beth tells me to hurry home. At first I'm scared, you know? Like I'm asking myself 'did another person die or something?' I ask her what it is, but she won't tell me. So I rush home. Driving down the highway at like ninety miles an hour, lucky enough I was in my cruiser or I'd be pulled over by one. I get there and search the house looking for her. She's not there..." Harlowe stopped as an attractive, thirty-something, redheaded waitress approached the table.

"Are you guys all set or would you like a few more

minutes?" She asked.

Harlowe looked at one of the paper menus. "I'll go last. You guys must be good by now."

Gale looked at the waitress. "Yes, I'm going to have the chicken sandwich, plain, with fries please. And a cup of coffee. Decaf."

"And for you, sir?" She asked as she turned to Hank.

"The turkey club platter, extra mayo. And to drink I'll have a water with lemon."

She wrote down Hank's order and looked at Eronie. "I'll have the ham sandwich. Fries as well. A regular coffee too."

Harlowe put down the menu and looked at Eronie. "I'm upset. All you guys have different sandwiches and I'm going to seem like I'm copying Dan." He looked at the waitress. "Same as him," he said, pointing across the table at Eronie. "Except I'll have a diet cola to drink."

The waitress smiled. "I'll be right out with your drinks guys."

"Okay, so continue with your lame ass story," Eronie said with a smile.

"Yeah so where was I?"

Hank spoke, "You got to your house and your wife wasn't there."

"Oh yeah. Thanks Hank. So I get there and I'm looking all around and I can't find Beth. So now I'm all nervous. I'm screaming her name and she's not answering. Finally I find her in, of course, the last room I checked. The bathroom. She has her hand behind her back. And I'm being serious right now, for a split second I thought maybe she was holding a gun. For a moment I even thought she may have been the 'Vandermeer Slasher,' that I may be the next victim. So I get all tense and shit. And she smiles and slowly pulls her arm out from behind..." He stopped again as the waitress came back with the drinks.

She placed them down on the table. "Your meals will be out shortly."

Hank knew Harlowe would ask where he left off again, so he told him before he could ask. "She pulled her hand out from behind her back," he said as he put a straw in his water.

Harlowe laughed. "Wow we think alike. It's like you knew I was going to ask. So yes, Beth pulls her hand out from behind her back..." He paused again. "This isn't even going to have the same drama as it would have when I began. I was excited to tell you this story and I got stopped too many times for it to be good."

Eronie was laughing. "No Jon tell us. I'm on the edge of my seat," he said sarcastically.

"The reason you're on the edge of your seat is because your fat ass can't fit on it," Harlowe answered back.

Gale chuckled softly. Hank did as well.

"So as I was saying. Beth pulls her arm from behind her back and in her hand is a pregnancy test. It was positive."

Hank would have been excited for Harlowe, but he hardly knew him. He only offered a congratulatory pat on the back.

"Wow that's really great Jon. Good for you," Eronie said.

"Yes. You'll make a great father," Gale added.

"Thank you."

Hank turned to Harlowe. "So this will be your first, huh?"

"Yes. Do you have any?" Harlowe asked.

"Two. A boy and a girl." Hank thought about how much he missed them. How much he wanted to go back home. "Keith and Anna. You're in for it. I'll tell you that much. They're a handful." He looked at Eronie. "Do you have any children?"

"No. I don't even have a girlfriend. It's just me, but I kind of like it that way. If Detective Gale can do it then so can I," Eronie answered.

Gale sipped his coffee then responded, "I don't have as much time on my hands as you do to find myself someone. Plus I'm an old man. You really should be married though. What are you thirty-six now?"

"No Detective, I'm thirty-four and you should be talking. I work just as much as you do and I'm only about ten years younger. You still have plenty of time. As do I."

"I was just playing with you. Take a joke," Gale said.

"My girl is my Jacuzzi. She's hot. Always wet. Let's me go in her whenever I want. And even when she's steaming, she doesn't have the ability to yell at me," Eronie responded, laughing hard.

Hank looked at Eronie, disgusted. *So this is how they act when they aren't working? Maybe I was better off staying at the hotel.*

The waitress came to the table holding a tray full of food. She gave the four men their plates. "Is there anything else I can get you gentlemen?"

Gale looked at her. "No I believe we're all set. The check will be fine."

She nodded and walked away.

In about ten minutes time the men were almost finished with their meals.

Gale put his last piece of his sandwich in his mouth. He chewed a few times and then swallowed, wiping his mouth with a napkin. "Our agenda is full today folks," he said. "We have to get back to the station look at anything new that may have been faxed to us by the Clermont Police. And then we're going to solve this thing. We have six more days to do so."

Hank looked puzzled. "You're serious about the week off thing, huh?"

"Yes I am. He will strike in six days. That's his design. I'm as sure about this as you are about the alphabet," Gale replied.

"What about that Zucker kid? If these four murders are related he cannot be a suspect any longer. Is he getting out or do they think there may be more than one murderer collaborating?" Hank asked.

"Good question. I never even thought that there's the possibility of two killers and that Zucker may be one of them. I would assume it's only one though. Serialists don't usually work together. Too easy to get caught. It doubles the odds. And I suppose if Zucker was in on this he'd have given up the name of his accomplice by now. He would have nothing to lose in doing so. But anyhow, I spoke with Jeffrey Gunderson earlier this morning and he said he would take care of it. I gave him all the details we know so far and he said if it checks out he'd see to it that Zucker gets out. My gut tells me that he was probably in the wrong place at the wrong time. Knowing that kid he probably will have considered being in prison the best thing that ever happened to him. Maybe a good book idea."

"I still have so many questions about him that I can't even begin to start asking them now," Hank responded.

"Well you can ask them when we get back to the station," Gale replied.

Hank put his hand behind his back and reached for

his wallet. Gale stopped him. "It's on me. Don't worry about it. You were my guest. You can cover me next time."

"Thank you."

Gale looked at Harlowe. "You too. Consider it a new father gift."

"What about me?" Eronie asked.

"Maybe next time." Gale put thirty dollars down on the table. He reached inside his jacket's interior pocket and pulled out a pen. "I actually do have something for you." Gale picked the check up off the table and flipped it over to the blank side. He wrote down something and placed the check back down.

Eronie looked at what Gale had written.
Daniel Eronie, 555-9087
Call Me.

30

Tom arrived back at his house feeling even more alone than he ever had been before. He knew he didn't deserve to be in prison for a murder he didn't commit, but he also knew why he was put there. In more ways than one it was a place where he could hide. A place where he got the chance to get away. Away from the realities he'd have to go through.

The realities he understood the moment he stepped foot near his doorway.

He knew that as alone as he had felt in the dirty prison cell, in a way it was better than returning back to reality. Prison was his fantasy. His book. And at least he had comfort that went beyond the luxuries his house held. He had a way to forget about all that had happened. A way to forget about Calverly.

A way to forget about the murders.

Now, however, he had a constant reminder. As he fumbled to get the door open he remembered not having closed it the night Calverly was murdered. He trembled at the thought. The kitchen reminded him of the precious time he spent there eating, instead of helping. The bathroom brought the memories of not hearing her calls for help, being oblivious to any that there may have been. But the room he could not enter at all was the one that housed the most pain. The one that the crime took place in.

He cringed at the sight of his bedroom's door and walked past it quickly and into the living room. Even the living room was a useless solace. The bloodstain on the couch made Tom feel more uneasy. And the name 'living' just didn't seem to fit. He didn't know what to do. In a way he wished he were back in prison. He felt safe there.

Safe from the images in his head.

The ones where Calverly's head lay on his lap, dying or dead.

At least there he had the writings on the walls. They were calming to him. There he had the drunks and druggies, prostitutes and whores. But here he had real evil. It was as if Tom became adjusted to his prison stay. He did what he didn't want to do and adjusted.

Now he would have to adjust to his own life.

He felt more caged in his own house than he ever had behind bars. He was dirty,

but the shower's memory would corrupt his mind. So he refrained from using it. He had hundreds of book ideas, but they were worthless to him now because they would be too real. Too memory-jogging. He had an urge to call the Calverlys and offer his condolences, but they wouldn't want to hear from him. Not now. Not after all the finger pointing. Not after he had been a suspect.

He only sat. Alone. Empty.
Dead inside.

31

"Okay so here's where we are now," Gale said as he entered his office with a few manila folders. He handed one to each of the other men. "Walter Dunfellow, fifty-three-year-old, retired construction worker. He recently started a landscaping business and he was from DeWitt, Kentucky."

Hank was unsatisfied that Dunfellow's occupation didn't fit the killer's script. Neither did the Vandermeer. *He wasn't playing the game fairly. He was cheating.*

Gale continued, "No wife. No kids. But get this," he looked directly at Hank. "This is the kicker. Dunfellow was down on vacation, visiting his family..."

Eronie interrupted. "Let me guess, one of his sisters or brothers married a Vandermeer?"

Gale glared back at Eronie, ashamed of his childishness. "Not quite," Gale replied as he turned back to Hank. "But they did marry a Calverly."

Hank was completely shocked. *So he did fit.* "He was Calverly's uncle?"

"That's what Clermont just told me."

"Holy shit," Eronie exclaimed. "That poor family."

"I know," Harlowe agreed. "They just hear that their daughter was killed and now they had to find out about this."

Hank was still in shock at the information. He was almost scared at how right he had been. Aside from the occupation, everything fit. This would have to be the game. *These were his rules. Vandermeer, alphabet, neck, and me.*

"It's going to be very difficult. We know he's going to strike soon. Six days, if you're correct Detective. And we know the next is an 'E' with a connection to the Vandermeer. But now the connection is not as simple as it was before. The next victim could be anyone, ranging from an employee or guest to a family member," Hank said.

Eronie smirked. "You are quite the investigator," he said as he patted Hank on the shoulder.

"But we do have six days notice in advance. Anyone *at* the Vandermeer, in relation *to* the Vandermeer, anyone that happens to have walked *by* the Vandermeer, is going to be looked at if they fit the criteria. Let's call there now and see what we've got," Gale said.

Gale picked up the phone and dialed the Vandermeer quickly. He knew the number by heart these days.

"Hello, can I speak to a manager please. This is Detective Gale."

"Oh certainly Detective," the man's voice on the other end replied. "Hold on just a second."

A few seconds later Fullmer picked up. "Hello, Detective. What can I do for you today? Maybe answer some more questions?" He asked in a sarcastic, fed up tone. "I've been answering questions for the past two weeks. I'm starting to get a little irritated now. I started a while ago actually. What do you want to know that you don't already know from me?"

"It's understandable that you've been having a rough two weeks, but don't you think we all have? This won't take long anyhow."

"That's what they always say," Fullmer answered.

"Yeah. We're the big bad guys now. We're the ones out to get you. You want to answer my questions now or would you rather just come down to the station? Better yet, maybe you just want more publicity for your hotel. You could easily get that if this madman strikes again," Gale replied.

"How many madmen are out there? I thought this was done. I thought you found the guy."

Gale ignored Fullmer. "Are you by a computer right now?"

"Yes. I'm in my office. Why?"

"Just find out what guests have an 'E' last name for me. That's all I'm asking. Simple stuff, Mr. Fullmer. Simple stuff."

Fullmer seemed to have calmed down. "Hold on." He typed in the letter 'E' on his computer. A list popped up on the screen. "Forty-seven people came up."

Gale covered the phone and looked at the other three men in his office. "Forty-seven 'E' names."

Hank looked up from one of the photographs in the folder. "Ask him to find out where they are from. Lessen the load."

Gale looked back quizzically at Hank and nodded. "Is there a way to tell me where they are from?" He asked into the phone.

"Yes. I told one of your men that already anyway. Is that what this is about?"

Gale looked at Hank, he knew it must have been him Fullmer had told.

"No," he said into the phone. "Just do it for me."

Fullmer typed in 'E' under the 'address' space on the computer. Four names popped up on the screen. "Four people fit that search criteria."

Gale looked at the other men and smiled before talking into the phone again. "Give me their names and their hotel phone numbers. I would like to talk to each of them."

Fullmer looked at the list on the screen. "Alyssa Eddy, room extension number 234. Christopher Edgecomb, room 378. Lyle Englewood, room 101, and Harold Ennis, room 352."

Gale wrote down each of the names and turned the paper around so that the others could see. "And one more question, Mr. Fullmer. Can you tell me if any of your employees fit that search?"

"Hold on." Fullmer typed in the criteria. One name popped up. "Just one."

"Who might that be?" Gale asked.

"Jennifer Elkind."

32

Jen was unable to do much of anything since she returned home from the Vandermeer the night Calverly's news report played. Jen's mother broke the news to her as soon as she arrived home from work. It sent Jen in an emotional tailspin. She didn't know how to handle what had happened and just locked herself in her room.

She had been inside ever since 8 p.m. It was now 2:12 p.m. of the next day.

Jen had cried all the tears she could and when she had finished she didn't even know what she was crying for. It was pointless. No amount of tears would bring her best friend back. Calverly's life would not be miraculously restored once a certain teardrop quota was met. It was lost.

Forever.

Jen didn't want to accept the fact that she'd never get to see Calverly again, but she had to accept it.

Jen wiped her eyes one last time. At least for now. There would be more tears. But for now they needed to replenish themselves.

She finally unlocked her bedroom door and walked down the hallway and into the bathroom. She looked at her face. It was swollen. Her eyes were bloodshot. Her lips chapped. If Jen's heart wasn't beating as fast as it was, then she would have looked as dead as the others.

Jen rubbed her swollen cheeks and turned on the sink faucet. She dipped her hands into the warm water and splashed her face gently. The water sprayed everywhere. She looked at her reflection in the mirror and turned off the faucet. The refreshing droplets of water dripped down Jen's forehead, eyes, cheeks, mouth, and chin.

She dried her face off, but water still dripped downward, spattering against the porcelain sink.

Not water, but tears.

More tears.

Jen jumped as she heard her mother call her name. "Jen. Are you okay honey? It's good to see that you finally came out of your room. I made you pasta. It's on the table. I'll be back in about fifteen minutes; I have to pick Zach up from school. We'll talk when I get back."

Jen could hear the muffled sound of the door shutting in the distance.

She looked at herself in the mirror again. The tears were flowing more than ever before. "Why Katie?" She asked. Jen looked down at a soapdish that was atop the sink counter. She picked it up and held it tightly in her hand. Without hesitating she threw it at her reflection.

The mirror didn't shatter, but instead formed a spiderweb-like crack that slowly stretched outward. Jen bowed her head and cried some more.

The bathroom door slowly creaked open.

"Ahh," Jen screamed as she saw the suited man standing before her.

33

Hank walked into Gale's office. He had been in another room calling up one of the possible targets. The men had decided to split up the duties.

"So I didn't get a hold of Eddy or Edgecomb, which is not unusual considering the time. They're probably out doing something better than just lounging around their hotel room," Gale said.

Hank thought about how that was all he did. The past two weeks had been hell and he had nothing better to do than to wallow in his notes and thoughts.

"Yeah I got through to the Elkind house. The mother told me Jen had a rough time with Calverly's death. Apparently they were best friends," Hank said.

"Well there's another connection for you," Gale replied.

"Yeah." Hank wasn't pleased. He was sick of connections. Sick of the game. "The mother said she'd tell her daughter to call us back a little later. I told her to ask for you."

"Okay good."

"What about the other two? Did they happen to get through to anyone?" Hank asked.

"I don't know. I was just headed to Jon's office now actually. I'm sure we'll find out when we get there." Gale got up from his chair and walked over to Hank. "Right this way."

"I know where it is," Hank said.

Harlowe was on the phone when Hank and Gale arrived at his door. He waved them in.

Eronie nodded to them. "He's talking with Ennis right now," he said softly. "I didn't get in contact with Englewood. What about the other three?"

"Not yet," Gale responded.

"Okay so I hope you have a safe trip back home then. Thanks for your help," Harlowe said as he hung up the phone. He looked at the others. "Well one down. Four more to go."

"What did he say?" Gale asked.

"Well he is leaving the Vandermeer as we speak actually. Headed back to Elmira, New York. So it can't be him," Harlowe answered.

"You never know anymore. Seems like whoever is doing this is mixing things up all the time. Maybe this time it won't be a week off. Maybe it will be today or tomorrow. Or as we speak," Hank said, sounding paranoid.

"I doubt that. But even if it were, we're doing all we can," Gale replied.

That was true. Hank knew it. If someone did strike before the time was up, it's not as if no one tried. "I know. I know."

"We do, however, still have a lot of work for us to do. These are just the typical victims right now. There are still the unusual ones. Like Dunfellow. We have to find out if anyone fits the pattern of just knowing someone at the Vandermeer. That will be tricky," Gale said.

Hank thought for a moment. "Not really," he said. "The only people who would even know the people at the Vandermeer and not be staying there themselves, would be the friends or family of the employees. That's what we'd have to do. Talk to the employees. Ask around. He can't be mixing up his plan too much. To have someone too vaguely connected to the Vandermeer would only make this guy look less clever. And I don't believe that's what he wants us to think."

34

"Oh, honey I'm sorry to have scared you. I heard a noise and came to check up on it. You okay?" The man asked. He looked at the mirror. "What happened here?"

"I'm sorry dad. I did that. I don't know what got into me." Jen began rubbing her arms and swaying side to side. She started to cry.

Her father walked over to her and gave her a hug. "Oh it's okay honey. I know. It's alright. You're going through a lot right now. Don't worry about it." He looked at the cracked mirror. "Nothing a little masking tape won't fix," he joked.

Jen didn't laugh.

"Honey. Everything will be alright. I promise. It's tough. These things are difficult, but everything will be alright."

Jen shook her head. "Yes." She put her head on his shoulder and squeezed him tightly.

"It's okay," he repeated. "Your lunch is on the table. Go eat it. You need some food in your stomach."

"Okay." She pulled her head off her father's shoulder and wiped her nose and eyes with her hand. She sniffed.

Her father grabbed a tissue from nearby. "Here."

"Thank you."

She blew her nose.

Jen walked out of the bathroom with her father and sat down in the kitchen. She picked up a fork that was set on the table and pulled the plate of pasta over to her. She slowly stabbed the fork into the noodles within her plate.

She cringed at the thought of anything stabbing another. She thought about how the two Vandermeer victims were brutally killed. Cut and stabbed.

She put down her fork and pushed the plate away.

She couldn't eat.

Her father walked over to the refrigerator and grabbed some orange juice from inside. "Want something to drink?" He asked.

"No thank you," Jen replied.

Her father closed the refrigerator door and then read the reminder note that was stuck to it. He pulled it off and handed it to Jen. "Mom must have left this for you."

She read the note.

Tell Jen to call Detective Gale, Orlando Police Department.

35

Gale pressed the flashing red hold button on his office phone.

"This is Detective Gale speaking."

"Hello, Detective. This is Jennifer Elkind. I got a message to call you."

"Yes. I have some questions for you. Nothing big."

"Okay," she answered.

"You work at the Vandermeer, is that correct?"

"Yes I do," Jen replied.

"Okay. I know you've probably been asked hundreds of questions lately…"

"Oh don't worry about asking them."

"Good," Gale replied. "You were a friend of Katherine Calverly's?"

"Very good friend, sir. Yes," Jen answered with teary eyes.

"I see," Gale replied. He didn't really know what to ask her because he was caught off guard with her phonecall.

"Does this have to do with her?"

"In a way, yes. Where are you from Jen?" Gale asked.

"I live in Edgewater, sir. Why?"

"You live in Edgewater?" Gale rubbed his forehead, even though he knew from Fullmer that where she lived began with an 'E.' "And you work at the Vandermeer? Isn't that a bit far to be driving every day?"

"It's kind of far, but it's manageable. Takes me about an hour to get there, but I don't work everyday. I only work four times a week."

"What do you do with the rest of your days?"

"Nothing. I used to go to school, but that didn't work out so well."

"Should you be working today?" Gale asked.

"Tonight, but I don't think I'm going to go in. I'm not feeling very well."

"I wouldn't think you would be. It's a terrible thing to lose a friend. It's a terrible thing to lose anyone you love."

A tear fell from her eye and caressed her cheek until it dried up. "Yes."

"Are you working tomorrow?" He asked.

"I'm scheduled."

"I see. Well can you do me a favor and not work for a little while? I know that seems weird coming from me, but I think it may be best," Gale said.

"I don't think I will be going to work for awhile anyway. I don't know if my parents would like that idea themselves. And I'm not feeling like I like it either. I used to feel safe there with all the police and stuff, but I just don't know anymore. And I know they locked up Tom, but..." she couldn't finish.

Gale ignored the Tom statement, not knowing if he'd be let off or not. He figured if she thought he was the murderer at least she'd feel better thinking he was locked up. "I understand. I think it would be best to just stay at home. Spend time with your family. But could you do me a favor?"

"What?" Jen asked.

"If you do think about going back to work any time soon, let me know first. Okay?"

Jen found it odd that Gale would want her to do that. "Yeah sure."

"So is anyone home with you now?"

"Yes, my father is. Would you like to talk to him?" She asked.

"Oh no. Not necessary. So is it safe to assume that most of the day either your mother or father is home with you?"

"My mom doesn't work so she's home all the time," Jen answered. "Why do you ask?"

Gale didn't know how to make his reasoning behind the question sound acceptable. "I just think it would be good to have people around you for a little while. You know, not be alone?" Gale knew that sounded awkward, but he couldn't just outright tell her that she may be a possible victim.

"I understand."

"Okay, Jen. I will talk with you later. Hope you feel better soon. Goodbye."

"Bye."

He hung up the phone.

36

Two murders later and the small apartment had changed only slightly. There weren't any new bags of bloodstained clothes to keep the others company. No added newspapers that were dancing on the floor alongside the yellowed rest.

But that didn't mean the house was empty of sin.

It didn't mean it was void of evil.

As unchanged as the house had remained, it was apparent someone walked on the wooden floors recently. It was obvious that a murderer showed up to confess his transgressions. And it was clear that he had come back to wash his sins down the drain.

The two bloodied towels were still in a pile on the floor, long since dried. A new one was draped over them, protecting them from the pain. Hiding them from the hurt.

It was clean.

The last two murders weren't bloody enough to corrupt the white towel with color.

Another clean towel was thrown over the top of the door. It was waiting to be used. Waiting to dry off the damp skin of evil.

The sink was dirty. Not by blood. By something else.

Something different.

The mirror's crack had stretched even further. It almost extended from one end of the mirror to its diagonal counterpart, but it hadn't yet made it that far. Instead, it slowly crept closer towards the finish line.

Closer to the edge.

Eventually it would be victorious.

But not yet.

The suit was missing again. The hanger no longer grasped onto the knob. Instead it lay twisted on the floor. Curled up in terror.

The kitchen had been left alone once again. It seemed as if the killer didn't need to eat. The old ham sandwich no longer looked like it had ever been an edible meal. The bread was grayed from mold. The meat was an assortment of colors. It was slowly decaying. Eventually time would take its toll even further.

Everything had a time.

The kitchen didn't appear to be the haven for hunger. It was more of a refuge for remorse. It was full of emptiness.

Empty stomachs.

Missing hearts.

The infamous small room that looked out to the Vandermeer still accommodated the weapons and tools that were shut inside. The rope and dagger were missing, but the many others still remained. They wondered which was next to go.

They wondered which would be used to strike the next victim down.

They were all viable options. One hadn't been picked yet.

It was either too early or the murderer was too unsure.

No weapon lay next to the torn image of Garrison.

None slithered towards the paper or stabbed his likeness. The room was full of possibilities.

Was it something that lay among the wreckage? Was it one that trembled in fear, not wanting to be picked? Was it one that jumped for joy at the mere option of taking someone's life?

Or was it something even more ingenious than what piled in the room?

There was still time to decide.

37

Tom watched the sun slowly descend into the ground. He remembered how he once could watch the sun set and think it was so calming. So peaceful. Not very long ago he had watched it set and thought it was beautiful.

Not now.

He stared out the window and followed the sun, as it sunk deeper and deeper into the horizon. Now all Tom could think of was how the sun seemed to be dying. It was being put in its grave. Just like the others.

Just like Calverly.

But unlike the others who died, the sun would rise again. Tom knew that in the morning the sun would prevail. But Tom also knew that by then the sun, like himself, would have changed. It would not be the exact same sun it had been when it took its nighttime bow. It would have become different, even if only slightly.

Everything changes.

Nothing is the same as it were yesterday. Nothing is the same as it were today. When tomorrow arrives, everything will have changed.

If tomorrow arrives.

Tom couldn't take his eyes off the gradually dipping sun. He watched closely as the day turned into night. As a clear blue sky fell victim to a darkened, star-speckled backdrop.

He knew that in the morning nothing would be the same again.

Tom got up for the first time since sitting on the couch. He had a pain in his stomach and an even sharper one in his head, yet the biggest pain was the one in his heart. The others could easily be fixed, but not the pain that missed Calverly. If he were looking for a way to ease that pain he was in the wrong place. The house Calverly was murdered in could do nothing more than create more sorrow. He knew that.

He also knew that it would be impossible to run from the pain that haunted him. It would constantly follow. He couldn't just pretend it never happened, but he also couldn't wallow in shame either. It wasn't his fault she was murdered.

It wasn't his fault.

Tom pushed open the bathroom door and stepped inside. The image of Calverly screaming jumped into his head.

It wasn't my fault, he thought.

He moved closer to the sink. The mirror above it showed his sad reflection.

Another image of Calverly flashed in his head. The rope squeezing tighter against her throat, blocking the air.

He shook it away. *It wasn't my fault.*

He stepped closer.

Another image. The stranger opening the door and lurking inside his house. Waiting.

It wasn't my fault, Tom's head chanted.

He finally reached the sink. His reflection unchanged. He reached over and turned on the faucet.

The hot water splattered all over.

Tom looked into the mirror.

"It's not my fault," he said loudly.

Tom's head was pounding with thoughts and images. His stomach ached, as it screamed to be fed. He bent over and opened up the cabinet under the sink.

He looked at the assortment of items that were lined up inside.

Toilet paper. Toothpaste. Bandages. Pills. Mouthwash. Tampons. Soap.

He closed the cabinet, not sure what he was looking for.

Tom stood back up and turned off the water. The mirror was fogged up. His reflection had become blurry.

It had become vacant.

He placed his hands against the edge of the counter and bowed his head.

"Why?" He asked.

He shook his head as the images invaded. Hundreds of horrible images.

Tom closed his eyes. It only made them worse. More clear. More vivid.

He squeezed his eyes tighter.

They still remained.

Tom slowly bent over and opened up the cabinet again. He reached inside and grabbed the bottle of pills.

He stood up and shook his head, then stopped abruptly.

"It *was* my fault."

He glanced at the pill bottle in his hand.

38

It was already a little after 6 p.m. and only Elkind and Ennis had been contacted. Hank impatiently waited in Gale's office as Gale tried to get a hold of Alyssa Eddy. It would be his third time calling. Hank wanted to leave; he realized he worked better alone, and at least in his hotel room he had his own place to sit and think. He felt like an onlooker when he worked alongside Gale and the others. Gale was the man taking charge and Hank wasn't used to that. He didn't mind Gale, Eronie, or Harlowe, but he needed to get away after spending all day with them. Even still, he had the urge to wait until one more person had been contacted. He would feel safer.

"Hello," Eddy answered.

"Hi. Is this Alyssa?" Gale asked.

"Yes. Who is this?"

"This is Detective Charles Gale of the Orlando Police Department. I would like to ask you a few questions. It shouldn't take very long."

"The police department? What is this about?" Eddy asked.

"Nothing in particular," Gale answered. "We're just doing a check on the people staying at the Vandermeer. I guess you could say we're a bit on edge with all that has happened there lately."

"I can understand that. I'm glad you have finally caught the guy who did all that."

Even though Dunfellow's murder had happened the night before the FBI had urged the news stations not to air the report until further notice. Gale realized the news report had not made the news yet. Everyone still believed the criminal had been found. Everyone thought they were safe again.

Everyone had been wrong.

"Yeah," Gale answered. "So would it be okay if I asked you a few questions?"

"No problem at all," Eddy responded.

"Well then…how long have you been staying at the Vandermeer?"

"I actually just arrived yesterday afternoon. I was supposed to stay here all this week, but the news scared me off. It probably scared a lot of people off because this place is pretty empty. But then when I read that the suspect was in custody I decided to leave the hotel I was at and come here. I've been here before and it is quite wonderful," Eddy replied.

"That's what I am told," Gale said. "So far you feel safe there, huh?"

"Yes. No reason not to be. Everywhere I turn I see a police officer. A bit intimidating, but at least I know there won't be any problems."

"Well that's good," Gale replied. "So what brings you to the Sunshine State? Vacation? Business?"

"I guess you could say a little of both. The weather has been amazing lately so it feels like a vacation, but I really came here on a business trip," she answered.

"Is that right? What type of business?"

"Well I'm a pharmaceutical sales rep, so you know how that goes," Eddy responded.

"Not exactly, but it sounds important."

Eddy started to laugh. "Well I won't bore you with the details."

"How long will you be staying?"

"I go back in three days," she answered.

Gale let out a sigh of relief. *It couldn't be her.* "Are you alone or with family? Husband? Boyfriend?"

"Sadly alone," she replied. "My boyfriend is at home."

"And where might home be, Ms. Eddy?" Gale asked.

"It would be in New York."

Eronie walked into Gale's office and started to say something, but stopped when Gale put up a finger.

"Where in New York?"

"Buffalo."

Gale didn't understand. He thought she was from somewhere beginning with 'E.' That was the whole point. "Buffalo?"

"Well I actually just moved not very long ago. I was originally from Endicott."

Now it made sense.

"Well I don't want to waste anymore of your time. I will let you enjoy the rest of your vacation." Gale didn't know what else to say. He couldn't just tell Eddy to watch out for a possible murderer. Even if he did strike early, he couldn't scare everyone who fit the criteria.

"Oh it wasn't a waste of my time at all Detective. Have a goodnight."

"I'll try. Goodbye."

Gale hung up.

"Sir, Jon wanted me to tell you that he had to head out. He'll call you a little later," Eronie said as soon as

Gale said 'goodbye.'

Gale looked at his watch. "Head out for what?"

"Beth no doubt. You know how he is. Always leaving and stuff," Eronie answered.

"Yeah, yeah, yeah. It's not like this is community service and you can leave as you wish. This is his job," Gale said, a bit irritated.

"He was in some sort of rush. I was calling up Englewood so I didn't hear why he was leaving. Maybe it had to do with police work."

"So did you get in touch with that guy?" Gale asked.

"No. I think I'm just going to call him again at my house, if that's okay with you."

"Well I'd rather you stay here and finish up the work. You off soon?"

"As we speak Detective," Eronie replied.

"Okay. What's his name again? I'll just call him. I still have to call up…" Gale looked at his notes, "Chris Edgecomb, anyway."

"Lyle Englewood. Room number 101."

Gale wrote it down. "Okay, I guess I'll see you at the restaurant in the morning then."

"I shall be there," Eronie said. "I'll see you two tomorrow."

Hank and Gale said 'goodbye' as Eronie left.

Finally Hank felt as if he could speak. "So anything useful?"

"She said she was leaving in a few days. So that's a good sign. I couldn't just outright tell her to watch her back."

Hank didn't agree. He knew he would do more to keep any possible victim safe. But then again he couldn't be sure anything would be able to assure safety. "So we have two left?"

"Yes." Gale looked down again. "Edgecomb and Englewood." He looked at Hank. "You look pretty beat. You want to just head out. Maybe you should get some rest. You did enough, I mean without you where would we be? Letter 'J'? Maybe 'P?'"

Hank did look tired. His eyes were droopy and his face was pale. He hadn't gotten a full night's sleep in over two weeks and he had a feeling that one wouldn't be coming any time soon.

"I'm a little tired Charlie, but if you need help I can stay," Hank said.

"No. It's not a problem really. Like I told you before, I'm a night owl, I stay up until everything is finished."

"I hear that. I'm no different. I'll probably get to the hotel and stay up until four o'clock anyway."

"Well as long as you're at the restaurant in the morning I don't care how much sleep you get tonight," Gale said with a smile.

"I'm invited again?"

"Of course. You're part of this investigation. Plus this time you can pay." He laughed loudly.

"Same time?"

"Yes. Same as today," Gale answered.

Hank got up from his seat and stretched. "Well, then I guess I'll be going then."

"Alright, I will see you tomorrow morning."

Hank headed to the door, but then stopped and turned back to Gale. "You should call Jeffrey Gunderson and tell him to get some guys to try and find anyone at the hotel that know people that fit the victim profile. It makes our job a lot easier. You do know it would be impossible to do this all on our own. That's what the Bureau is for."

"Yeah I was going to do that. In fact I will do it

now." Gale picked up the phone. He looked at Hank. "We're going to get this fuck."

Hank nodded. "I hope so."

Gale dialed up Gunderson's number.

30

The killer's apartment was cold. The chill in the air was a constant reminder of how lifeless it was. Although outside had been over seventy degrees, inside felt as if it were a freezer.

The lights of the Vandermeer seemed to be smiling off in the distance. It was warm there. Life was housed there.

But it would be the old apartment that would be smiling soon.

It was begging for more bodies to be massacred. Begging for more blood to be spilt. It needed more. The more deaths that tallied up meant the more company the apartment would have.

Without death it was alone.

Alone and cold.

But with death came company. The killer returned after death. This was *his* place. Only when a murder had occurred would anyone walk along the floorboards. So until then anything housed inside would be alone.

The bloodied clothes that sat on the couch waited for the killer to return. They wanted a third bag to grace its soft cushions.

The towels that piled onto one another waited for the evil to come back. They needed another one to be placed atop of them. They begged for another to blanket them.

The tools and weapons waited to be picked. They waited for a plan to be devised. They wanted to be held in the gloved hand of the murderer. At least then they would be free, no longer shut away in a room.

Even the window that looked out to the Vandermeer waited. It waited for the dark. Because in the dark death prevailed over life. Evil triumphed over good.

'Bang. Bang. Bang.'

All remained still as a knock was heard at the door.

'Bang. Bang. Bang.'

No answer.

'Bang. Bang. Bang.'

The killer was early.

40

Eronie turned off the air blowers in his Jacuzzi and stood up. The water slowly returned to the calm it had been before the bubbles had erupted from the blowers. He reached over and grabbed a dry towel then stepped out of the Jacuzzi and dried himself off.

It had relaxed him after a long day at work. He felt better now. Any stress had subsided and any tension had decreased. He walked out of the small Jacuzzi room and walked into the bathroom. He threw his wet towel into a corner.

Eronie flipped his hands over and saw how wrinkled they had become. He had been in the Jacuzzi for a long time. He lifted his forearm up to his nose and smelled it. "Chlorine," he said. He walked over to the shower and turned the handle to the middle. The water sprayed violently from the showerhead. Eronie grabbed the nozzle and turned it slightly.

The water calmed down.

He quickly took off his bathing suit and strung it on the doorknob. It needed to dry for its next use.

Eronie got inside of the shower.

After Eronie was rinsed off of all soap he turned off the water. He smelled his forearm again.

No more chlorine.

Eronie grabbed a clean towel on the side of the shower, draped over a metal bar. He threw the towel over his head and rubbed it hard and quickly against his hair. He then dried off the rest of his body. Shoulders, chest, stomach, thighs, lower legs. He wrapped the towel around his waist and stepped out of the shower.

Eronie walked over to his bedroom and opened up his dresser drawer. He took out a pair of plain black boxers and some white tube socks. He unwrapped the towel from his waist and tossed it onto his bed. Eronie put his feet into the boxers then pulled them up to his waist. Then he pulled on his socks, hopping on one foot to keep balance. He opened up another drawer and grabbed a t-shirt and basketball shorts. He quickly put them on.

Eronie grabbed the towel he had thrown on his bed. Its dampness had seeped onto the comforter. He ran his hand over the wet spot. "Damn," he exclaimed.

He walked a few steps out of the bedroom, towel in hand, before he stopped. Slowly he walked back and flung the damp towel over the bedroom door to dry.

41

"Sorry I'm late Brian," Donnelly said as he opened the manager's office door. "I had car trouble. Did you get my message?"

Fullmer was typing on a computer. He looked at his watch.

7:33 p.m.

Donnelly was a half hour late.

"Yeah, Mike told me you'd be late. Don't worry about it, I had to finish up with office work anyhow," Fullmer replied.

"I'm really sorry though," Donnelly reiterated.

"It's okay. You couldn't help it if your car was having problems."

Donnelly sat down in one of the leather swivel chairs in the office. "Yeah. The piece of junk just wouldn't start for the longest time."

"What year is that thing?" Fullmer asked as he typed something into the computer.

"Nineteen-eighty-seven."

Fullmer snickered. "A classic."

"Certainly not in my eyes," Donnelly said.

"Why don't you just get a new one? It's rather sad that you have a car from nineteen-eighty-seven when you're a manager at this place."

"I probably should," Donnelly responded. "But, until today, I hadn't found the need. She'd gotten along alright so far."

Fullmer pressed one more button on the keyboard then pushed hard at the desk and rolled with the chair. "Done! Well if this becomes a habit I won't be too happy. I work too much as it is."

"Well, like I said, I'm sorry. Did you have to be home for anything important?"

"Not really. Today I would consider it a blessing that I stayed later than I needed to because the wife has been on my case recently. At least being here I'm able to take my mind off of that," Fullmer answered.

"I can understand that."

Fullmer got out of the chair and walked to the door. "Now it's time to face reality," he said as he turned the knob.

"I'll see you later Brian," Donnelly said.

"Have fun Ed," Fullmer replied, shutting the door behind him.

Fullmer took off his sportscoat and threw it onto the passenger's seat before getting inside. Once in he loosened up his tie and buckled in his seatbelt. He then stuck the key in the ignition and turned it. The car made a roaring noise as it started up. Fullmer pushed in the 'power' button on his stereo and classic rock started to play.

The stereo clock flashed 7:42 p.m. when Fullmer finally pulled out of his parking space.

He took a right turn out of the Vandermeer parking garage and headed home.

Fullmer turned the volume on higher as he sang along to the old song that was playing. The high volume drowned out his voice and his thoughts. As the song neared its end Fullmer turned the power off and thought. His face got serious and he realized he needed to do something.

Something unexpected.

Something that would be a surprise.

It would never be seen coming.

He took the first exit he saw off the highway and drove a few miles before pulling into a small store. He turned off his car and got out. A smile graced his face as he opened up the store door.

This will be good, he thought.

Within a few minutes he came out of the store holding a bag. Something pointy was inside.

Whatever was inside looked sharp.

He opened his door and gently placed the bag atop his sportscoat in the passenger's seat.

He started up the car and turned the radio back on. He sang louder than ever, this time the music wasn't loud enough to drown out his voice at all. He seemed happy. At ease.

Complete ease.

Fullmer kept singing to the music. The wheel was being used as a drum as his hands tapped hard against it. He was a one-man band.

The stereo clock flashed 8:12 p.m. when Fullmer finally pulled into a driveway. He turned off his headlights quickly, as if not to be seen, and grabbed the bag on the seat beside him. He left his sportscoat inside and quietly opened his door, shutting it without making a sound. Fullmer took a deep breath and softly trotted along the paved walkway to the front door.

'Bang. Bang. Bang.'

He put his hand into the bag and waited for someone to answer.

42

Once again Hank sat at his desk. A box of pizza lay directly in front of him with two slices remaining inside. The manila folder was opened and his eyes were glued to its pages. He had solved just about everything he could, but still something was missing.

Hank pulled out his notes and wrote on the top of one page in all capital letters.

WHAT IS MY CONNECTION?

Hank underlined 'connection' a few times. There had to be some greater connection than the murderer just wanting to beat Hank at the game he'd won so many times. No matter what the killer would eventually be caught. Hank had caught every killer he was set out to find.

All except one.

The one that shot him.

However, Hank knew that this could not be the same murderer. For one thing the murders that were committed in Massachusetts were nothing like the recent ones. That killer wasn't as clever. He wasn't as sharp. He wasn't playing a game with Hank like this one was. The murderer from Massachusetts just got lucky. He got away.

But no one can run forever.

Hank popped the tab of a soda can and poured the cold beverage into his mouth. He placed the can on top of the pizza box. It wobbled a bit before settling.

There has to be a connection to me, he thought. *The alphabet is the game, but why am I involved? What purpose do I serve? Does he just want me to lose? To fail? Or is it more than that? I'm the missing piece to the puzzle. What is my connection?*

Hank circled 'connection' on his paper a few times and put his head in his hand. He rubbed his temples trying to think of the possibilities.

The reasons.

The murderer had recruited Hank to play the game. But why?

Hank stopped rubbing his temples and reached into his back pocket. He pulled out his wallet and threw it on the desk. It was hurting his back, making him sit lopsided. Now he felt more comfortable.

He pulled at the folder and turned to some of the pictures. He picked out the ones of Dunfellow and placed them in a line next to one another. Hank leaned back in his chair and folded his arms. He stared at the photographs.

It looked like Dunfellow had lived for at least a few minutes after he was cut across the neck. Hank scratched his head and thought.

He was left to die. The first two were killed probably within seconds, then the bodies were mutilated afterwards. Calverly was strangled until she took her final breath of air. But he was left to die.

Hank flipped to the other victims' pictures. He looked at the one of Calverly.

What would have happened if Zucker caught the murderer midway through strangling her? How did he know Zucker wouldn't be back? Did he open the door and come inside after Zucker was in the shower?

"No," he answered the question in his head. "He couldn't have."

That would be too risky. He was already inside.

Hank flipped to Tom's testimony and skimmed the write-up.

He had left the door unlocked. It doesn't make any sense. Why play such a risky game? Everything had to go perfectly for him to strike. If he wanted Anderson he had to know the room he was in. Or follow him. If he wanted Barkley he would have to have followed her too. Same with Calverly and Dunfellow. This guy's playing more than just a deadly game. He's taking chances.

Hank looked out the window and into the darkness. He watched as some cars drove by.

This guy plays with each one of them. He knows their every move. He follows them. It wasn't a coincidence that all the victims fit the same profile, at least alphabetically.

He continued his thought aloud, "But it *is* a coincidence that the deaths were a week apart. He doesn't plan when they die. He just does it when he can. When he's able to."

Hank was onto something. *If Zucker were in the bedroom that night, instead of taking a shower, Calverly wouldn't have been dead. The killer would have to come back. It was just a coincidence that it was a week later. It could have been a day later. Or a month.*

"This game doesn't have a time. It just has an order."

Whoever is next could be killed at any time. Hank looked at the photographs again. *And if I'm part of the game...*

Hank's eyes darted from side to side. "Then he's

also following me."

The words made Hank uneasy. He hurriedly put the photographs into their folder. The can atop the pizza box shook and quickly tumbled onto the desk. The soda spilled everywhere.

Hank quickly picked up the folder so it wouldn't get drenched.

His wallet dropped to the ground, its contents also spilling out.

Hank ran over to the nightstand and grabbed some tissues. He dried up the mess and then turned his attention to the wallet lying on the floor. A few bills had sprawled out. He picked them up and then opened his wallet and placed them inside. He stopped doing the task for a moment and stared at his license.

For the first time he had realized what his connection was. He was surprised that he had figured out so much and yet had no clue what his purpose was to the whole thing.

Now he knew.

It was in front of his face all along.

Hank's eyes grew big as he stared at the license.

He had been wrong about one thing, and he knew that now. Hank wasn't just a *part* of the game.

He *was* the game.

43

Eronie cringed as the machete forcefully came down upon the victim's head, nearly splitting it entirely in half. The body dropped to the ground as blood poured out of the wound like a waterfall. The machete was wedged so deep into the skull that it was difficult to pull out. Two gloved hands grabbed the handle and tugged at the weapon.

No avail.

A boot violently stomped on the victim's torso hard, cracking some ribs. It needed leverage. The hands pulled on the weapon again.

Nothing.

The boot caved into the victim's chest, the skin could be heard being torn apart. Blood sprayed everywhere. The boot lifted up off the chest. Guts were draped over it. Blood dripped from it.

It crashed back down into the open chest with great force.

Thump.

Then it hit the soft entrails, the stomach and intestines. It sounded like it was stepping in mud.

The machete was finally pulled from the victim's skull.

But the horrible murder wasn't finished yet.

The large, bloodied blade violently came down across the victim's leg, tearing away at the skin and muscle until it finally struck bone.

It was pulled out. Blood dripped from it like tears.

It was brought back down. Another wound.

Up again.

Then back down.

After several wounds were inflicted on the already dead body the machete was dropped. It lay on the ground as the bloodied boots trudged over to the victim's bathroom.

Probably to clean up.

But the mess was far too great to clean. No one would be able to flee from such a horrendous crime. Even with gloved hands they would eventually find the culprit.

The bathroom door opened slowly. Someone was in the shower.

The water was too loud to be able to hear the intruder.

The gloved hands punched the mirror above the sink. The glass shattered everywhere.

The sound was loud enough to worry the person inside the shower. The water shut off and the curtain was pulled back. The naked girl stared in horror as a jagged piece of glass cut across her neck.

'Bang. Bang. Bang.'

Eronie jumped at the knocking at the door.

"Who the hell is this?" He asked himself as he turned off the violent movie.

Eronie looked out the window and smiled. He walked over to the door and unlocked it. He slowly turned the knob and pulled it open.

"What a surprise. So what brings you to my neck of the woods?"

44

Tom finally woke up from his drug-induced slumber. The pills didn't have the effect on him that he thought they would. They knocked him out, but not forever. Instead he woke up on the bathroom floor a few hours later, all groggy.

He rubbed the back of his head. He felt the large bump that he had acquired from his fall. Tom pressed in the soft mound of swollen flesh.

"Ow! That fucking hurts like hell," he screamed.

He didn't understand why he woke up. He thought he'd be dead. He wanted to overdose on pills, not wake up in a stupor.

Nothing in my life can go smoothly, he thought. "Not even my death," he said aloud.

He slowly sat up and looked at his legs. His jeans were completely soaked.

He had pissed his pants.

Tom shook his head at the sight and thought. *No one lives after overdosing in the movies. No one does in books. Why the hell am I the one who has to? Why can't my life be like a fucking book? It would make for a pretty good one. It seems just as unrealistic as those stupid mystery novels that sell off the shelves.*

He touched the wet spot between his legs. "I pissed

my fucking pants. Holy shit, what else can go wrong?"

Tom got up and looked at himself in the mirror. "Ugh," he groaned.

Tom's eyes were puffy, his cheeks were flushed, and he had scratches all over his face. He brought his fingers to one of the cuts just under his left eye. "How?"

He looked at his urine-stained pants again and then quickly took them off. The inside of the jeans stuck to his thighs. Tom threw the wet pants into the bathroom hamper.

He walked over to the shower and turned on the water then slowly got undressed. *Maybe it was a good thing that the pills didn't do their job,* he thought. *Maybe I wasn't meant to die. Maybe it wasn't my fault.*

Tom turned off the water after only a few minutes. The thought of staying longer reminded him of the night Calverly died. If only he had taken a quick shower then she'd still be alive.

Or even if he hadn't taken one at all.

Then everything would be okay.

Tom grabbed a clean towel from a folded stack close by. He quickly dried off his body and then wrapped the towel around his waist. He got out of the shower and walked over to the sink.

If only I didn't take a shower, Katie would be here. If only I stayed with her in the room. I could have saved her.

The thoughts were awful. Just when he believed maybe they had subsided, that maybe the pills had at least done something right, they just as quickly came back.

Tom closed his eyes and rubbed his forehead to ward off the thoughts. "Ow," he exclaimed, as he happened to rub one of the cuts on his head.

He looked in the mirror. A small amount of blood fell from the scratch.

Tom kneeled down and opened up the sink cabinet. He reached in and grabbed a few bandages. He looked stunned at what he saw inside.

The bottle of pills was still there.

He dropped the bandages and reached inside for the pills. He shook the bottle.

It was full.

"I don't understand," he said.

The bottle hadn't been opened.

Tom shook his head in awe at the situation. "I *didn't* take them?" He asked. "I put them back?" He tried to make sense of it all.

But why don't I remember?

He tried to think of what had happened. He couldn't remember putting the pills back, but they were definitely there.

Tom's eyes squinted, his forehead creased. He was deep in thought. He was confused.

"Why don't I remember? What the hell is wrong with me?"

He looked at the hamper and his wet pants inside. He touched the scratches on his face then the bump on the back of his head.

He didn't remember what had happened, but he understood what probably did.

"Did I pass out again?" Tom asked himself.

He didn't know the answer; instead he shook his head slowly in disbelief.

45

Fullmer stood outside the door as it slowly opened. "Surprise!"

Amy put her hand on her chest. "You scared me Brian," she said. "Why are you knocking? Did you forget your keys?"

"No," Fullmer said as he pulled out a bouquet of roses from the bag. "I wanted to surprise you."

Amy looked at the flowers. She smiled. "Are you trying to get on my good side?"

"I don't know. But if I were, would it be working?" Fullmer asked as he stepped inside the house.

"Maybe."

He handed her the roses. "Watch out for the thorns, they're sharp. I almost got pricked when I picked them out for you."

"This is very sweet of you Brian. And certainly unexpected." She kissed him on the cheek. "I'll put these in water right away."

Fullmer closed the door and made sure it was locked. He walked right behind Amy, following her into the kitchen.

She opened up a cupboard and pulled out a vase. "So why did you do this?"

"No reason. Why does everything have to have a

reason? Maybe I did it just because."

She put the vase under the sink faucet and turned the water on. The vase slowly filled up. "With you everything has a reason. Just because of what? Because we fought yesterday?"

"Well maybe that had something to do with it. But I figured I should do more stuff like this anyway. Sweet stuff, like I used to do when we were younger. Remember all the stuff I did?"

The vase was three-quarters full when Amy turned off the water. "Of course I do. That's why I fell in love with you. You were romantic." She placed the roses in the vase.

"I still am," Fullmer replied.

Amy chuckled. "Well I suppose you can be if you put your mind to it."

Fullmer smiled. "I suppose." He walked over to Amy and kissed her on the lips then wrapped his arms around her. "I love you," he whispered in her ear.

"I love you too." Amy was slowly released from Fullmer's embrace. "I don't think you can get off the hook this easily mister," she said jokingly.

Fullmer smiled. "What do you mean?"

"Well for one thing you're home almost an hour late. Didn't you get off at seven?"

"Yes, but Ed had car troubles and came in late. I didn't get out until after 7:30. And before you ask me why I didn't call you, I'll save you the breath and tell you. I wanted it to be a surprise. If I called you then you would have known it was me knocking at the door."

"That doesn't really make any sense. If you called me I would have been less worried about where you were and I still would have been surprised you got me the roses," Amy answered.

"Well the next time I want to surprise you I'll make sure I tell you first," Fullmer said.

"Ha. Ha. Very funny." Amy poked her husband's stomach a few times. "Hey is that blood on your shirt?" She asked, pointing to a red spot near his tie.

He nervously looked down at the stain. "Maybe." He looked at his fingers. "I guess I did get pricked."

46

Hank was waiting in the same booth for the others to arrive. He had gotten there early because he was anxious to tell them the missing piece to the puzzle. He was also curious what Gale would think.

The same redheaded waitress came over to the booth. "Are you waiting for the others, sir?"

"Yes I am, thank you. But I guess you could get me a water with lemon please."

"Certainly."

Gale walked in soon after the waitress had left the table. "You're early Hank."

"Not really," Hank replied.

"So did you get a good night's sleep?"

"Not at all. Too much on my mind. And I've been wanting to tell you all about it since I figured it out," Hank hurriedly replied. "But when I tried to call you last night your line was busy. You must have been talking with the other possible victims."

"I probably was, and by the way they all checked out. Both leave today."

"I'm not so sure that even matters anymore," Hank said.

Gale ignored Hank's statement; he was more interested in what he had said earlier. "So what did you figure out?"

The waitress came back with Hank's water. "Here you go, sir. And would you like something to drink?" She asked, turning to Gale.

"A decaf please."

"Sure."

"I figured out what I have to do with this game the murderer's playing. I realized why he leaves the papers," Hank said.

Gale was disappointed with Hank's response. "Didn't you already figure that out? Didn't you tell me before that he wants you to fail at what you're good at, and that he wants to watch you do it?"

"I think that's a reason too. But last night I came to the conclusion that there's more to it than just that. My wallet happened to fall on the floor and when I picked it up everything became clearer to me."

"What exactly do you mean?" Gale asked.

Hank reached into his back pocket and pulled out his wallet. He took out his license from inside the clear plastic slit. Hank handed it to Gale.

Gale was curious. He didn't quite understand what Hank was doing. "And your license made you figure out your connection *because*?"

Hank pointed to the address on the bottom left hand corner of the license. "Look where I live."

Gale read it aloud. "Gloucester, Massachusetts."

The waitress came back and put down the steaming cup of coffee. "I'll come back when the other two have arrived."

Gale looked at her. "That would be good. They should be here any minute."

"Don't you see Charlie? He wants me. I'm on his victims list. 'G' for Garrison 'G' for Gloucester. I was supposed to stay at the Vandermeer."

Gale understood. His eyes got big. He realized he

had a connection too. "Hank do you know where I was born? Where I lived before moving here?"

"Maine?" Hank answered.

"That's correct. But do you know where in Maine?" Gale questioned.

"No Charlie. Why? What point are you trying to make with this?"

"I was born in Gorham, Maine Hank. Gale from Gorham. I'm just as much connected as you are. Maybe he wants me. Maybe I'm on his list and you're not. He could still want you to watch me die. He could still want you to fail. He may not want to kill you. Wouldn't that seem too easy? If you're dead then you couldn't watch him finish the alphabet. That's what he wants to do, right? He *wants* you to watch him win."

Hank realized that Gale had a good point. Gale could just as much be on the list as Hank. They both fit the profile, but Hank was convinced it was himself that would be the target. "How do you fit into the Vandermeer? You don't have a strong connection. I stayed there."

"My connection is just as strong as Dunfellow's was. He was Calverly's uncle. I'm on the case. That means I have some connection."

Once again Gale was right. The murderer sometimes played unfairly. Maybe even the mildest connection was good enough. Maybe there didn't have to be a connection at all.

"Well if it is me or you he wants, then we have a good idea what to expect. We don't have to wait for death, but we do have to suspect it," Hank said.

"But you also must realize that he's still stuck on 'D.' He hasn't moved passed 'D' yet. Even if you or I were on his list, we'd catch him before then," Gale responded.

Hank was irritated. "I'm not worried about being on his list, Charlie. Like I said, if anything it makes it easier to figure out. If he wants me then I must have some connection to him. I must see him. He probably follows me. Knows where I live. Knows what I do with my time. Hell he's probably outside right now, waiting." Hank looked around the restaurant. "He's probably inside waiting."

"He has a schedule Hank. He strikes at intervals. If it's you or me he wants then he has to finish off two before he even gets to us. We'll find out who 'E' is before he strikes, nevermind 'F.' Nevermind us."

"That's the other thing Charlie. There is no schedule. It wouldn't make sense. How could he know when the perfect time to kill someone was? How could he know Anderson wouldn't be doing something the day he was murdered? That people wouldn't have surrounded him? Or Barkley? Or Calverly? How did he know Zucker would be in the shower? How did he know Dunfellow would have to pull over to check his car?"

"So you're saying there's no predetermined schedule for him to strike?"

"That's exactly what I'm saying. He strikes when he can. When he's least likely to get caught. There's just an order, the rest falls into the hands of the victims. For all we know 'E' and 'F' could be dead. We may just not have found the bodies yet. This guy knows what he's doing. He's a step ahead of us," Hank said.

"Not any longer. We know his possible moves for 'G.'"

"Well if that's true then he's not a step ahead. He's even."

Harlowe walked into the restaurant and sat down beside Gale. "Sorry I'm late. I was posting some more eviction notices. Boring job, until I get to knock down the doors and see what's inside."

"Where's Dan?" Gale asked.

"He didn't come with me. I thought he was with you guys."

"We both came here separately. I thought maybe you'd have picked him up," Gale answered.

"No. I didn't think he needed a ride. I was scheduled to work earlier than him so I couldn't have picked him up anyway. He'll be here," Harlowe said.

"Oh I don't doubt he will. It's just a little odd. In all my years knowing the guy he's never been late. He's always the first person to be somewhere," Gale said.

"Especially the buffet line," Harlowe replied.

"Maybe he's nervous because of the note you left the waitress last time," Hank said.

Gale and Harlowe laughed. "Probably," Gale replied.

"I'll give him a call." Harlowe took out his cellphone from the clip on the side of his belt.

It rang five times before the voicemail picked up.

'Hey this is Dan. You know what to do.'

'Beep.'

"Yeah Dan, this is Jon. I don't know if you just forgot to show up or not, but we're at the restaurant. Hopefully you're on your way because we're going to order without you." Harlowe hung up.

"How far away from here does he live?" Hank asked.

"Not very far. Probably ten minutes," Harlowe responded.

The waitress came over and took the men's orders. They all ordered the same as the last time.

Harlowe tried calling Eronie again after a half hour

had elapsed and they had finished their meals.

It went to his voicemail again.

'Beep.'

"Hey I don't know where the hell you are, but we're going to come by your house to get your fat, lazy ass up. If you get this soon give me a call back. If you're headed to the restaurant now, it's too late. We're leaving." Harlowe hung up the phone.

Hank put ten dollars on the table then looked at Gale and put another ten dollars. "It's on me."

Harlowe threw down some cash and stood up. "Should we stop by Dan's, see if he's there?"

Gale slid out of the booth. "Yeah, may as well. It's on the way. We're not going to take three cars there though."

Hank got out of the booth and stood near the other two. He grabbed his knee. "I think I'm just going to head back to my hotel for a bit. I'll see you back at the station in two hours or so."

"You sure you don't want to come with us? It won't take long," Gale asked.

"No it's fine. I need to rest my knee and make some phonecalls anyhow. Talk to my wife."

"Whatever you say Hank. I'll see you at the station then."

Hank limped over to the exit. "See you later."

Gale turned to Harlowe. "You can drive."

"No problem," Harlowe said.

47

Hank sat in his hotel bed and threw his cellphone onto the pillow. He had just gotten off the phone with Carol. Everyday he missed her more and more and he was beginning to regret not having left for home a while ago. But he knew that he was too involved now. He knew it would be impossible to leave. He had figured out so much and he was so close to finding out all the answers.

He knew the victims' profile.

He knew the game.

And now he even knew his part in the game.

The only thing he needed was the murderer.

And he knew that would be difficult.

Hank lay back on the bed. His legs still dangled over the side. He placed his hands under his head for support and turned to the pillow. He reached over and grabbed his cellphone.

He dialed Victor's number.

"Hey Victor, it's Hank. I have to ask you some questions."

"Well I hope I can answer them," he replied.

"I hope so too. I think I'm getting closer to finding out who this murderer is. I'll tell you one thing; he's by far the smartest one I've ever been assigned to. He does things carefully. He doesn't leave any good evidence. And the stuff we find, like the papers, is to mess with my head. Everything he does has a purpose in his grand scheme."

"Sounds like your kind of man," Victor said. "So what is it you'd like to know?"

"Well I've been wondering if Zucker is still in custody. And I'm also a bit confused as to why there hasn't been a story about Dunfellow's murder the other night. By the time they show it there could be a few more."

"Well let's hope that's not the case," Victor replied. "Zucker was released. Florida's Bureau and the Clermont Police had nothing against him. He was just as much a victim as the girl was…"

"Did Gale know about this?" Hank asked.

"What? About Zucker's release?"

"Yes."

"I would assume he did. He's the Orlando detective, right?"

"Yeah that's him," Hank answered.

"Well Jeffrey Gunderson must have told him. Probably last night I'd imagine," Victor said.

"Okay. I was just curious because I didn't have a clue. Maybe Gale thought I knew. It just seemed like a pretty big thing to slip someone's mind. What about the Dunfellow story?"

"Um…as far as I know it will break tonight. FBI urged the stations and papers not to air or print anything the day after because there were still a lot of things to go over. They didn't want another story about a possible killer being caught, like they had with Zucker. It wouldn't have been fair to Zucker or the people involved. I think they have enough now to put up a good story, based on fact, rather than assumptions," Victor responded.

"Well I guess that's all I wanted to know then," Hank said.

"Well I see. So anyway, how are you doing with everything?"

"Not bad. I just wish this whole thing were over. I don't like not being confident. I don't like not knowing more than the criminal. It makes me feel uneasy."

"Well I would think that's normal. But I also know this is what you were born to do. You'll get the job done."

"I hope so. The question isn't whether or not I can get the job done, because I think I can. The question is whether or not he'll get his job done first."

Victor was puzzled at Hank's riddle-like answer. "What does that mean?"

"I think he wants me dead too…"

48

Gale and Harlowe pulled into Eronie's driveway.

"He must be here," Harlowe said. "His car's here."

Gale laughed. "What a sleuth you are Jon. Great deductive reasoning."

Harlowe put the car in park and turned it off. "Well let's get that fat ass of his out of the house." He opened the door and got out.

Gale did the same.

They quickly walked up to the door and rang the bell.

No answer.

Harlowe pressed the button a few times in a row.

Nothing.

"Should we break down the door?" Harlowe asked, jokingly.

"He's probably in the bathroom," Gale responded.

"He's probably in his Jacuzzi is more like it."

Harlowe rang the bell a few more times.

Still no answer.

"Maybe it's unlocked," Gale finally said. "One thing I learned in the past couple of days is people tend to forget to lock doors."

Gale's hand grabbed the doorknob and turned it.

It opened.

"How strange?" Harlowe asked. "You'd think people would learn after all that has happened around here lately."

The door slowly swung open. Gale stepped inside. He immediately covered his nose as he caught a whiff of the odd-smelling aroma inside. "Ugh it smells absolutely terrible in here."

Harlowe took a whiff. "Smells like burnt meat."

Gale walked over to the living room. "Dan!"

No answer.

"This place reeks," Hariowe said as he got a stronger scent.

"I wonder what the hell it is," Gale replied. "Dan!"

No answer.

"It kind of smells like chlorine, maybe his Jacuzzi blew up," Harlowe said. "Chlorine and shit."

Gale looked at the living room. Something seemed to be missing.

"Doesn't this room look empty to you? Has he changed it since the Superbowl party?" Gale asked.

"I'm not sure I haven't been here in awhile." Harlowe looked around the room. He saw the empty spot that Gale must have been talking about. "Yeah I remember now. That little stupid T.V. that he kept on the side of the big one isn't there. He probably threw it away. Why would he even want a little T.V. when he has that enormous sixty-four inch one?" Harlowe looked at the huge television.

Gale smiled. "It was good when the halftime show came on. We could watch something else at the same time."

"So where is that fat fuck?" Harlowe asked as he walked over to the Jacuzzi room and peered inside. "Oh my fucking God. Charlie!"

Gale walked over to Harlowe. "What?" He didn't

have to wait for an answer as

he saw Eronie's body half inside the Jacuzzi and half out. Eronie's head was at the bottom of the Jacuzzi. The water was up to his waist.

His legs dangled over the side.

Gale and Harlowe were speechless as they looked at their dead friend.

Harlowe finally broke the silence, "He was the next victim."

Gale walked to the opposite side of the Jacuzzi and spotted an extension cord. He followed the orange line from the plug across the room to the inside of the water. "I believe so. 'E' for Eronie." He looked at the small television that was at the bottom of the Jacuzzi. "'E' for electrocution."

Harlowe quickly pulled out his cellphone and dialed up the police.

Gale took a closer look at Eronie's body. His skin was peeled off of his face. It looked as if it had melted off. His eyes were almost completely out of their sockets. They looked like nothing more than two globs of goop.

There was something floating under Eronie's chest. Gale watched as it slowly spun around and came into plain view.

Another newspaper.

Garrison Saves the Day.

49

Hank was awakened by his ringing cellphone. He was trying to catch up on some much needed sleep before heading to the station.

"Hello," he answered as he sat up and rubbed his eyes. He had only been napping for less than an hour, but it seemed like an eternity.

"Hank, you were right," Gale said on the other end.

Hank was still in a dazed state of mind, having just been awakened. "What? What was I right about?"

"There's no set time, Hank. The fucking killer doesn't set a time for the victims to die. He doesn't strike every week. He strikes when he thinks he can."

"What are you trying to tell me, Charlie? What are you saying?"

"Dan's dead," Gale replied. It was all he could muster up.

Hank shook his head. "What?"

"Dan's dead. Jon and I found him in his hot tub. He had been electrocuted. 'E' for Eronie. He was next. The connection can be small. The killer didn't think we'd suspect him. He was the last guy we'd suspect. He knew it. He knew we'd try and look for other victims, but Dan slipped our minds," Gale answered.

"Are you still at the crime scene? Should I meet

you there?"

"No. Jon and I just left. We stayed until forensics, homicide, and the FBI showed up. We got as much information as we could. There's no evidence that was left. Just the newspaper article he always leaves. A way to sign his work. I would have called you earlier, but to be quite honest it hadn't crossed my mind. I was in shock. I'm still in shock. I can't believe he came after Dan. That sick bastard. I can't believe it."

Hank didn't believe it either. Eronie hadn't even crossed his mind. Although his last name did begin with an 'E,' Hank had never thought about the possibility. Once again the killer's next move was right in front of his face and he never saw it coming.

"I'll meet you at the station in twenty. We'll discuss more there," Hank said.

"Yeah, sure. See you there."

The phone hung up.

Hank arrived in Gale's office just when he said he would. Harlowe and Gale looked as if they were in a deep conversation, discussing something that seemed important. They stopped as soon as Hank entered the room.

"So he's killed another victim far sooner than we had imagined," Hank said.

Gale looked at him. "Just the way to do it too. He knows what he's doing. This guy is a professional. I just can't believe I didn't see this coming. Dan was always right here. He fit the profile as well as anyone else and I didn't even see it."

Hank sat down, grabbing his knee. It had been acting up on him recently. "You can't blame yourself. Dan knew about the whole 'E' connection. Maybe he should have known himself," Hank replied.

"Yeah, but until this morning I didn't believe he'd

strike early and I doubt Dan did either. He probably never knew that there didn't need to be a strong connection to the Vandermeer. That just showing up there would be good enough in the killer's eyes," Gale said.

"There is one odd thing, sir," Harlowe said to Hank. "Dan has lived in Orlando his whole life. He didn't come from a town that began with an 'E.'"

Hank didn't understand. *The murderer couldn't just be using the order of last names to kill people. It wasn't clever enough. This guy was clever.*

"Are you sure?" Hank asked.

"I've known him for years and he's always told me he was born and raised here in Orlando," Harlowe answered.

Hank was still in disbelief. *The murderer could not have switched the rules of the game that drastically.* "Are you sure he was murdered?" Hank didn't mean to ask the question, but it slipped out. He tried to find a way to make the connection fit. "Couldn't he have mistakenly electrocuted himself?"

Harlowe and Gale looked appalled. "I probably would have thought the same knowing what you know Hank. But if you had seen his body you wouldn't have even thought about asking that question. He *had* been murdered. There wasn't a doubt in anyone's mind. It's not like he was in the tub with his bathing suit on and a television found a way to jump inside with him. He was fully dressed. He was half in and half out of the Jacuzzi. He was definitely murdered," Gale responded, angrily.

Hank knew he had asked the wrong question. Gale and Harlowe were good friends of Eronie's and to top it all off he insulted their intelligence. "I'm sorry. I just think there has to be some sort of connection. How can he be the only one who doesn't fit the profile a hundred percent?"

Gale looked Hank directly in the eyes without blinking. "Let's not go through this again. Sometimes things don't always have to fit. Sometimes you have to scratch your head and wonder why. This time is no different. Dan didn't fit the profile entirely, but on the other hand he did fit it. He was an 'E.' He was electrocuted. He was connected to the Vandermeer. What more could you possibly ask for, besides a note from the murderer telling you that he was going to forget about the whole born in an 'E' town this time around?"

Hank knew it would be worthless to argue with Gale. "Did he happen to have a neck wound?"

Gale smiled. "You don't get it quite yet do you? Not every little thing you find with the first four murders is because the killer intended it to be that way. The first two were vacationers, but Calverly wasn't. The first three had jobs that began with the same letter as their last names did, but Dunfellow and Dan didn't. The first three worked or were staying at the Vandermeer, but Dunfellow and Dan weren't. The first two were cut, Calverly wasn't. Then Dunfellow was. But no, Hank, Dan did not have a neck wound."

Hank was even unhappier. He thought, *How could I have been so wrong? I had never been wrong before. First it was with the occupations, then people staying or working at the Vandermeer. Now it was the place of birth and neck wounds.*

A single thought had grabbed his attention. *Places of birth.*

Many people think that where someone lives as a child and where they are born are one in the same, but that isn't necessarily always the case. Some people are born in a hospital out of the town they grew up in. Some places don't have hospitals. Orlando had many, but who knows if Dan's mother gave birth elsewhere.

Hank couldn't back down. "Okay so maybe I was wrong about the neck thing, but I can't just forget about the place of birth thing. If not for the places the victims are from beginning with the same letters as their last names, we only have the alphabet working for their names and the weapons used. The murderer wouldn't do that."

"Why not?" Gale asked.

"Because he's better than that. If it were only those two things then he could find anyone. There wouldn't really be a victim profile. But this guy doesn't take the easy way out. He wants us to be on to him and there would be no way on Earth that we could be on to him if he just used people's last names as his only criteria. There would be too many possibilities. He likes it when we have an idea as to what his next move might be. That's why he plays the game," Hank answered.

"But we wouldn't know any of his moves until we found the connection that you did. Early on we'd have no idea of any possible victims. We wouldn't have been able to target any," Harlowe said.

Hank had the answer. "I know. The killer just used the first few murders as a stepping-stone. They were a way to have us figure him out just a little. Now we're able to file down the victims. That's what he wants. We couldn't then, but we can now. That's why Dan must have been born somewhere other than Orlando. Maybe he came unexpectedly. Maybe his parents were in another town or city at the time."

Gale understood Hank's reasoning. "Maybe." He picked up his desk phone and pressed in a button.

"Hillary can you call the City Hall and see if they could find Daniel Eronie's birth abstract. Find out if he was born somewhere other than here?"

"Sure Detective Gale," she answered.

"Thank you." He hung up the phone.

"If you are right Hank this guy will surely pay for what he's done. He's playing with matches, but soon enough he will get burned," Gale said.

"I hope soon comes early," Hank answered.

Hank tried to figure out anything he could. There was a lot he had missed by not being at the crime scene. There was so much he wanted to know.

"Was Dan wounded at all? I don't understand how he was thrown into the Jacuzzi without putting up a fight. He didn't go in on his freewill. But if he wasn't wounded beforehand then how did the murderer get him inside the water? Dan wouldn't have gone in on his own, just waiting to be electrocuted."

"They found a large contusion on the back of his head. Some of the investigators on the scene said it looked like he had been knocked unconscious first then thrown into the water. The television was thrown in afterward," Gale replied.

"The way the body was actually looked like Dan had been leaning over the Jacuzzi to test the water or something before he was hit," Harlowe added.

"So the killer must have already been inside then," Hank responded.

"Why do you say that?" Gale asked.

"Because if Dan had answered the door and the killer was waiting outside then the blow to the head to knock him unconscious would have been in the front. But it wasn't," Hank replied.

"So you think he was already inside when Dan got home?" Harlowe asked.

"Well I don't know, but it would seem like that would be the case. If not inside waiting to strike, then invited in at some point," Hank answered.

"Well the door was unlocked when we arrived. So the killer may have just snuck up on Dan," Harlowe said.

"That doesn't seem right either. If someone had come up from behind him he would have noticed. He wouldn't have been leaning over the Jacuzzi," Hank replied.

"Well I just said it looked like he had been doing that. Just so you could get an idea," Harlowe responded.

"But it would make sense if he were doing that. It would take too long to drag the body into the tub after he was knocked out. And there would be the chance Dan would come to by then. It would take too much strength to carry his large body over to the Jacuzzi and throw him inside. And if someone did do that I think Dan would have been more than just halfway in the tub. You say he wasn't."

"So you're implying that what Jon believes is true? That Dan was feeling the water when he was knocked out?" Gale questioned.

"In a way. He may not have been feeling it, but he was facing it. The placement of his wound would indicate that. Maybe he was showing it," Hank said.

"Showing it? Dan was showing his Jacuzzi to the murderer?" Harlowe asked.

"Whoever it was he didn't suspect him to be the murderer. I think Dan knew whoever killed him," Hank said.

Harlowe and Gale were stunned at Hank's statement.

"Are you serious?" Gale asked.

"Yes I am. By the way, did you find the weapon that created the wound?" Hank asked.

"They didn't find the weapon. Maybe it was the

T.V.," Harlowe answered.

"Too heavy and it would take too long. Dan would have noticed," Hank said.

"Well whatever it was they haven't found it yet," Gale replied.

"That's a bit odd because so far he's always left the weapon," Hank said.

"I thought so too, but then again I don't know many weapons that begin with an 'E.' I think he took it with him because the weapon this time was the electricity," Gale responded.

"Well whatever it was we'll find out some viable options when forensics tells us more," Harlowe said.

Hank nodded. His eyes turned to the blinking red light on Gale's desk phone. "I think someone's trying to reach you Charlie."

Gale looked at the light. He picked up the phone and pressed in the blinking button.

"Hello."

"Yes, Detective Gale. I'm sorry it took so long. City Hall was busy the first few times I called. They did find Detective Eronie's birth abstract."

"Okay. So where was he born?" Gale asked.

"Elkton, sir," she answered.

Gale's eyes widened. "Thank you, Hillary."

"You're welcome, sir."

The phone hung up.

Hank knew something important would be told. "Was I right?" He asked.

"Apparently he wasn't born in Orlando, but in a place about two hours from here."

Hank wanted to know. "Where?"

"Elkton."

Hank was happy that his victim criteria still worked.

Harlowe was amazed at how correct Hank had been. "Who would know such a thing? Who would know he was born there?" He asked.

Hank looked at Harlowe. "I was thinking the same thing. And the answer is quite obvious."

"Who?" Harlowe asked.

50

Tom woke up on the living room couch. He had fallen asleep there the night before, still not wanting to enter the bedroom. He had a strange feeling inside the pit of his stomach. It may have been from the lack of food or something else. His head kept telling him to turn on the television. He looked at the clock on the VCR.

3:05 p.m.

He had slept for over fourteen hours. Tom was amazed, but he also found it to be necessary. He hadn't slept in a long time, barring the two-hour episode on the bathroom floor. He listened to his head and turned on the television.

Mallory, the news reporter, was in mid-sentence. *'The FBI have now joined in on the search for what has become to be known as the 'Vandermeer Slasher.' The originally suspected, twenty-five-year-old, Thomas Zucker has been released on lack of evidence. He was in custody at the time of the fourth murder, which occurred two nights ago. The victim was the fifty-three-year-old, Walter Dunfellow, who was on vacation from Kentucky. This has been a terribly stressful and scary last couple of weeks and the FBI urges everyone to decrease their vulnerability by not being alone. If there is any light at the end of this dark tunnel it would be that famed, New England-based, serial investigator, Hank Garrison is also on the case. The heinous crimes...'*

Tom turned off the television. He had recognized Dunfellow's name.

He was Katie's uncle.

How is Katie related to all of this? She worked at the hotel the others were murdered at, then she was killed, and now her uncle. What is this all about?

The thoughts made Tom uneasy. He had no answers to any of them. Although he had always admired Hank's ability to figure out crimes, even using Hank's past for *The Assault*, he certainly didn't carry that same gift. He was only a writer. Nothing more.

But Tom knew that he'd never be able to live with himself if he didn't get the opportunity to find out what Hank believed about the crimes and their connection to Calverly. He didn't want to contemplate suicide every night because he surrendered to his awful thoughts. The thoughts that told him he had something to do with Calverly's murder. He didn't want to be so stressed out that he couldn't help passing out at random moments. He didn't want to be afraid of his house anymore. Afraid of being killed.

But most of all, Tom didn't want to be afraid of his life.

51

"The killer, like everything else that has happened in the last two weeks, is right in front of us. We've seen him before. We've probably spoken to him before. For Dan's murder to make any sense at all, he would have to have known the murderer," Hank said to the other two.

"If what you're saying is correct, then what would you suggest?" Harlowe asked.

"Well I didn't know Dan as well as either of you…"

Harlowe jumped in before Hank had finished. "You can't be serious. You think we did this? I didn't know where he was born. I don't even know if *he* did. We have a business-like relationship. I hardly see him other than at work. Except for a small party at his place every now and then."

Hank was a bit suspicious at Harlowe's uneasiness. He had never suggested it was Harlowe. "I didn't point fingers. I'm not saying it's you. I'm not saying it's anyone. I just think whoever it is would know Dan pretty well."

Gale leaned forward in his chair. "But what about the other murders? How would someone that knew Dan know about where they were born? What if they were all born in different locations than where they resided?"

"That's a good question. I suppose we could have each one checked, but why try to find a flaw in the criteria?" Hank asked.

"Well that's what you just did. Dan didn't fit, what *you* believe to be, the killer's ultimate plan," Gale answered.

"I tried to make it fit. I didn't try to make it *not* fit. The killer didn't know the other victims. It would be impossible to have known them all. They were from all over. The killer didn't care if they were born in a different city than what their license said. He used them to draw us…" Hank stopped, then continued, "To draw *me* closer. Once I know his next move he mixes it up a little."

"So if he strikes again, what will he do?" Gale asked.

"Maybe the same thing as before. Maybe Dan was just to throw us off. It worked, but I don't think it did as well as he had hoped. Maybe his next move will be just like the first couple. Maybe it will be entirely different. But whoever it is we know it begins with an 'F,'" Hank answered.

"So, if it is someone Dan knew, we need to find out who that is. And fast," Harlowe said.

"Yes. And you two have to help me with that. You both knew him far better than I did," Hank replied.

"I know of a Josh and a Gary," Harlowe said. "I spoke with them at the last Superbowl party Dan had."

"Last names?" Hank asked.

"I have no clue." Harlowe looked at his watch. "But I have to do some more evictions soon, so I'm sure the investigation is still taking place in his house. I could just stop by and get his cellphone. The numbers of all his friends would be in there."

"That's a good idea. But they wouldn't just let you take something from a victim's house. I could go with you. They'd understand more if FBI was present," Hank said.

"Sure."

Hank's eyes were drawn to the flashing red light on Gale's desk phone again. "Someone is calling, Charlie."

Gale picked up the phone and brought it to his ear then pressed the button.

"Hello," he said.

"Yes, Detective. Tom Zucker just called for Agent Garrison. He said he'd like to speak with him about Katherine Calverly," Hillary said.

"Is he still on the phone?"

"No. He said he wanted to speak with him in person."

"Where?"

"Well he left his number, he said he could meet Agent Garrison wherever he wanted."

"Okay. Thank you." Gale hung up.

"What was that about?" Hank asked.

"Zucker called. He wants to meet you somewhere to discuss Calverly," Gale answered.

"Is he still on the line?"

"No. He left his number with Hillary. She's at the front desk," Gale replied.

"That's strange," Hank said.

"Maybe he has something good. A lead or something," Harlowe responded.

"Hank, I can go with you," Gale said.

Hank shook his head. "No, I think it may be best if I'm alone." Hank turned to Harlowe. "What time do you figure you'd be at Dan's?"

"I could swing by there in no more than two hours.

I don't have too much work to get done," Harlowe answered.

"Well that sounds about right. I can meet you there around then."

Harlowe grabbed a pen from his pocket and a paper off of Gale's desk. He wrote down the directions to Eronie's house.

"Okay, so we'll all meet there in two hours," Hank said.

Harlowe handed Hank the directions. "Here you go."

"Thank you. Hey that light is flashing again," Hank said, pointing to the phone.

"What the hell is this? A telethon?" Gale picked up the phone and pressed in the button.

"Hello."

"Sorry to bother you again Detective, but a Dean Wilson from forensics would like to speak with you. He's on hold now, sir."

"Thank you Hillary."

Gale pressed the 'hold' button.

"This is Detective Gale."

"Yes, hello Detective. This is Dean Wilson down in forensics. I just wanted to let you know that we didn't find anything worthwhile on the victim. No fingerprints or hairs. Nothing. Pretty much another clean murder. However, the contusion on the back of the victim's head was made from a small, thin object. Something heavy and strong. A bat or a metal pipe. The force was extremely powerful and the mark shows that it was with an upward thrust. This would lead us to believe he was near the Jacuzzi before the blow to the head. It would have knocked him unconscious and he would have fallen into the water. Had the head trauma occurred somewhere else in the house there would certainly be blood somewhere, but there wasn't any traces other than what was in the water."

"Thank you. That may all be very useful," Gale responded.

"You're welcome. We'll keep in touch."

"Yes we will. Goodbye."

Gale hung up the phone.

"That was forensics. They said that the blow to Dan's head was made from some sort of bat or lead pipe. Something strong."

"So whatever it was he still has it on him," Hank said.

"He certainly does. Or it's somewhere we haven't searched yet," Gale replied.

52

As soon as Hank got into his car he dialed Tom's number. He didn't have the slightest idea what Tom wanted, but it was a great opportunity to talk to the man who was connected to two of the murders. Barkley was reading his book and Calverly was his girlfriend. He had wanted to talk with Tom for a while and now was his chance.

"Hello, is this Tom Zucker," Hank asked when a voice picked up.

"Yes this is. Is this Agent Garrison?"

"Yes. I was told you wanted to meet me to talk. Can you tell me what this is all about?" Hank asked.

"Well yes. It has to do with the murders, Katie in particular. I've just been on edge recently and I thought that maybe you could straighten things out for me. I need to know some things. I was hoping that you could help me. I really have no one else I can turn to right now," Tom answered in a scared voice.

Hank didn't understand why Tom wanted his help. He was suspicious. He was cautious. Deep inside Hank was wary of Tom's intentions. "You know I can't just give out information about the murders. That can't be done."

"It's not like that, Mr. Garrison. I need to talk with

you about stuff related to the murders, nothing specific. I know what you can and cannot tell me."

"Do you know something?" Hank asked.

"I know that there are connections. I need you to tell me why," Tom replied.

Hank was interested. "What kinds of connections?"

"I'm at Teddy's Diner. We can discuss all that further here. Do you know where it is?"

Hank knew the place well. It was the same diner he ate at with the others. "Yes. I'll be there shortly."

"I'll be waiting."

The phone hung up.

Hank arrived at the diner in ten minutes time. When he walked through the door Tom flagged him down. Even though Hank was suspicious of Tom, he felt safe inside the diner. There were too many people around.

And if Tom were the murderer, there would have to have been two all along. Dunfellow was killed when Tom was in prison. It would have been impossible for Tom to have killed him.

But Hank had never even considered the possibility of two murderers. It didn't seem right. Not clever. Too movie-like.

Too unreal.

As Hank limped slowly over to Tom's table the possibilities crossed his mind.

Maybe Zucker is here to get me and the other killer is out to get the other victim. Out to get the letter 'F.' Hank shook off the thoughts. *No, Zucker is not the murderer, I'm just paranoid.*

Hank scanned the people in the diner. Each face looked like it could have committed a crime. Each pair of eyes seemed to be set on his own. To Hank they all looked like killers.

Killers or victims.

I just have too much on my mind. Zucker wants something else. He wants to know something. He doesn't want to kill me.

Hank finally reached the table. He slowly sat down, grabbing his knee. "So what is it you want to know?"

Tom was shaky. "I've been feeling really strange lately. Ever since Katie was killed. Ever since I was put in jail. Hell, ever since I've been released. All I see is death. All I see is connections. I faint and I have no idea why. I do things I don't remember doing and I didn't do things I remember doing. I need your help."

Hank didn't know how he could help. Tom seemed to have experienced a lot of what Hank once did. Awful thoughts and numerous connections. "How am I supposed to help you?"

"I need to know some things."

"You know I can't do that. I told you that I can't," Hank replied.

"I don't need you to tell me confidential things," Tom said. "I just want you to tell me if what I know makes sense. My mind's all messed up and I need to know if it makes sense to you."

"If what makes sense?" Hank questioned.

"My connections."

"Why me? Maybe you need a psychologist or something. I work for the FBI, I'm not a doctor," Hank said.

"I know what you do. I know who you are. I know a lot about you. I wrote a book about you. You solve crimes. You put killers away. I need to see what you think, because in a way I'm just like you."

Hank was uncomfortable with Tom's remarks. The newspaper clippings found at the murder scenes flashed through his head.

He admires me.

"What is it you want to tell me?" Hank asked.

"I'm not a detective or a Federal agent, or whatever you want to call it, like you, but I have been looking into the murders. When I watched the news today I saw that Katie's uncle had been murdered too. He was number four. It just made me wonder what's going on. Each one is connected to Katie. The first two were staying at the Vandermeer, then she was killed, and now her uncle. There's something strange going on. I'm afraid that the killer is still going to strike the people Katie has a connection to. Maybe her family, maybe her friends, maybe the people that she works with, maybe…"

"You," Hank finished for him.

"Yes. Maybe me. So I want to know why her? What is her relevance to all this?" Tom asked.

Hank thought for a moment before answering. "I'm not sure she has any relevance. I found connections with each crime a thousand times over, but I realized it was just my mind playing games with me. For a while I was afraid of what was happening to me. Every time I closed my eyes I saw a connection. I saw death. And as soon as I opened them I saw even more. I couldn't even block the images if I tried. I was just like you. And it wrecked me. The thoughts bore me down. But now I know that sometimes you can make it seem like there's a connection to anyone. There's a definite connection to me. There's one to you. There's one to everyone staying or working at the Vandermeer. There's probably even one to the man eating Key Lime Pie over at the counter. Everywhere you turn there's a connection."

Tom felt more at ease. "So how do you figure out

who's next?"

Hank thought about the question. It was the most important thing and the one thing he couldn't answer.

Time was running out.

A waitress finally appeared at the table. "I'm sorry to keep you waiting, sir," she said to Hank. "I didn't see you walk in. Can I get you anything?"

"No thank you. I just came here to talk," Hank replied.

Tom stared at Hank. "Are you sure Mr. Garrison. I'll pay if you're hungry."

Hank smiled. "I appreciate the offer, but I just ate not very long ago. I'm full." Hank's eyes became blank as he listened to what he had just said.

Full. 'F' for Fullmer.

"I'm sorry Mr. Zucker, but I have to head out. We can continue this conversation another time." Hank quickly slid out of the seat.

Tom didn't understand. "Where are you going?"

"I'm going to solve a crime," he answered as he hobbled out the door.

Hank started up his car and drove out of the diner parking lot. He picked up his cellphone and looked at its call log to see if he had Fullmer's number.

Nothing.

He called up the Vandermeer.

"Is Mr. Fullmer working tonight?" Hank asked as soon as someone picked up.

"He left for home about an hour ago. Is there a question you would need to ask a manager?"

"Um…." Hank tried to think. "Yeah, sure."

"I can get you Mr. Donnelly. Hold on."

"Yes."

"Hello, this is Mr. Donnelly."

"Hi, this is Agent Hank Garrison again. I got Mr.

Fullmer's address off of you before."

"Yes, I remember," Donnelly replied. "What can I do for you?"

"I just need his home phone number," Hank answered.

"Hold on just a second while I check the computer." Donnelly typed in Fullmer's name.

All his information popped up on the screen. "Do you have a pen?"

"I'll remember," Hank said.

"Okay. It's 555-3467. Can I help you with anything else?"

"Actually, yes, you may be able to. You wouldn't happen to know where Mr. Fullmer is from? He didn't always live in Orlando, did he?"

"No he moved here about a year and a half ago. He's originally from Georgia."

"I see. Do you know where he lived in Georgia?" Hank asked.

"That's a good question. He's told me so many times too. He always talks about going to visit his old friends back home. I can't remember it though. It's right on the tip of my tongue. Fairfield. Franklin. Farmington. It begins with an 'F.'"

"Fuck." Hank hung up the phone without another word.

58

The small, second floor apartment was still cold and lonely. It had been waiting for the killer to appear again. Waiting for the murderer's next visit.

The last couple of murders had no blood to clean up.

Nothing but sin to be washed away.

The small weapons' room had not been rummaged through since the dagger had been released from its clutches. The newspaper of Hank was just as ripped as it had always been. The window still looked out to the lively world below.

A car pulled in.

The two bags still sat, side-by-side, on the old gray and black plaid couch. Its two gloomy colors had become tainted by reds and browns.

Blood and guts.

The yellowed newspapers still infested the floorboards. They were pasted to the wood by the sticky blood that had dripped onto them.

The downstairs door opened up.

The towels on the bathroom floor were still bunched up in a corner. A new one hadn't been added.

'Creak.' A foot stepped up the first stair.

The crack on the mirror was less than an inch from

the edge.

'Creak.' Another step.

The sink was full of dried up spots. They hadn't been cleaned off.

'Creak.' Another step.

The suit was back on the twisted hanger and hooked onto the doorknob. It didn't look like anyone had been to the apartment recently, but someone had. Someone had returned the suit.

'Creak.' The last step.

The kitchen was just as big of a mess as it always had been. The dishes still remained in the sink. The flies still adorned the floor and table. However, the sandwich was finally gone. Someone had thrown it away.

The apartment's doorknob rattled.

Every bit of death inside the house seemed to wait for the guest to enter.

The door slowly moved forward.

The two bags flapped with the breeze of the opening door. They looked like they were clapping. The papers fluttered around on the floor, as if jumping for joy.

The door finally opened completely.

Harlowe walked inside.

54

Hank was a few miles from Fullmer's house. He had been trying to call him for ten minutes, but it was always busy. He tried again.

Nothing.

"Where the hell is he?"

He called again.

Still nothing.

Hank's eyes grew big as he looked out the window. A few miles up the road dark black smoke clouds gathered.

"Shit!" Hank hit the steering wheel with great force. "Shit! Shit! Shit!"

Hank knew he was far too late.

'F' is for fire, he thought.

He pulled in behind a few fire trucks and some police cars.

"What the hell happened here?" He asked the first police officer he saw.

The man looked at Hank funny. "A fire," he answered callously.

"I can see that," Hank said. "When did it happen? Did anyone get out?"

"Who are you?" The officer asked.

"Hank Garrison, FBI."

The officer was taken aback. His attitude changed. "I just got here myself. Some of the other police officers say it happened about fifteen minutes ago. It was an explosion. Probably a gas leak or something."

Hank knew that it was more than that.

"Did anyone get out?" Hank asked again.

"Not that I know of. Neighbors say a man and his wife lived there. The explosion came from out of the blue. It was unexpected. I doubt anyone survived. Look at the place."

Hank looked. It was nothing more than ashes any longer. If Fullmer had been inside he wouldn't have had a chance.

Hank didn't figure it out quick enough. His time was ticking.

He was next.

Hank walked over to his car. *Who is it?* Hank looked around at everyone watching the smoke rise into the air. *It could be anyone here.* He thought about what he had said earlier in the office. *It's someone Dan knew. And someone that knows me.*

Hank pulled out his cellphone and dialed Gale's number.

"Charlie," Hank said as soon as Gale answered.

"Yes, Hank."

"Where are you?"

"At the office, just headed out to Dan's place to meet up with Jon."

Jon, Hank thought. *It makes sense. For once something makes sense. It was Jon. He was never around. He always showed up after murders took place. He could have done them all. He knew Dan. He knows me. He even left today. Jon is the murderer.*

"Charlie, I think the murderer *is* Jon," Hank bluntly replied.

"Are you serious? Where did you come up with that conclusion?"

Hank ignored the question. "I was headed to see the Vandermeer manager because I had a feeling he would be next. I wanted to warn him. 'F' for Fullmer. 'F' for the place he was from in Georgia. 'F' for fire."

"What are you talking about Hank?" Gale asked. "Fire?"

He still wasn't paying attention to Gale. "When I got to his house it was burned down. He was inside. He was the next victim."

Gale was astonished. "So that's where the fire was. I heard a call on the radio just a little while ago about that. But what does this have to do with Jon?"

"Jon fits it all. He's never around. That eviction shit he talks about, his pregnant wife, that's all bullshit. He's the murderer. He knew Dan. It's him. I have a feeling. I have a gut instinct," Hank answered.

"Well he's probably at Dan's now. I'll meet you there. If it's him we won't let him know that we know. There should be plenty of cops there still."

"I doubt that. It's getting late. They'd be done by now. Call for some backup. If it's him we both need to be safe. You or I may be next," Hank said.

"I'll call for some. How long will you be?" Gale asked.

"Twenty minutes, probably."

"Be careful Hank," Gale said.

"You too."

The phone hung up.

Hank got into his car and drove off.

'Ring. Ring. Ring.'

Hank picked up his phone and looked down at the caller ID. It wasn't a number he recognized. He opened up the phone and placed it to his ear.

"Hello," Hank answered.

The voice on the other end was muffled. Hank couldn't make out the words that were being said.

He hung up and looked at the screen.

No service.

Why didn't I see it? Why didn't I realize all this sooner? Why does it have to fall into place now? I should have known.

Hank stopped his mind from asking any more questions. "The game ends tonight," he said loudly.

55

Hank pulled into Eronie's driveway earlier than he had told Gale. It was rather empty. No other cars, except for Gale's, Eronie's, and his own, were present. Not one other car. Not a single police car.

Hank was suspicious. He had told Gale to call for backup a while ago.

They would have showed up by now, he thought.

Hank hobbled over to the front door. It was open. He walked inside.

Gale was a few yards away from Hank, his back facing him. He was talking on the phone.

Hank slowly hobbled closer to him. He didn't hear Gale saying anything on the phone. It was just silence.

Hank hoped the police were on the other end. Harlowe would be there soon and without backup maybe the next victim would be easy.

Hank was within a few feet from Gale's back.

Gale spun around quickly, just before Hank had reached him. "Hank!" He shouted as they faced one another.

Hank jumped. Gale had caught him by surprise. He didn't expect him to turn so abruptly.

Gale realized that he had frightened Hank and laughed. He shut his phone. "I'm sorry to have scared you. It's funny because you'd think *I* would be scared. You're the one that snuck up on me. I guess sometimes you just never know."

Gale sounded different. Just slightly, but different nonetheless.

He looked Hank in the eyes. "I just got off the phone with Jon. He'll be here soon. If you're right we'll know tonight Hank. And we'll both be here. He can't get both of us. It's a pretty ballsy choice, you assuming it was Jon. He does fit. It does make sense, but why would he do such a thing? Why was he playing a game with you? Are you sure it was him?"

Hank didn't understand why Gale hadn't called for backup. *Was Charlie the murderer and not Jon?* He didn't know what to do. He was once again suspicious of everyone. *No. It was Jon. It makes sense.* His thoughts invaded. *But so does Charlie.* "Where's the backup?" Hank asked as he slowly moved backward, as if shying away from Gale.

Gale smiled. "They'll be here."

Hank didn't like Gale's grin. It looked too wise. Too happy.

"Charlie, I told you to call for backup twenty minutes ago. They should have been here already. If it's Jon we'll need backup." Hank looked both scared and angry. He took another step back. "So where is the backup?"

Gale just smiled. He remained silent.

Hank was worried.

He felt alone.

"Charlie this isn't funny. This isn't a game..." Hank paused when he realized what he had said. *Game.* He pulled out his cellphone and began dialing the police. "I'm calling for backup."

Gale walked closer to Hank and then quickly swatted the cellphone from his hand. It crashed to the ground and slid a few feet away. "Backup?" Gale asked in a wicked voice.

Gale reached into his suit pocket and pulled out a latex glove.

Hank just stood still, as if mesmerized at what just happened. In awe of the game. In awe of the player.

Gale slipped the glove onto his right hand and then reached into his holster and

pulled out his gun. "What backup?" He asked with a smile.

Hank was still in shock. *Charlie,* he thought. *No one ever would have known.*

Hank spun his head to face the door. Gale noticed.

"I doubt you will be able to run anywhere. Not with that knee of yours."

He aimed the gun at Hank's bad knee and then slowly moved it to his good knee. "Inney."

He brought the gun back to Hank's bad knee. "Meeny…"

Back to his good knee. "Miney…"

Now his bad knee again. "Moe…" Gale took a deep breath and smiled. "Remember playing that game as a kid?"

Hank didn't know what to do. The door was close by, but Gale was right, he wouldn't be able to run. Not with his knee.

He remained still and quiet. He was slowly being backed into a corner. There was nowhere else to go.

Nothing else to do.

The gun jumped to his good knee. "Out…"

Now the bad knee. "Goes…"

Good knee. "'Y'…"

Bad knee. "'O'…."

After the back and forth battle Gale's gun had with

Hank's knees he finally stopped on the good knee. "'U.'"

A loud noise erupted as the gun fired a bullet. It tore right through Hank's knee.

Hank fell to the floor. "Aahhhhhhhh. What the fuck?" He screamed in pain.

Now it was *impossible* to go anywhere.

Gale inched closer to the pained Hank. He now had the gun aimed at Hank's head.

Hank was grabbing at his knee. His face was contorted in pain. His eyes were glossy. Hank's hands were placed tightly against the wound. Blood dripped through his fingers.

Gale kicked Hank's aching knee. "You see Hank," he started, "Sometimes a guy comes along who is smarter than you. Sometimes a murderer is better than those who track him down." Gale smiled. "Fuck, sometimes a murderer actually *is* the one who tracks him down."

"You'll be caught. If not by me than by someone else," Hank said through clenched teeth.

"Oh I assure you my dear friend it won't be by you. You'll be dead. And as far as I know there isn't another famous FBI agent out there. If you couldn't figure it out, then how could anyone else?"

"Why did you do it?"

"I would love to sit here and chat with you, but I really ought to be heading out. I wouldn't want to be caught at the scene of a crime. That's not my style."

"Why did you do it?" Hank asked again, this time in more of a whisper. He was trying to buy time. There was no other option.

"Simply to prove that I was better than you. That someone out there was better. I was getting sick and tired of reading about the great Agent Garrison. Then I read about you coming down here on vacation, that's when it all clicked. But enough about that. You didn't figure it out in time. It just goes to show you that you can't always win Hank. Sometimes you're meant to lose. This is just one of those times."

"How did you do it? How did you plan out all the victims? How did you find out their places of birth?" Hank's voice was now hoarse.

Gale laughed. "Are you fucking serious? You're asking me how? I'm about to shoot your fucking brains out and you're asking me how? Well there's a little thing called technology Hank. And let's just say cops can pretty much do anything. Some…" Gale stopped and smiled. "Even seem to get away with murder. Ain't that the shit, huh?"

"What are you out to accomplish?" Hank asked.

Gale ignored the question. "This isn't a movie Hank. This isn't like all those fucking unrealistic movies where the guy tries to escape death when there's a gun to his head. You *can't* escape this. 'G' is for Garrison…Time's up."

A gunshot sounded.

56

Gale fell to the floor. His head hit the ground hard and ended up a few inches from Hank's knee. His eyes quickly became lifeless. Blood poured from the bullet's exit wound, which was centered on his forehead, and dripped to the ground.

Hank looked up at Harlowe. He must have entered through another door. He didn't even realize he was there.

Not until Gale fell.

Hank winced in pain. So many questions took control of his head, but only one came out. "How did you know it was him?" Hank asked.

Harlowe walked over to Hank. He ignored the question. "Are you okay Hank? That wound looks bad. Are you okay?"

Hank didn't answer. "How did you know it was him?" He asked again.

"Maybe I'm better than you," Harlowe answered, jokingly.

Hank grinned. "Maybe you are. So tell me how."

"Well," Harlowe began, "I went to evict someone at an old apartment building. The best thing about doing that is being able to see what's inside. I think I told you that before."

Hank nodded.

"Well oddly enough, inside of that shitty place was a whole bunch of newspaper clippings about you, just like the ones that were left at the crime scenes. There were also bags of bloodied clothes and a whole shit load of tools and weapons. But it was the bathroom that gave it away. Inside was a suit I saw Detective Gale wear not that long ago. I tried to call you. I tried to warn you that it was him."

Hank remembered the phone call that he didn't understand.

"I can't believe he did all this. Why do you think?" Harlowe reached around his belt. His metal baton fell out of its loop and hit the back of Gale's lifeless head, before dropping to the ground. He pulled out some gauze from his belt's side compartment and pressed it against Hank's wound.

"He wanted to win," Hank answered.

"Don't we all? Backup should be here any minute. I called them right before I came inside through the back door."

Within seconds Hank heard some police cars pull up outside.

"Talk about good service," Harlowe said. He helped lift Hank off the floor. "Come on. Let's get you out of here."

Hank uttered a painful sounding laugh as he was pulled to his feet. "It's kind of funny. All this. This game."

"How's that?" Harlowe asked.

"Because Gale is from Gorham and you killed him with a gun."

"Uh huh," Harlowe said with a smirk. He propped Hank against the wall then bent over to retrieve his baton. "That is a bit strange."

Printed in the United States
39968LVS00001B/34-42